THE MANIFESTOR PROPHECY

ALSO BY
ANGIE THOMAS

FOR YOUNG ADULTS
Concrete Rose
On the Come Up
The Hate U Give
Find Your Voice: A Guided Journal for Writing Your Truth

THE MANIFESTOR PROPHECY

ANGIE THOMAS

BALZER + BRAY

An Imprint of HarperCollins*Publishers*

Balzer + Bray is an imprint of HarperCollins Publishers.

Nic Blake and the Remarkables: The Manifestor Prophecy
Text copyright © 2023 by Angela Thomas
Illustrations copyright © 2023 by Setor Fiadzigbey
For information address HarperCollins Children's Books,
a division of HarperCollins Publishers, 195 Broadway, New York, NY 10007.
www.harpercollinschildrens.com

ISBN 978-0-06-322513-8 (trade bdg.) — ISBN 978-0-06-331949-3 (int.)
ISBN 978-0-06-329495-0 (special ed.)

Typography by Jenna Stempel-Lobell
23 24 25 26 27 LBC 5 4 3 2 1

First Edition

In honor of Virginia Hamilton
and all of the ancestors who knew we could fly

CONTENTS

ONE

HELLHOUNDS, HAINTS, AND HAPPY BIRTHDAYS

When my best friend JP turned twelve, his parents bought him a phone. It was a super big deal, 'cause one, JP loses everything, and two, his parents think phones are "quick access to the Devil." (I didn't know the Devil had a phone.)

For her twelfth birthday, Alabama McCain down the street got a sweatshirt once worn by a member of her favorite K-pop group. Weird, but not as weird as being named Alabama even though you're from Mississippi.

Sean Cole got a four-wheeler for his twelfth. Now he likes to ride around the neighborhood, knocking over trash cans. His mom says he's being a boy. I say he's being a butt.

For my twelfth birthday, I've got them all beat. My dad's gonna teach me how to use the Gift so I can finally be a real Manifestor. First I've gotta catch a hellhound.

I tiptoe through the woods so the leaves don't crackle under my feet. In yesterday's homeschool lesson, Dad said hellhounds can hear sounds from hundreds of miles away. I think I can *smell* a hellhound from hundreds of miles away. Wherever this thing is, it's filling the forest with a strong odor of boiled eggs and Fritos.

"Remember what I told you, Nic Nac," Dad says. His voice is around me, like he's speaking on an intercom. "Look for the signs. Hellhounds always leave a trail."

A trail of what, funk?

I wipe my forehead on my arm. You'd think eight in the morning was too early to sweat, but it's normal for late May in Mississippi. The sun glares through the trees, and the air is thick and sticky; it feels like walking through toffee.

I grip the handle of my net. The mesh is made from Giants' hair, one of the strongest materials on earth. Although I zoned out for most of Dad's hour-long lecture, I do remember that Giants' hair is one of the few things that hellhounds can't chew through. I also remember that hellhounds breathe fire. So I search for signs. Burnt leaves, scorched earth . . .

Smoke. Up ahead, a pillar rises into the air. Where there's smoke, there's a hellhound.

I tiptoe in that direction, and bam, there it is in the clearing—a hellhound with brown fur that stands on end. It has horns, which means *it* is actually a *she*. She's the size of a tiger, and she gnaws on a bone big as she is. Hey, better that bone than me.

Now to catch this thing. If only I knew how to use the Gift, this would be a breeze. But nooo. "You're too young to learn," Dad said. "It's nothing to play with," he said. "Wait until you're twelve," he said.

"Those rules stink," I said.

Lucky for me, I'm twelve today and that means goodbye rules, but at the moment all I've got is my net. I raise it above my head as I inch closer to the hellhound. Good doggy. Don't worry about this live, three-course meal walking toward—

Aaaand she sees me. I freeze.

"She can smell fear, Nic Nac," Dad says. "Don't be afraid."

Says the guy who isn't three feet from a hellhound.

Nope, I'm not going out like this. One of us is gonna attack first, and it's gonna be me.

I take a step.

She growls and takes one too.

I take another step.

She charges.

I nearly pee my pants.

She tackles me to the ground.

Hundreds of pounds of hellhound pin me down. The stench burns my eyes. I'll never tell Sean he stinks again. If there is an "again." I'm probably seconds from pearly gates and angels.

But suddenly the hellhound shrinks. She smells like cheese—not great but not bad—and instead of biting my head off, she licks my face. The woods dissolve, revealing my backyard, and that fire-breathing, gigantic hellhound is a tail-wagging little hellhound pup.

Dad's standing over on the patio, laughing. "Happy birthday, Nic Nac."

He waves his hand, erasing the rest of the illusion he drew, along with the concealment mojo that kept our neighbors from seeing that our backyard had become a forest. My dad's a pretty good Manifestor. He managed to make this furball look ten times her size. In reality she's no bigger than a shoebox.

I wipe her warm slobber from my cheeks. "Is she mine?"

"I'm not saying names, but somebody *has* been bugging me for a hellhound or a dragon. Since a dragon ain't happening, a hellhound it is."

I grin. "See? I knew you'd get the hang of things."

"You may wanna hold off on that celebration, Nic Nac. Please believe there are rules if you wanna keep this pup."

"Name them."

Dad raises his eyebrows. "Who are you and what you done did to my kid? Because the Nichole Blake I know hates rules."

"Apple." I point at myself. "Tree." I point at him.

He laughs. "Touché, Miss Blake. Tou—"

"What are you guys doing?"

Dad and I jump.

"JP," Dad says with a deep breath. "Good morning to you too."

My best friend peers over the fence that separates our backyards. JP's only the second friend I've ever had in my life. The first was this girl Rebecca who was in my home-school group in Atlanta. We bonded over Oreos. I thought I'd never have a friend like her again until JP strolled along. When I first met him, he wore a dress shirt and bow tie like he was ready for church on a Sunday instead of fourth grade on a Tuesday. Nobody forced him to dress that way either. JP just likes bow ties. He held his hand out and said, "I'm Joshua Paul Williams. You can call me Joshua Paul."

We call him JP. Sometimes Pastor JP because of the bow ties. Plus, JP's dad is a preacher, and JP has a freckled face, round belly, and short brown hair just like him.

JP's the only Black kid on our street besides me, but that's not why we're friends. JP's the one kid who doesn't think I'm the weird homeschooled girl. Also, I'm not 100 percent sure JP could survive without me. I'm not saying that because he's an Unremarkable either (aka doesn't have the Gift or any supernatural ability—mostly everyone around here is Unremarkable). I'm saying that because he's a hot mess.

He adjusts the holder straps on his glasses. "Sorry I scared y'all. My momma says I'm sneakier than a snake in slippers."

"Uh, snakes don't have feet," I say.

"Yet I somehow get what she's saying," Dad adds. "How long you been standing there, li'l man?"

JP shrugs. "Not long."

5

Thing is, a majority of Unremarkables don't know about the Gift or know that Remarkable creatures really exist. On top of that, they can't see that stuff. But illusions are so powerful that they're the one Remarkable thing Unremarkables can see. Luckily the concealment mojo should've kept JP from seeing the illusion Dad drew, and my puppy should look like a normal puppy to him. But there's a teeny, tiny chance that he saw *something*. Unremarkables have those moments. They usually explain it away by saying their mind's playing tricks on them.

"Mr. Blake, my momma asked if Nic is going with us to the book signing tonight and if I can go to the museum with y'all tomorrow?" JP says. "She would've asked herself, but she gets shy around you 'cause she thinks you're cute. Don't tell my daddy I said that."

Ewwwww! "JP! You don't say that out loud!"

"It's the truth!"

Dad shakes his head. We've lived in ten neighborhoods so far—I keep count—and Dad's had a fan club in every single one. He's tall and lean with a dimpled smile, dark brown skin, black locs, and tattoos covering his arms. Know what it's like having the cute father in the neighborhood? Disgusting. I wanna vomit on the regular.

"Nic can still go," Dad says. "And you can still come with us tomorrow. Tell your momma I said thank you for taking her tonight."

"Yes, sir. I can't believe we're gonna meet TJ Retro."

"*And* he's gonna sign our books," I add. JP and I are

the unofficial-but-should-be-official leaders of the TJ Retro fan club (along with official editors of his unofficial wiki). We've read his Stevie James books a hundred times. They're about this foster kid, Stevie, who finds out he's a magician and attends a magical prep school with his best friends, Kevin and Chloe. One day he will have to battle the evilest magician in the world, Einan.

The magicians and their magic remind me of Manifestors and the Gift a little bit, but in real life, the Gift is more powerful than magic. You see, the Gift is an innate power that lives in us Manifestors. Magic, on the other hand, is a corrupt form of the Gift. It's hard to control and super destructive. Also, magic in real life can only be performed with a wand, and the magic in wands runs out after a while. We Manifestors don't need wands.

So although the Stevie books aren't accurate, they're cool. The third book in the series came out last week, and Mr. Retro's making a book-tour stop in Jackson tonight. JP and I have held off on reading the new book, and we're avoiding all spoilers until we get our copies signed. That's discipline right there.

"Good ol' TJ Retro and his inaccurate books," Dad mumbles.

"How could books about magic be accurate, Mr. Blake?" JP asks. "Magic isn't real."

"Yeah, Dad, how could they be accurate?" I say.

He side-eyes me, and I grin. Dad hates books about magic. He calls them "fabricated tales written for profit."

Technically all fiction books are fabricated tales written for profit, but I let dude have his moments.

He clears his throat. "They're just not my thing, JP."

"In other words, he's got no taste," I say.

Dad puts me in a light headlock. "What you say?"

"Get off!" I shout, and laugh. He plants a big wet kiss on the top of my head.

"I got taste," he says, letting me go. "The best taste. Remember that."

"You wish," I say as my hellhound jumps up my legs. "Check it out, JP. I finally got a dog."

Since JP is an Unremarkable, he can't see the smoke she lets out as she squeaks or the small horns on her head. But JP barely glances at her. "Uhhh, I better go. Vacation Bible School only waits for Jesus. Happy birthday, Nic!"

He disappears from the fence, and I frown. "What's that about?"

"With JP, who knows?" Dad says. "C'mon. We gotta get started with your school day."

The other kids in Jackson got outta school for the summer earlier this week, but Dad homeschools me year-round. Today that's A-okay by me. It's Gift lesson time, baby. Time to finally become a real Manifestor.

You see, although we Manifestors are born with the Gift inside of us, we still have to learn how to use it, and there are lots of ways to use it, too. The easiest is with mojos and jujus, which control the elements. We can do stuff like form fire in our hands or make water shoot from the ground. If we do it with good intentions, it's a mojo. Bad intentions, it's a juju. We can also use our minds to summon objects or create illusions and tons of other things. It can take years to learn to master the Gift, plus Manifestors are still discovering new ways to use it. I don't have to know a ton of stuff, but geez, I'd like to know how to do *something*.

My puppy scuttles behind us into the house. We've lived in Jackson for two years now. It was New Orleans before this, Memphis before that, Atlanta, Charleston, DC, New York. Basically, we've lived a lot of places. Dad let me choose our new city this time, and I picked Jackson. I can't explain it, but it felt like the place we needed to be.

I gotta say, I made a good decision. This is one of my favorite houses so far. It's got an upstairs and a basement, and it's in an artsy neighborhood called Fondren. Once a month, there's a neighborhood-wide festival, and on Sundays Dad and I walk to the diner a few streets over for milkshakes and cheeseburgers.

It feels like we've found a home here, but any day now Dad could say, "Hey, you up for a change of scenery?" That really means, "Hey, an Unremarkable caught me using the Gift, so let's get out of here." That happens a lot.

In the kitchen, a deep growl rattles the door to the basement. I sit at the counter. "Is that the demon you caught at the governor's mansion?"

Dad waves his hand, and a light glows under the basement door. The demon squeals. "Yep. Second one in two weeks. I swear, demons can't stay away from that place."

Dad's a handyman here in Jackson. Unremarkables don't know that eighty-five percent of their household problems are the result of haints, demons, ghouls, and other Remarkable creatures. Twelve percent of what's not caused by creatures can easily be fixed with the Gift. The remaining three percent require a screwdriver and a prayer.

"A'ight, Nic Nac," Dad says. "Quick quiz—when did we Manifestors first receive the Gift?"

Aw, man, here he goes with this. I'm ready for Gift lessons, not a quiz. But I gotta do what I gotta do. "Our ancestors were first blessed with the Gift while they were enslaved," I say. "It was given to them so they could escape to freedom."

"You sure about that?" Dad says.

Oh shoot. The fact that he asked makes me not sure. "Uhhh . . . I think I am?"

"Sorry, baby girl. You got this one wrong today. Remember what I always tell you—nothing about *any* Black people started with slavery. For us Manifestors, the Gift was first given to our ancestors, the Wallinzi, in Africa. We're focusing on them for today's lesson."

"What? But . . . but I thought you were about to teach me how to use the Gift. Today's the day I'm supposed to learn, remember?"

Dad frowns. "It is?"

"Yes! On my eleventh birthday, you said I could learn

10

when I turned twelve. Before that, you said on my tenth birthday that I could learn when I turned eleven."

"I don't remember—"

"Aaaand on my ninth birthday, you said I could learn when I turned ten."

"That was a while ago. You sure?"

I press my lips together. "Dad, this isn't fair. You told me you learned to use it when you were ten."

"I did. I also grew up thinking it was a quick fix for everything, but it's nothing to—"

"Play with," I say.

"There can be real—"

"Consequences," I say.

"You could hurt yourself or—"

"Somebody else," I finish. I've heard this a million times. "I just wanna know how to use it for simple stuff, like to draw an illusion to make my room look clean or ways to use it on a gamer troll."

"Orrrr you could actually clean your room. Please do. I caught a whiff of some serious funk in there the other day. I'm definitely not teaching you how to use the Gift on a gamer troll. You'd mess around and make some poor kid's teeth fall out."

I widen my eyes. "You can do that with the Gift?"

Dad purses his lips. "Like I said, the Gift's not a quick fix for when you're in a bind, baby girl. Besides, it ain't got nothing on this." He taps the side of my head. "Your brain's the only gift you need. *You're* the only gift you need.

Everything you need is inside of you."

"Well, since the Gift is inside me, don't I need to know how to use it?"

He smirks. "You're persistent, I'll give you that. I think we should wait another year, Nic Nac."

I wanna tell him to give me a chance. That I'd be careful, I promise I would. That I wanna know that I can do it, that I'm a real Manifestor.

But Dad won't listen. He never does. I sigh. "Yes, sir."

He kisses my forehead. "Let's get this Wallinzi lesson out of the way so we can head to Ms. Lena's."

After about two hours of homeschooling, we hop in Dad's pickup truck—me, Dad, and my hellhound pup. I think I'll name her Cocoa. She's the color of a cup of hot chocolate. The demon Dad caught at the governor's mansion sleeps in a cage in the bed of the truck, and on the back seat there's a crate holding blue-glass bottles with the smoky forms of haints swirling around in them. Dad caught them in various houses this week. When he hits a pothole on our street, the bottles clink against one another.

"You gotta be kidding me," he says. "Another one?"

Jackson has potholes galore. Sometimes people turn them into pools and flower beds. It's cool and sad at the same time.

I glance back at the one Dad rode over. "Was that there yesterday?"

"Nah, I don't think so. Them things pop up real fast

though. Bet it's got something to do with that volcano under the city."

Most people don't know that Jackson is built on top of an inactive volcano that's only a few thousand feet below the city. The opening is said to be right below the Mississippi Coliseum. I'm just glad it's inactive. Trust me, I wouldn't have told Dad we should move here if it was active, although the Jackson culinary specialties of caramel cake and chicken on a stick are worth the risk of volcanic eruption.

We hit potholes the whole way to Farish Street. In one of our history lessons, Dad said that it used to be *the* spot for Black folks in Mississippi. It was one of the few places where they weren't discriminated against. I found some old pictures online that showed people crowding the sidewalks to go into the shops and restaurants.

Today, most of the buildings on Farish Street are abandoned. That's how Ms. Lena's seems to Unremarkables. They don't know that the boarded-up door is only an illusion hiding a steel door with ancient markings on it.

Dad holds the cage with the demon in it as he opens the door. The sounds of blues music and chatter drift outside, along with the aroma of fried foods. The place is packed today, but Fridays usually are. That's when Ms. Lena serves her famous fried catfish and Cajun fries.

The lights in the juke joint stay dim to keep people from seeing how run-down it is, but the Remarkables light the place up a bit thanks to the Glow, different-colored auras that tell you the kinda Remarkable they are. Only other Remarkables see it, but Dad says Unremarkables sense it. They usually say that person has "it" or something special about them.

We Manifestors have a golden Glow that's a little brighter than other Remarkables' Glows. It's probably not a coincidence that we're some of the most powerful Remarkables there are. Don't get me wrong, Rougarous, Vampires, Giants, Fairies, Merfolk, and other Remarkables are powerful, but they don't have the Gift like us.

A couple of Manifestors at the bar are being served by a small purple-glowing Aziza with brown skin, glittery wings, and pointed ears. That's Ms. Sadie. Don't call her a Fairy or she'll tell you that Fairies are from Europe and Azizas are of African descent and Azizas are stronger than Fairies. They're able to pick up things a thousand times bigger than them.

A Manifestor at a booth shows a red-glowing Vampire a suitcase with small leather bags in it. The Manifestor is Mrs. Barbara, and she's a salesperson for Miss Peachy's Marvelous Mojo and Juju Bags. The slogan shimmers on the suitcase in glittery letters: "If you're wise, you'll open this surprise!" Remarkables love them, 'cause they're filled with the Gift, but you don't know what a bag can do till you open it up. It could be a mojo bag that rains money and gold, or it could be a juju bag that turns off the gravity in the room or makes it rain actual rain. It's like a Remarkable version of scratch-off tickets. People will spend all their money trying to find the mojo bags with money or gold in them, and most of those are worth no more than ten dollars. It's rare to find one that's worth millions. Dad says nobody's getting rich but Miss Peachy.

Over at a table, a dark-skinned Rougarou with a gray Glow talks to a Shapeshifter (orange Glow) and a Vampire as he shows them pictures on his phone.

The Rougarou, Mr. Zeke, spots us. "Hey, it's the birthday girl!"

I grin as it's echoed around the juke joint. This is a lot different from how it used to be. Before Dad and I moved to Jackson, we didn't go around other Remarkables much, and if we were around any, Dad told me not to talk to them. He's kinda over the top when it comes to stranger danger. Once we got to Jackson, he met Ms. Lena and started coming to the juke joint to sell her the creatures he caught on jobs. He was super hesitant to talk to folks, but over time, the regulars became like our family.

I get swarmed with birthday hugs. Ms. Sadie promises me a root beer float with a drizzle of caramel. Mrs. Barbara gives me a Miss Peachy's bag and claims she has a good feeling that it may be a gold-raining mojo. I stick it in my pocket. Would be just my luck that it's a juju bag that rains frogs instead.

We go over to Mr. Zeke, and he wraps me in his wooly arms. I can only imagine what he looks like during a full moon. "Happy birthday, Nic! How's twelve treating ya?"

"The same as eleven so far."

"Wait till you hit the hundreds," says the Vampire, Mr. Earl. "Not a thang feel different. I went a year thinking I was a hundred and ten, and I'm a hundred and eleven."

"You a hundred fourteen, Earl," says Mr. Zeke.

"Well, dang. See what I mean?"

"I see somebody got a hellhound," Ms. Casey, the Shapeshifter, says with a look at Dad.

I grin. "Yep! He had to cave eventually."

"Yeah, yeah, yeah. You won't be grinning when you're cleaning up all that hellhound poop," Dad says. "How was the trip, Zeke?"

"Amazing don't describe it, man. I was showing Earl and Casey the pictures. I got as close as I could."

Mr. Zeke takes a trip every year to a Remarkable city or historic site. This year he went to Africa to see the Garden of Eden. Well, the outside. Nobody can go in. According to Dad, the Wallinzi, the tribe we descend from, live in the city that surrounds the garden. Mr. Zeke shows us a picture of himself outside the garden's gates. The ivory wall is hundreds of feet tall, and two angels in golden armor stand guard.

"How was the city?" Dad asks. "As beautiful as they say it is?"

"More so," Mr. Zeke says. "Those Wallinzi, though . . . interesting folks."

"Funny, I just started giving Nic homeschool lessons on them," Dad says.

"You oughta teach her that they ain't real welcoming to

outsiders," Mr. Zeke adds. "Especially not to us 'less gifted' Remarkables. You know how some of y'all Manifestors are."

Mr. Earl and Ms. Casey grunt in agreement. Some Manifestors like to make sure other Remarkables know that we're the most powerful Remarkables. Dad says it's silly; that as Black folks we've seen people like us get treated as inferior and we shouldn't do that to others.

"I'm sorry you had to deal with that, man," he tells Mr. Zeke.

"It is what it is, Maxwell. I'll deal with them over LORE any day."

There go the grumbles around the juke joint. In Ms. Lena's, you should never mention LORE, the League of Remarkable Efforts, aka the Remarkable government. It's mostly run by Manifestors, and they monitor Remarkables to make sure we don't mess with Unremarkables. In any major way, at least. I mean when Mr. Earl broke into the Jackson blood bank, he had to deal with the Unremarkable police. But if he were to go on a rampage and bite a bunch of Unremarkables, LORE would step in. LORE also oversees the secret Remarkable cities in North America, including Uhuru, where Dad and I were born.

I haven't been to any of the Remarkable cities since I was a baby. Dad and I are exiles, Remarkables who don't live in Remarkable cities. So is everyone in Ms. Lena's. Half of them left LORE cities on their own; some say there are too many rules to follow in the cities. The other half got kicked outta the cities. Dad says he chose for us to live in the Unremarkable world, but sometimes I wonder if he really had a choice. I mean, with the way we move around so much and how Dad never went around other Remarkables, it's as if he had something to hide. Then again, I can't imagine he'd do anything to get kicked outta anywhere.

"Speaking of LORE, anything I need to know?" Dad asks.

Mr. Zeke glances at me—so quick I almost don't see it—then says, "You know how it is this time of year."

Uhh, what does that mean?

Dad nods. "Thanks, man."

Mr. Zeke holds his fist out. "Hey, we exiles stick together."

Dad bumps it. "Always. C'mon, Nic Nac."

I follow him toward the back. "What happens this time of year?"

"Grown folks' business," he says. That's also what he calls politics and what happened to Mr. Earl after he broke into the Jackson blood bank.

Dad raises his hand to knock on Ms. Lena's door, but the door swings open before he can. Shelves cover every wall of the office, holding cages filled with creatures and vials of tonics in every color. An older Black woman sits at the desk in the center. Gold rings adorn her fingers, and her skin is bathed in a bronze Glow.

Ms. Lena is a Visionary, a person who has visions of the future. That's different from a Prophet. Prophets hear divine messages about certain people's futures, seek them out, and relay the messages. Prophecies aren't super detailed and can get misinterpreted by the recipients. Visionaries see flashes of things that will happen. It's apparently like seeing pieces of a puzzle but not the picture the puzzle creates.

"Ah, my best supplier," Ms. Lena says. Her New Orleans accent makes me think of walking around Uptown with Dad. "I see you brought that hellhound back. I told you, ain't no refunds."

I should've known Dad bought Cocoa from Ms. Lena. She's the go-to for everything from hellhounds to lightning birds to tonics.

"Oh nah, we're not bringing her back," Dad says. "Just brought her along for the ride."

"Uh-huh. She only breathing smoke? I gave her a tonic to stop that fire mess, but I ain't responsible if she burn your house down."

Um, what?

"Just smoke," Dad says. "No fire."

"Uh-huh," Ms. Lena says. I think that's her favorite non-word. "Well, stop wasting my time. Show me whatcha got."

Dad sets the cage on her desk as the demon claws at the metal bars. It's maybe a foot tall and has red bumpy skin and beady green eyes. Ms. Lena uncaps a vial and splashes a clear liquid on it. The demon howls as its skin sizzles like water thrown on a hot skillet.

"Holy water," Ms. Lena says. "He gets too unruly, I'll hit him with some oil."

She pronounces oil like *earl*. That's how some folks from New Orleans say it. Ms. Lena was born and raised down there, but then this hurricane called Katrina hit. She spent three days on a roof until some Swampfolk—the bayou cousins of Merfolk—rescued her.

"How many haints you got for me, Maxwell?" she asks.

"Ten, including a real angry one from Madison."

"Oooh, chile! You done made Ms. Lena's day. We 'bout to make some good money!"

"Who buys haints from you anyway?" I ask.

Ms. Lena sets her hand on her hip. "Who wants to know?"

"She didn't mean any harm, Ms. Lena," Dad says.

Ms. Lena puts her hand up. "Nothing wrong with a curious child, chile. If you must know, Miss Nosey, there's some rich Remarkables out here who like to collect haints. Don't ask me what they do with 'em. It ain't my business long as they pay up."

Weird. If I was rich, I'd buy something useful, like a pet dragon trained to attack my enemies. Practical stuff.

"Your daddy said that hellhound's your birthday gift," Ms. Lena says. "How old are you?"

"Twelve."

"Ohhh." She flashes her gold-capped teeth in a smile. "I remember that age real well. You oughta let me try and fetch you a vision. I don't usually do it for free, but for your birthday I don't mind."

"Nah, that's okay, Ms. Lena," Dad says. "I don't want you going out your way."

"Oh hush, Maxwell. It's not a problem."

"No, really," Dad says. "Don't."

Ms. Lena reaches for my hands. "Why not? It'll take a min—"

Our fingertips barely touch.

A strong gust of wind whips past me. Dad, Cocoa, and Ms. Lena disappear, and I'm in a darkened tunnel.

I frantically glance around. "What the—"

Another flash. I'm in a gigantic cave, but everything around me is blurry. There's something big and dark up ahead; I can't make out what it is. Then someone shouts, "Nic, run! It's behind you!"

I'm about to turn around to look, but another gust of wind whooshes past me, and I'm back in Ms. Lena's office.

She lets go of my hands and shouts, "How you do that?"

I hold my throbbing head and blink stars out my eyes. It's moments before everything gets in focus, and once it is, I see Ms. Lena staring at me, horrified.

I'm just as horrified, looking at her. Her Glow flickers as if someone is flipping a light switch on and off.

"What you do?" she shrieks. "You better tell me, li'l girl!"

Dad doesn't let me respond. He grabs me and Cocoa and hurries us outta the juke joint.

TWO

THE ADVENTURES OF TYRAN J. PORTER

Dad speeds home, hitting every pothole. "Tell me exactly what happened, Nichole."

I start from the beginning. Our fingers touched, there was a gust of wind, then the tunnel, the cave, the voice. "Was that a vision?"

"It sounds like one," Dad says, and there's this expression on his face that I've only ever seen once or twice. He's terrified.

Holy moly, he's terrified. Dad's not scared of anything, so if he's terrified, I should be planning my funeral. "What does it mean?"

"Calm down, baby girl."

"How did I see her vision?"

"I don't know."

"What *was* the vision?"

"I don't know," he says.

My chin trembles. "Did I hurt her?"

"Hey, hey. Calm down. You didn't do anything wrong."

"But her Glow, Dad. It was flickering."

"I'm sure there's an explanation," he says. "As much as we know about the Gift, there's so much we *don't* know, but I promise that you did nothing wrong, you hear me?"

He says that, but his face tells a different story. He hasn't stopped frowning since we left Ms. Lena's.

There's something wrong with me . . . or worse, I did something really bad.

Dad pulls into our driveway and shuts off his engine. We sit in silence, and he runs his fingers along a tattoo on his forearm. V.XXVII, the Roman numerals for May twenty-seventh, my birthday. It's technically two tattoos, one on top of the other, so it almost looks like it's 3D.

"You know," he says, "I think it's best if you don't go to the book signing tonight."

"But you said I didn't do anything wrong!"

"You didn't, but you shouldn't be around so many Unremarkables."

My eyes sting. "You think I'm gonna hurt somebody?"

"No!" he says quickly. "No, baby girl."

"Then why can't I go? Meeting Mr. Retro is one of my birthday gifts!"

"Nichole," he says, in that tone that warns me to watch *my* tone. "Look, Mrs. Williams and JP can get your books signed for you. We'll have our own birthday celebration here. I bought cake, and I'll go pick up a pizza from Sal and Mookie's. Then we can—"

I jump outta the truck and march into the house, crying my eyes out.

I spend most of my birthday alone in my room with Cocoa.

I overheard Dad call Mrs. Williams and tell her I'm not feeling good. He said it was nothing major, but he wants to be sure, so he's keeping me home tonight. It's got me thinking that something really is wrong with me.

My tablet beeps somewhere in my room. Cocoa stops playing with a pair of socks and goes straight to the heap of dirty clothes in the corner. I dig around in the pile for my tablet. I've got three texts from JP.

My momma told me the news!

Nic, it's TJ Retro!

Illness can wait!

I plop back on my bed. The worst part about being friends with Unremarkables is that you can't be like, "I'm not really sick. I did something to a Visionary today and my dad is more afraid than he wants to let on."

Not happening, so I write: I wish I could go. Can you get my books signed for me?

Of course, JP writes.

I'll get a selfie taken for you.

Technically it's for me since I'll be in it and not you.

But I'll think of you the whole time!

Am I making things worse?

YES, I write and toss my tablet back into the clothes pile.

Cocoa hops on the bed and rests her head on my stomach. She looks up at me with those big red eyes like, "Master, how may I assist?"

I scratch behind her ears. "At least I got you today. Some birthday this is."

There's a knock at my door, and Dad peeks around it. "Mind if I come in?"

"It doesn't matter, you're gonna come in anyway."

"True, but I think I got two good reasons."

I sit up. Dad walks in holding two small birthday cakes covered in thick, tan-colored frosting. Caramel cake. I'm kinda in love with caramel.

But instead of giving in, I lie back down.

"That didn't do the trick?" Dad says. "A'ight, bet. How 'bout this?"

He sets the cakes on my nightstand and rubs his palms together. With the wave of his hand, my ceiling disappears and a night sky takes its place. One by one, Dad draws stars in midair. Little twinkling ones, big glowing ones that resemble diamonds. They float up to the ceiling. A couple of them shoot across the room.

Dad grins at me. "I told you that you deserve the stars."

I fold my arms. "Nice illusion, but no."

"Aww, c'mon, Nic Nac! You keep pouting, and I'll bust out singing."

"I'm not pouting, and you can't sing."

"You sure? I've got some pipes on me," he says.

"No."

"I think I feel a song coming on."

"Dad, no!"

"Hap-py birth-day to ya!" he sings, off-key. He tries to dance, and Cocoa growls at him from the bed.

Before I know it, I'm laughing. "Okay, okay! Please stop."

He dances over to me and holds out one of the cakes. "Make a wish, and nah, wishing that I stop singing and dancing don't count."

"I need a prayer for that," I say, and close my eyes. Every year I wish that on my next birthday, it won't just be me and Dad. As much as I love the guy, I wish we had other family too. Then I imagine that I'm surrounded by a mom, grandparents, aunts, uncles, a brother. I've always wanted a brother. I close my eyes tight enough, and I can almost see them. Their faces are blurry, yet they seem real.

I wish for them again and blow out the candles.

Dad looks at the other cake. Every year he gets an extra one to commemorate surviving another year as my father. Rude.

"Happy birthday," he says, sounding a little sad. He blows out the candles.

I lick frosting off a candle. "What's wrong, old man? Upset that I'm growing up?"

"*Old man?* Can't I have a moment without being judged?"

"Nope!"

"Hater. So, whatcha wish for?"

I never tell him about my family wish. I don't wanna make him think he's not enough. "That we figure out what's wrong with me so I can go to the book signing."

"Oh," Dad says, sounding real guilty. As. He. Should. He brushes my hair. "Whatever happened earlier, we'll figure it out. As far as tonight, it's for the best, baby girl."

"I still don't like it."

Dad has the nerve to smile. "You're just like your momma."

There's an ache deep in my chest. I get one whenever Dad brings her up, as if my heart is missing something. But it doesn't happen a lot. Dad rarely talks about her.

My mom's not dead. I think she doesn't wanna be around for me. Dad says that "sometimes adults make decisions that they think are for the best, but they're not." I'm afraid to ask more, because who wants to find out that their mom doesn't wanna be their mom?

I wish I at least remembered her. Then when I made my birthday wishes, she wouldn't be so blurry. I think I remember her eyes; I see them in my dreams. They're big and dark brown like mine, and they gaze down at me as she sings me lullabies.

"Some days, you may not understand the things I do, the things I've *done*," Dad says, "but protecting you is my priority. A'ight?"

He just had to go there. The caramel cake and silly

dance moves were bad enough. Now here he goes with the protection talk. "All right."

"My girl." He kisses my forehead and snuggles up against me. "You know, I vividly remember the first time I held you."

"Daaad," I groan. "No more mush, please."

"I think I sat there for hours, staring at you. I wasn't sure I could be the father you deserved. Still don't." He sits here quietly for a moment, then abruptly hops up. "You want pizza for dinner?"

"Pizza's fine. You okay?"

"Yeah, baby girl, I'm good. How 'bout we go pick one up from Sal and Mookie's? We can grab some ice cream too, while we're at it."

I almost tell him yeah, but it hits me: it takes about ten minutes to get to Sal and Mookie's, then you gotta wait for the pizza. That would be more than enough time to . . .

"Can I stay here?" I ask. "I kinda don't wanna be around people."

"Whatever you want, baby girl."

"That should be a daily rule."

"Hah! Not happening," Dad says. He whistles at Cocoa. "C'mon, girl. Let's go get you some food."

She follows him out. Really, I think she's following the cake.

I wait until Dad's footsteps thump against the staircase before I grab my tablet. When I blew out my candles, I made an extra wish: to meet TJ Retro. I don't need a wish when I've got a dad who's leaving, giving me the perfect opportunity to sneak out.

I text JP.

It's a miracle! I feel better.

Looks like we're both meeting TJ Retro tonight.

Dad leaves minutes before Mrs. Williams and JP do. The timing's so perfect that it seems like I was destined to grab my Stevie books, sneak next door, and ride to the book signing with them.

I'm pretty sure Dad won't see it that way, but it's a chance I'm willing to take.

The Williamses' minivan has "New Life Christian Church" written on the side, along with the address, service hours, and a picture of the first family—Pastor Williams, Mrs. Williams, JP, and JP's older sister, Leah. I don't know a lot about her. She died before we moved here and JP doesn't talk about her much.

"I'm so glad you're feeling better, Nichole," Mrs. Williams says as she drives. She's a short, chubby woman who wears her hair curled. "When your daddy told me you were sick, it broke my heart. Nobody should spend their birthday sick."

"Yes, ma'am. It's a miracle!" I don't know where "lying to a pastor's wife" ranks on bad things, but I bet it's up there.

Mrs. Williams throws her hand up. "Hallelujah! You know, Joshua Paul is leaving for the vacation Bible school camping trip this Sunday after church. You should join

29

them. It'll be two weeks in the wilderness with no phones, no video games, no computers. You'd *love* it!"

She can't mean me. That sounds like torture.

Lemuria Books is on the second floor of a small shopping center next to one of Jackson's interstates. Above the entryway of the shop, a statue of hands holds a giant book. The store is cozy inside, thanks to the books in every nook and cranny.

The long line of TJ Retro fans stretches out of the store and down the staircase. Mr. Retro smiles from a poster in the shop's display window. He's a Black man about Dad's age, with twists in his hair. He's holding a copy of his latest book, *Stevie James and the Soul Scythe*, which shows a Black boy on the cover, pointing a wand at a hooded figure. An employee says Mr. Retro will be here soon.

"Joshua Paul, why don't you and Nichole go grab us some goodies from the bakery?" Mrs. Williams says, taking our books. "I'll save your spot. Don't go too far now."

"Yes, ma'am," says JP. He's real quiet tonight, and trust me, JP and quiet don't go in the same sentence. He's been nervously chewing on his lip since I got in his mom's minivan.

We go downstairs to the bakery, and I nudge his side. "Hey, don't be scared about meeting Mr. Retro. Long as neither of us burps, farts, or falls, it'll be fine."

"Gee, that's helpful. But I'm not nervous about meeting him."

"Then what is it? Another one of your challenge videos

30

didn't go viral?" JP loves doing those weird online challenges, like recording himself walking up milk crates or eating a piece of spicy candy. The things Unremarkables do for fun.

"My latest challenge video is doing extremely well, thank you," he says.

"Okay. Did you accidentally read a spoiler about *Soul Scythe*? Bruh, it's fine. One spoiler won't ruin the whole book."

"Stevie, Kevin, and Chloe take Einan's soul scythe."

I gasp. "What? You can't just tell me that without a warning, dude!"

He folds his arms. "I thought one spoiler doesn't ruin the book."

"It . . . it doesn't. I'm just surprised. How do they get it? What do they do with it?"

"I'm not giving you any more spoilers, but that's not what's bothering me."

"What's up then?"

"I can't tell you. You're gonna think I'm weird."

"I already think that. But!" I quickly add, 'cause he gasped, "I'm weird too. We go together like peanut butter and potato chips." Aka the best sandwich known to humankind.

"No, I mean you're gonna think I'm out there. Way, way, way out there. In space, past Pluto, in another galaxy." He looks down. "I can't lose anyone else."

I rub his shoulder. JP may not talk about his sister, but

it's obvious that he misses her big-time. "You won't lose me," I say. "Just tell me what's up."

"Okay. This morning, when you and Mr. Blake were in your backyard, I saw—" Something behind me grabs his attention, and he gasps. "Nic, look! Look!"

I turn around and follow his pointed finger to the bakery windows. A black SUV just pulled up outside. A Black man in jeans, a T-shirt, and sneakers climbs out the back.

JP tugs at my shirt. "That's . . . that's him, Nic. That's him!"

My mouth falls open, but not because I'm finally staring at *the* TJ Retro. It's because *the* TJ Retro has a golden Glow.

My favorite author is a Manifestor.

JP grabs my hand and races us back upstairs to join his momma in the signing line. Moments later, TJ Retro comes up the staircase to a round of applause.

He smiles and waves at everyone. When he sees me, he does a double take. I'm the only other person here with the Glow, the only other Manifestor. This close, there's no mistaking his. It bathes his brown skin in a golden light.

He's about to speak, but one of the bookstore employees whisks him away.

"He almost spoke to us!" JP says. "Think he recognized us from online? We do comment and message him a lot."

JP and I aren't obsessed, we're persistent. Difference.

"You know, I can't put my finger on it, but there's

something special about that man," Mrs. Williams says. "He has 'it,' whatever it is."

Typical Unremarkable. Don't know a Remarkable when they're standing two feet away.

Look who's talking. I can't believe I didn't realize that Mr. Retro is a Manifestor. Then again, the Glow doesn't show on Unremarkable pictures and videos. I wonder what he's gonna say to me. There's not a lot he *can* say with so many Unremarkables around, but he could be like, "Let's keep in touch." Then we could text each other, and he'll think I'm so cool that he puts me in his books. Stevie could use another friend.

Okay, maybe I'm reaching . . . or not. I gotta talk to him.

Of course, now that I'm super excited to meet him, the signing line moves ridiculously slow. I guess it's for a good reason—Mr. Retro takes his time with every kid who comes up to the table. Some of them are dressed up as Stevie, Chloe, Kevin, and other characters. A couple have stacks with international editions of the books. Mr. Retro signs every single copy.

Eventually, there's eight sets of people between us and the front of the line. Five. Three. One person separates us from TJ Retro.

I clutch my books to my chest. I'm surprised everyone can't hear my heart pounding. "What do we say to him?"

"Oh no!" JP turns to his mom. "What *do* we say? I don't remember how to talk!"

Mrs. Williams chuckles. "Giving him your names

would be a good start."

"What *are* our names?"

"You're Joshua Paul, and this is—"

"Nichole!"

Oh no.

No, no, no, no, no.

Dad marches into Lemuria, zeroed right in on me. Judging by his glare, I won't leave the house until I'm twenty-five.

"Nichole Blake," he growls. "You've got five seconds to—"

"Calvin?" Mr. Retro says.

Dad looks past me. "Ty?"

Calvin? Why would he call my dad that name? And who is Ty?

Mr. Retro approaches Dad with careful steps, then hugs Dad tightly. "Dawg! I thought I'd never see you again!" he says.

Dad slowly wraps his arms around him in return. "*You're* TJ Retro?"

My dad is hugging my favorite author. My dad. Is hugging. My favorite. Author.

Mr. Retro pulls back. He's shorter than Dad, so they aren't quite eye to eye. "It's a pen name, long story. Where you been?"

Dad glances around nervously. "This isn't a good place to—"

"Cal, it's cool," Mr. Retro says. "They're not here."

They *who?* I'm so confused.

"We should go," Dad says.

"But Nichole hasn't gotten her books signed," Mrs. Williams chirps. Beside her, JP stares at Mr. Retro, wide-eyed and mouth open. I'm not sure he's breathing.

Mr. Retro notices me. "Oh my God! Is this—"

"Nichole? Yeah," Dad says.

They share a look, as if there's a silent conversation between them.

"Wow, Nichole," Mr. Retro says. "I haven't seen you since you were two! You're almost as tall as me now, which obviously doesn't take a lot to do, but—"

"You *know* me?" I ask.

"I was there when you were born and helped you take your first steps. Changed a couple of diapers. I'm probably embarrassing you by bringing it up. Point is, I'm your godfather."

Pause. Rewind. Replay. "You're my *what?*"

"She'll have to get her books signed another time," Dad cuts in. "We have to go."

"C'mon, Cal. I haven't seen you in years. You can't just leave, man."

JP, who is apparently five minutes behind, goes, "Mr. Blake, you know TJ Retro?"

"He was the brother I never had," Mr. Retro says.

Seconds pass. Finally Dad sighs. "You got a pen and paper?"

"Anybody got a piece of paper?" Mr. Retro calls out,

and everyone in line seems to rummage through their bags. Mrs. Williams digs in her purse and pulls out one of those long receipts that you get at the drugstore that has more coupons on it than anything.

Mr. Retro passes it and his pen to Dad, who quickly scribbles our address on it.

"Come by later," Dad says. "Make sure you're alone."

"Squad promise," Mr. Retro says, with a slight smile. Dad doesn't return it. Mr. Retro clears his throat. "Mind if I sign those for you, Nichole?"

"Sure!" That's the only word I can manage. Mr. Retro takes my books and scribbles in them. He grabs a copy of the new Stevie book and signs it too.

He hands the books to me. "Make sure you read the title pages. Later, Cal."

"Later," Dad mumbles. "C'mon, Nichole."

I follow him and glance back. Mr. Retro mouths, *"Look at the books."*

I open one. Where it used to say, "The Adventures of Stevie James by TJ Retro," it now reads, "The Adventures of Tyran J. Porter by Tyran J. Porter." Below that, he wrote: *And his best friend, Calvin Blake.*

THREE

*THE PEOPLE **CAN** FLY*

"Your name is Calvin, not Maxwell, you're Stevie James's best friend, and you didn't tell me?" I almost shout. Almost. This *is* my dad, you know?

He whips the truck around a pothole. "Calvin is my first name and Maxwell is my middle name, but to you I'm Dad. And I'm not Stevie James's best friend, I was *Tyran Porter's* best friend. Difference."

"But Tyran Porter *is* Stevie. He changed the name in my books. He also changed Kevin to Calvin. Aw, man." I groan as it hits me. "My dad is Stevie's cowardly best friend!"

Dad does a double take. "Hold up. Coward? *That's* how he wrote me?"

"You're practically afraid of your own shadow."

Dad hisses a word I can't repeat. "I wasn't like that! Half of what Ty went through, he wouldn't have survived without me! But he couldn't be bothered to put that in his li'l books?"

"What did you go through?" I ask. "Did you guys really travel into a realm of shadows when you were kids? Did you travel back in time?"

"It's not as cool as it—"

"Is Einan real? How did you defeat him? You must have done it since an evil Manifestor hasn't destroyed the world." I'm talking way too fast, but I can't get my head around all of this. "Never mind, don't tell me how it goes. I wanna finish the series first."

"Nichole. I know this sounds exciting, but some of the stuff we did was dangerous. We nearly died, more than once."

"Wow. Kevin would totally say that."

"Hey!" Dad says, all offended. "What's that supposed to mean?"

I point at one of the books. "Cowardly best friend, that's all I'm saying. Take it how you wanna."

"TJ Retro," Dad says mockingly. "What kind of wack name is that anyway?"

"Looks like he took his real initials and then spelled Porter backward without the *P*. Genius. I can't believe you're friends with him, *and* he's my godfather, *and* you're in the books!" I flip to a page. "Who is Zoe?" The truck swerves. "Whoa!"

"Tyran put her name in there?" Dad says.

"Yeah. It used to be Chloe. She's Stevie's other best friend. Who is she really?"

He squeezes the steering wheel tight. "A friend."

"Where is she? Have I met her before?"

"It's complicated, Nichole."

"More like incredible. I can't believe you did something this cool once."

"Hey! I'm cool!"

"Not with those busted sneakers you aren't. You really wore your Chucks with the holes in them in public, Dad? Those are supposed to be for yard work, that was the rule."

Dad's mouth makes a hard line. "I put on the first shoes I could grab once I realized that my barely twelve-year-old wasn't home where I had left her."

"Oh."

"Yeah, oh. You wanna explain?"

"Umm . . . it was my birthday wish?"

"Oh, so you wished to be grounded? Because that's what you're getting. When we get home, go straight to bed."

"But Mr. Retro . . . Stevie . . . Mr. Porter . . ." Geez, these names are hard to keep track of. "He's coming over."

"You should've thought of that before you snuck out."

That doesn't make sense! How was I supposed to know that he's best friends with my favorite author? In fact, if I hadn't snuck out, none of this would be happening.

Unbelievable.

When we get home, Dad does the Big Confiscation. My tablet, gone. Laptop, gone. TV and video game privileges, gone. For two weeks, I'm only allowed outside to take Cocoa to handle her business, which basically means I'm only allowed to pick up hellhound poop.

That's not the worst part. Dad takes my Stevie—*Tyran* books. I thought reading them would get me through my two-week sentence. Plus, Dad being a character in them changes the way I'd read them completely. Not happening.

"But they're a great way to get to know you better," I tell Dad. "Don't you want your dear daughter to learn more about her wonderful father when you were her age?"

"Good night, Nichole."

He closes the door in my face.

Great. I'm ending my birthday the same way I miserably spent it—alone in my room. At least before I had Cocoa for company, but she's asleep on my bed. Sticky caramel frosting coats the hair around her nose, and she licks her lips of the last bits of my birthday cake.

I put on my pajamas and my satin bonnet and climb in bed with her. Although I'm grounded, sneaking out was worth it. Otherwise, I wouldn't know that my dad is Stevie James's best friend.

Man. To be honest, I wasn't a Kevin fan like that, no offense to Dad. He's a whiny li'l brat sometimes. Chloe . . . *Zoe* is my favorite. I wonder who she really is.

I don't know how much time has passed when the doorbell rings.

I crack open my bedroom door. I can't see anything from up here, but I hear Dad say, "Anybody follow you?"

"Nobody saw me coming. Literally," says Mr. Porter. "I made an invisibility tonic—"

"Wait a second," Dad says.

My door snaps shut, and there's a loud pop in my room. It reminds me of getting out of a pool and getting the water out of your ears, except now it's as if my room is underwater. Everything outside of it is muffled.

Dad soundproofed my room.

"Good night, Nichole," his voice says all around me.

Having a parent with the Gift is not as great as it should be.

I wake up to Cocoa nipping my ear.

"Noooo, Cocoa," I grumble, and turn over in my covers. "A few more minutes."

She nips with more force.

"Ow!" I grab my ear. Those fangs are no joke.

Cocoa dashes over to my door and runs around in a circle. Dad did tell me Cocoa was house-trained. He didn't say she'd bite my ear to get me up in the morning.

I step into my slippers and twist my doorknob; it's not locked anymore. Cocoa bolts out, and I groggily go after her down the hall, down the stairs, to the kitchen, and out the back door.

The sun is barely up. Lights glow in windows around the neighborhood as people start their day. I wanna go back to bed, but Cocoa takes her sweet time, sniffing out a place to pee.

I stretch and yawn. "It's all the same, Cocoa. Just go."

She keeps sniffing. Gospel music blares over at JP's house. It's Saturday morning, better known as cleaning day in the Williams household. JP says his momma wakes him at the crack of dawn by turning gospel music on high, and he gets up and starts cleaning. I think Mrs. Williams wants to make the whole neighborhood clean their houses, as loud as she plays that music.

Cocoa freezes mid-step, and her fur stands on end. She starts to bark at a dot in the sky.

It looks like a . . . bird? Can't be, that's way too big. It gets bigger as it gets closer, and—

That's a person. A Black man in a T-shirt and jeans. It's Mr. Retro.

My mouth falls open. I've seen Manifestors fly before. Dad even flew me around with him when I was younger. But it's not every day that my favorite author flies toward my house.

Mr. Retro comes to a soft landing in our backyard. "Morning, Nichole! I brought you and Calvin breakfast. I didn't know if y'all were biscuit types or English muffin types, so I got a little bit of everything. You sleep okay?"

Cocoa jumps up his legs to get to the food. I oughta tell him how much I love his books. That Chloe is my favorite character 'cause she's a Black girl like me. Or that his books make me feel better about being different from everyone else.

But what do I say? "I ove your ooks!"

I cover my mouth. Oh no.

He smirks. "You love my books, is that what you were trying to say?"

I nod.

"Thank you. Did you get a chance to look through your copies?"

"Yes, sir. I saw that you changed the names."

"I love that you're polite, but don't do the sir and mister thing. Makes me feel old. Just call me Uncle Ty. Deal?"

Holy moly, I can call him Uncle Ty. "Deal! How long have you known my dad?"

He feeds Cocoa a sausage patty. "Since I was your age. We went to Douglass together."

"Where?"

"One of the Manifestor academies in Uhuru," he says. "He hasn't told you about it?"

"No. Dad doesn't talk about Uhuru much."

"I see," Uncle Ty says. "I'm guessing he didn't tell you about the stuff we did growing up either?"

"Nope. Is everything in the books true?"

"Somewhat. I had to switch things up a bit or LORE would've been on my back."

"So Einan is real?" I ask, and I instantly feel bad 'cause he goes still for a moment. "I'm sorry."

"It's fine. His name is Roho. Well, was Roho."

"You defeated him? That's so cool."

"Cool is one way to put it."

He's being humble, but forget that. "No, seriously. You should have a statue. Or better yet, a holiday. You're a real-life superhero."

"Not sure LORE would agree with you on that one."

"Are you an exile too?" I ask.

"I guess you could say that. I spent the first ten years of my life in the Unremarkable world, living in foster homes. Didn't know I was a Manifestor or anything about the Gift. Then one day I was approached by a Prophet. You ever met one?"

I shake my head. I want to, but they're some of the rarest Remarkables to cross paths with. Most of them live in seclusion until they seek out the people they receive prophecies about. I would live in seclusion too if people were always begging me to bless them with a prophecy. Plus, not every prophecy is good, and people get mad at the Prophets as if it's their fault. That's gotta be exhausting.

"Receiving my prophecy changed everything for me," Uncle Ty says. "I'll never forget it. 'You are chosen to defeat an evil force that will cause destruction.' Me, a nerdy li'l foster kid. LORE found out about the prophecy and whisked me off to Uhuru to prepare to fulfill it, but . . ."

He goes quiet.

"But what?" I ask.

"Let's just say that after everything that went down, I

44

decided it was best for me to come back to the Unremarkable world. I haven't been back to Uhuru in years."

"What went down?"

"Enough about me," he says, way too upbeat. "I got you a birthday present." He digs in his pocket and takes out what looks like an ink pen. "It's a G-pen, made with—"

"Giftech," I gasp. Gift-infused technology. You can only buy Giftech in Remarkable cities, and Dad's never taken me to one, so I've never had any Giftech of my own. Dad once told me it's a hundred times more advanced than Unremarkable tech. "What can I do with it?"

"You can write to anyone with it, and they'll see it wherever they are."

"Anyone?"

"Any Remarkable, of course," he says. "You simply think about the person and write to them in midair. Only they'll see the message. Watch this."

He writes in midair with the pen. The words "Happy Birthday, Nic" sparkle and float in front of me, then fade away.

"Whoa," I mutter.

Uncle Ty smiles and hands me the pen. "Man, it's hard to believe you're twelve. I still remember the day you were born. Cal passed out. I had to bring him to with an awakening mojo."

"Does this mean that you knew my mom?" I hate that my throat tightens at the mention of her. I shouldn't care about someone who left me.

"I . . . It's not my place to speak on that, Nichole. I'm sorry."

I swallow away the tightness. "Oh. Okay."

Cocoa jumps up his legs for more food. Uncle Ty feeds her another sausage patty. "Good girl," he coos. "I used to want a hellhound. How long have you had her?"

"Since yesterday. She was my birthday gift from Dad. He was gonna teach me how to use the Gift too, but I only got Cocoa."

"You don't know how to use the Gift?"

"Nope. Dad thinks I'm too young to learn. Meanwhile, he learned to fly at my age."

"He actually learned at ten. He used to fly to school— that doesn't help, does it?"

"Nope."

"Sorry. Look, I get it," Uncle Ty says. "When I first got to Uhuru, I was the only kid who didn't know how to use the Gift already. I thought I'd be the worst Manifestor ever."

"You started learning once you got there, didn't you? Dad says I can't learn until I'm thirteen. *I'll* probably be the worst Manifestor ever."

It's quiet except for the sound of Cocoa sniffing at the fast-food bags. Uncle Ty stares at me as if I'm the most pitiful thing he's ever laid eyes on.

He sets the food on the patio table. "You've heard the story 'The People Could Fly'?"

"Yeah. Hundreds of years ago, our ancestors in Africa

were kidnapped by slave catchers who used magic to curse them. They forgot the Gift, and they forgot who they were. They were brought to America, and the pain and suffering of slavery made them forget more. Until one day an old man named Toby appeared on a plantation. He wasn't enslaved, and nobody knew where he came from. Toby saw the ones with the Gift, the Manifestors. He whispered ancient words to them, and they remembered who they were. Then—"

"They flew off like birds to freedom," Uncle Ty adds. "The beauty of the Gift is that it helps us when we need it. It knew that our ancestors needed to fly, and it helped them do so. Nowadays, it takes a little more effort, but hearing the ancient words helps you do the first step of flying. Levitation."

"Wait, are you about to—"

Uncle Ty smiles and reaches for my hands. "Kum yali—"

Our hands touch, and everything happens in a flash. Uncle Ty's Glow goes out like a fire doused with water, and a jolt shoots through my palms, making my own aura glow so bright, it blinds me.

I gasp and let go of him. Uncle Ty's Glow returns to normal as he hits the ground with a thud.

Oh no.

I just killed my favorite author.

Uncle Ty's knocked out cold on our living-room sofa. After he dropped, I yelled for Dad. He used the Gift to pick

Uncle Ty off the ground, and Ty's lifeless body floated to the sofa.

I bite my nail and silently pray to God, Jesus, and all the saints for him to wake up. If he's dead, then I'm going to jail, and if I go to jail, my life is over. I'll forever be known as the girl who killed Tyran Porter. "Is he okay, Dad?"

Dad lifts Uncle Ty's eyelids, showing nothing but the whites. "He's breathing, so that's good. It's like he got hit with a knockout juju." Dad looks up at me. "What happened?"

I back up and tuck my hands behind me. "I—I don't know. I didn't mean—"

"Hey, hey," Dad says, moving toward me, but I back up more. I don't wanna hurt him too. "Calm down, baby girl. Tell me what happened."

"He was gonna help me levitate, and he took my hands, and then—" My voice cracks. "His Glow flickered, and he hit the ground. What did I do, Dad?"

He kneels in front of me. "We'll figure this out, okay?"

"*What* did I do?" I repeat.

He cups my cheek. "I don't know, but I promise it's gonna be okay."

Uncle Ty groans and stirs on the sofa. "Cal?"

He tries to sit up on his own, but Dad catches him and helps him the rest of the way. "Easy, man. How you feeling?"

"Like I got hit by an eighteen-wheeler and my limbs were turned into jelly."

"You always did have a way with words. What do you remember?"

Please don't remember that I almost killed you. Please, please, please don't.

"I flew over with breakfast," Uncle Ty says, and my heart sinks. "Nic and I were in the backyard, and I was gonna speak the ancient words so she could levitate. I took her hands and then . . . it's like a strong static shock hit me. My energy was sapped out of me."

"I'm sorry," I blubber. "It was an accident."

"It's okay. I know you didn't mean it." He holds his head. "What did you do, though?"

"That's the problem," says Dad. "We don't know."

The doorbell rings. Dad lifts a blind at the front window and peeks out. "It's JP."

He opens the door, and JP strolls in wearing a freshly ironed bow tie and T-shirt with civil rights leaders' names on it. "Mississippi Civil Rights Museum, here we come!" he says.

"Right," Dad says. "The museum."

He totally forgot about our homeschool field trip. I gotta admit, I did too.

"Thanks for letting me come, Mr. Blake," JP says. "My daddy's wanted to take me, but the congregation keeps him busy. You wouldn't believe the stuff people come to him about. There are some real sinners in our . . ." He notices Uncle Ty. "Church. You're TJ Retro!"

"The name's Tyran. You're JP, right?"

"You remember me from the book signing?" JP asks excitedly.

"Yeah, and from your comments and messages online."

JP turns to me. "See? I told you it worked, Nic!"

I try to smile, but I can't. I stare at my hands.

What's wrong with me?

FOUR

MUSEUM MAYHEM

There aren't a lot of people at the civil rights museum. Dad, JP, Uncle Ty, and I practically have the place to ourselves. Dad lets me and JP check out the museum on our own while he and Uncle Ty hang back and talk. Ten bucks says they're talking about what I did.

I stuff my hands in my pockets.

The Mississippi Civil Rights Museum tells the history of the civil rights movement in the state. JP insists on checking things out in chronological order, so he sets off. I go around and look at what's cool. There are life-sized cutouts of civil rights figures, black-and-white mug shots of people who were arrested for sit-ins and marches, and a replica of a jail and a police car like the ones those same people were forced into.

It's hard to focus on this stuff. In my head I can see Uncle Ty lying on the ground. I think about how his Glow left him and then my Glow got brighter, like I took the Gift out of him. But that's not possible . . . I think.

Ugh, why is this happening now? First Ms. Lena and now Uncle Ty. I've touched other Remarkables' hands before and never made their Glow flicker. Maybe it's a puberty thing, like acne and underarm hair. I'd rather deal with pimples.

Nearby, a mom, dad, and two kids check out the replica of an old schoolhouse. One side of it is made to look like the nice schools that white kids in Mississippi attended, and the other side looks like the rundown schools Black kids were forced to attend. The mom takes pictures of her kids as they sit at the desks in the replica of the school and smiles at them when they're not looking.

Moments like this, I wish I had a mom. She might know what's wrong with me, or she could give me a hug like JP gets from his mom. The kind that looks like it'll crush your bones, but it has the perfect amount of squeeze in it. Forget a hug, I'd be cool with talking to—

Wait a second. Uncle Ty said I can use the G-pen to write to *any* Remarkable; I only have to think about them.

I glance around. No Dad, no Uncle Ty in sight. I take the pen from my pocket, wrap my fingers around it, and think of my mom's eyes that I see in my dreams. I write in midair: **HI, IT'S NICHOLE, YOUR DAUGHTER.**

I stop, sigh, put the pen back in my pocket. I doubt

I could send a message to a complete stranger; and just 'cause she sees it doesn't mean she'll wanna talk to me. Besides, I'm supposed to be taking notes on the museum.

I wander into the central gallery. A huge sculpture that resembles fettuccini noodles is suspended from the ceiling. Lights flash along it to the rhythm of "This Little Light of Mine" that's playing from speakers. On the walls there are photos of civil rights leaders, and below the photos there are names of civil rights martyrs from Mississippi.. I can't help but wonder why Manifestors didn't use the Gift to help them.

I go to another gallery. There are more photos, life-sized cutouts, and artifacts. I walk up to one exhibit. A doorway leads into a small room where a video presentation is playing. Above the doorway, there's a large picture of a Black boy who doesn't look much older than me. He wears a brimmed hat and a tiny smile as he stares off into the distance. Below that, there's another photo of that same boy, sitting and smiling with a woman who looks a lot like him.

Dad comes up behind me and squeezes my shoulders. "That's Emmett Till and his mom, Mamie."

"Oh." Dad told me about Emmett and his mom. Emmett was from Chicago and visited Mississippi in 1955. He was accused of whistling at a woman. I didn't think it was that big of a deal, but Dad said that back then because Emmett was Black and the woman was white, some people *did* think it was a big deal. The woman's husband and brother-in-law kidnapped Emmett in the middle of the night and killed him. He was fourteen; a kid like me. It made me not wanna whistle anymore. Emmett's mom became a hero after his death by making sure the world knew what happened to her son.

"Emmett's death ignited the civil rights movement as we know it, baby girl," Dad says. "People got so upset about it that they decided enough was enough. Kinda like when people march and protest nowadays. Now, what do you think Emmett and the rest of these exhibits have to do with us Manifestors? Why do you think I wanted to bring you here?"

"For school stuff?"

"It's a little deeper than that. History shows what happens to Black people when we're seen as a threat, what *still* happens," he says. "I never want you to live in fear or think that every person who doesn't look like you hates you. But there are ignorant people who make assumptions about us because of the color of our skin. If those people knew what some of us are capable of, it could put a lot of innocent folks in danger. That's why we must use the Gift responsibly. Do you understand?"

I do, and I don't. "Why can't we use the Gift to stop some of this stuff? Couldn't Manifestors have saved Emmett? Or help people nowadays?"

Dad stares at the photo of Emmett and his mother. "A long time ago, LORE decided that we'd be putting ourselves in danger by helping Unremarkables. I get it, they outnumber us big-time. All it would take is a bunch of them getting ahold of wands to cause major problems."

Wands are dangerous. Witches and wizards use them, and they're usually those rare Unremarkables who do know about the Gift. Wands are as close as they can get to having it. Wands allow them to see Remarkable things as well, but once the magic in the wand runs out, they lose any magical abilities.

"The slave catchers who made our ancestors forget the Gift used wands," Dad adds. "That's a prime example of the kind of problems we would have. LORE believes that the preservation of Manifestors and the Gift is more important than helping Unremarkables."

I look at Emmett, and he kinda reminds me of JP. Now all I can think of is someone hurting my best friend the way they hurt Emmett, and that LORE wouldn't have helped him. What's the point of having the Gift if we can't help people who need it? Why call it the Gift if we're only gonna keep it for ourselves?

"I would've saved him," I say.

Dad drapes his arms over my shoulders. "I would've too, Nic Nac."

Uncle Ty wanders over while looking through a pamphlet. "Man. There are so many important people and stories we don't hear about nearly enough."

"Good thing the museum is depicting them accurately,"

Dad says. "Accurate representation matters when it comes to real folks."

Uh, I don't think this is about the museum anymore.

"Cal, I told you LORE was already mad that I wanted to write the books. I couldn't write everything exactly how it happened."

Geez, a whole government didn't want him to write his life story?

"Did you or did you not write the school a lot like ours, Ty?" Dad says.

"Yeah."

"And Chloe is a lot like Zoe?"

"Yeah."

"And the Einan character is like Roho?"

Uncle Ty sighs. "Yes."

"Then you could've written a better depiction of me," Dad says as his phone beeps. He looks at the text. "Shoot. A customer out in Rankin County has a leaky pipe. Bet it's a depressed haint. I'm gonna go set up an appointment with these folks. Be right back."

"For what it's worth, Kevin's a fan favorite," Uncle Ty calls after him, but Dad waves him off.

Now it's just me and Uncle Ty. He suggests we check out the special exhibit on the Underground Railroad. It's an entire wall showing a map of various Underground Railroad safehouses around the country.

"Dope, but not completely accurate," Uncle Ty says. "Wanna see something cool?"

I shrug.

Uncle Ty waves his hand, and new glimmering lines appear on the map.

"There were two Underground Railroads," he says. "The metaphorical Underground Railroad that Unremarkables famously used, and the literal Underground Railroad for Remarkables—an actual underground train system. Both railroads were used to get enslaved people to freedom. However, Remarkables used the literal Underground Railroad long after slavery ended, up until Roho . . ."

He goes quiet.

"You okay?" I ask. He doesn't respond. I tug at his shirt. "Uncle Ty?"

He gives his head a quick shake. "Sorry."

"You good?"

"Yeah. You ever heard of PTSD?"

I nod. When Dad and I lived in Atlanta, our next-door neighbor once saw her best friend get shot, and certain loud noises made her think back to it. Dad said she had post-traumatic stress disorder, or PTSD.

"I call what I have CO-PTSD," Uncle Ty explains. "Chosen One post-traumatic stress disorder. It's kinda hard to get over someone wanting you dead because of a prophecy. Being the Chosen One is not what it's cracked up to be."

"What's the Chosen One?"

He looks surprised. "You don't know the Manifestor Prophecy?"

My cheeks burn. He may as well have said, "Wow, another awesome cool thing you don't know? How sad."

I try to save face. "Of course I do. It's a prophecy about . . . about a Manifestor, yeah."

A laugh tugs at his lips. "It's okay if you don't know about it, Nic. I know more than most. Some might say I'm obsessed with it."

He stares off at nothing, and it's strange how he looks older and hardened. I believe he'd tear the someone apart with his hands if they crossed him.

"What is the prophecy?" I ask.

"Centuries ago, it was prophesied that one day there will be a Manifestor who will destroy the Remarkable world. This person is called the Manowari, the destroyer."

A chill crawls down my back. "How will they destroy it?"

"No one knows. That's why it's terrifying. The unknown is never kind to the mind. Remarkables have tried to predict what will happen, when it'll happen, how it'll happen for hundreds of years. When Roho rose, everyone assumed he was the Manowari."

"He wasn't?"

"LORE says he was, but I know better. There are twelve signs that will signify who the true Manowari is, and no one has fulfilled all twelve. Yet."

The "yet" makes me queasy. "What's this got to do with the Chosen One?"

"Well, according to the prophecy, only one Manifestor

may be able to stop the Manowari. This person is traditionally called the Mshindi, but most people call them the Chosen One."

"You're the Chosen One," I say, putting two and two together. "Geesh, you *are* a superhero." My face falls as it hits me. "I almost killed a superhero."

"You didn't almost kill me. I'm sure there's an explanation for what happened."

"Yeah, I'm a freak," I mumble.

"No, you're a twelve-year-old who's coming into the Gift," he says. "At your age, it can show itself in different ways. When I was ten, I accidentally turned myself invisible."

"So it *could* be a puberty thing?"

"Could be. Either way, don't let this get you down. I'm fine, you're fine." He lifts my chin. "Keep ya head up, kid."

I can't help but smile a little. "Thanks, Uncle Ty."

"Anytime." His phone rings, and he fishes it out. "It's my agent. I better take this. Be back in a flash." He puts his phone to his ear and walks off, saying, "Hey, Molly. What's up?"

I decide to search for JP since I haven't seen him in a while. He's not in any of the galleries, so I head for the café. It's almost noon, and JP always says his sugar drops drastically if he doesn't eat at exactly twelve on the dot.

I find him standing in the dining hall, just a few feet away from the café. The aroma of Mississippi-style gumbo, shrimp and grits, and peach cobbler cinnamon rolls is enough to make me hungry too, but JP doesn't seem to care about food. He's frozen, staring at the only person in the café.

"Nic," he says shakily, "you see that, right?"

The clerk at the cash register is too pale to be a normal person. Her eyes are sunken and red, and her skin . . . it sags off her bones like it doesn't belong to her.

That's because it doesn't. "That's a Boo Hag," I whisper.

Dad calls Boo Hags "Vampires' country cousins." They live off breath instead of blood. They climb on victims at night and suck the oxygen from their bodies, and sometimes they steal the person's skin. It's the only way they can survive sunlight, since they don't have any skin of their own. This one took some poor woman's skin, and her job in the café. Maybe the Boo Hag likes gumbo.

"What's a Boo Hag?" JP asks me.

"They're like Vampires except—" I stop. Hold on one freaking minute. "You can see it?"

"*You* can see it?" he asks. "Nobody else ever sees it!"

"Of course *I* see it! But *you* shouldn't see it!"

"I don't know what y'all see," a thick Southern drawl says, "but I see some new skins."

The Boo Hag makes her way around the counter and into the dining hall, the stolen pale skin dragging along like an oversized coat. "Lucky me, lucky me," she says. "It's a good thing I decided to take over the café today. I'm 'bout to update my wardrobe."

"Stay back!" I say.

"Or what? If you knew how to use the Gift, you would've used it on me already 'stead of just standing there. You gon' make a real nice fall wardrobe." She smiles. "Now, which one of y'all is gonna give Daisy your skin first?"

"D-Daisy?" JP stutters.

"My momma said I was pretty as a flower. Got a problem with that?"

Yeah, her momma lied.

What did Dad teach me that Boo Hags are allergic to? Sugar? Water? Salt, that's it! It'll melt the skin right off them and send it back to its owner. What do you know, there are saltshakers on the tables around the dining hall.

"JP," I say through my teeth, "we need salt."

"We're gonna die," he whimpers.

He's useless.

We back into a table, and the Boo Hag's grin widens. I reach behind me and feel around for the salt and pepper shakers.

"Stay back!" I point them at her. Boo Hags aren't allergic to pepper, but a little extra spice won't hurt. "Take one more step, and I'll season you!"

Now *she* backs up. "I don't want any problems!"

I advance, rattling the saltshaker. The Boo Hag shudders. Having power over someone is kinda awesome. "I'm gonna tell you once: Get. Out. That. Skin."

"No!"

My lips turn up. "Your call."

I fling salt at her.

The Boo Hag dodges it and leaps onto a wall on all fours. "You should aim better."

I back up, expecting her to lunge, but the floor shakes violently beneath us. The tables and chairs around the dining hall rattle so hard, they move out of place.

"Earthquake!" JP shouts, and crawls under a table.

Since when does Jackson get earthquakes?

The Boo Hag looks at me with panicked eyes. "What are you doing?"

"I'm not doing anything!"

"Liar!"

She lunges at me.

I fling the salt dead in her face. Seasoned Boo Hag, coming right up.

The effect is instantaneous, like salt on a slug. The Boo Hag screams as her nose melts away, revealing red muscle underneath.

"You foolish girl!" she says.

That little bit of salt won't get her completely outta the skin. I raise my hand to shake out more, but a forked tail tears outta her backside and knocks the saltshaker from my hand.

Uh-oh.

I back up as she crawls toward me. The floor shakes, and JP screams for his momma under the table.

"Not so cocky now," the Boo Hag snarls. "You're gonna make a lovely fall sweat—"

White light hits her with a crack. A geyser shoots outta

the floor, drenching me, the Boo Hag, and JP under the table. Some of it gets in my mouth, filling it with a briny taste. Salt water.

"Nichole!" Dad says as he rushes into the dining hall with Uncle Ty.

The floor steadies. The Boo Hag howls and thrashes as the skin melts into the tiled floor. Based on what Dad taught me, the skin will automatically return to its owner, who will wake up exhausted and won't remember a thing.

Once the skin is gone, it leaves behind a tailed creature that resembles a human muscle diagram from a health book. She dissolves into the puddle of salt water.

Dad takes me by my shoulders. "Are you okay?"

I'm shaky and I'm soaking wet, but I have my skin. "Yeah, I'm okay."

"Nic, did you or the Boo Hag cause the earthquake?" Uncle Ty asks.

I blink water out my eyes. I don't know how to start an earthquake. I didn't know it was *possible* to start an earthquake. "I didn't do it. I—I don't think."

Dad waves his hand, and a warm breeze dries me off. "Where is J—"

"How'd you do that?" JP shouts.

Dad and Uncle Ty turn to see him crawl from under the table.

"Do—do what?" Dad stammers.

JP points excitedly at me. "You dried Nic's clothes and made water shoot out the floor to hit the Boo Hag thingy!"

"You saw that?" Uncle Ty says.

"Ye—"

Red light zips into the dining hall and hits JP. He drops.

"JP!" I shout.

A lightning bolt comes next. It zaps Uncle Ty with a loud, sizzling crack, and he convulses to the floor. Another hits Dad and sends him into spasms as he drops.

A hooded figure with a golden Glow stands at the other end of the dining hall. The Manifestor takes slow, calculated steps toward me.

I force my feet to move backward. The Manifestor raises their hands, and my life replays in my head like a fast-forwarded movie. This is how it's gonna end, in a museum.

A loud *whoooosh* fills the dining hall, and a gust of wind knocks the Manifestor down. I watch Dad stagger to his feet. He drew the wind juju.

Uncle Ty coughs as he gets up. The mysterious Manifestor is already back on their feet.

Dad grabs me by my shirt and flings me behind a brick column. Flashes of light zip through the dining hall, but the Manifestor dodges every juju that Dad and Uncle Ty draw. Uncle Ty tosses a fireball, and with a snap of their fingers, the Manifestor puts it out. Dad flicks his hand, and a rope made of light appears in his grasp. He lashes it toward the Manifestor. They grab it, yank it outta his hand, and advance, forcing Dad and Uncle Ty back.

"You baby-stealing demon," they growl. "I should kill you where you stand!"

Dad and Uncle Ty stop dead. *"You?"* Dad says.

The Manifestor hits him with a flash of light, square to his chest, then hits Uncle Ty with one. The two of them drop lifelessly.

"No!" I run out from behind the column and rush the Manifestor, but they wave their hand, and ropes of light tie my arms and legs tightly together.

"Let me go!" I shout as I try to break free.

"Alexis, stop!" the Manifestor says.

I freeze. I know that voice. I don't know where I know it from, but I do.

"Who—" My mouth is dry. "Who is Alexis?"

The Manifestor pulls their hood down, and I lose my breath.

The woman has my face, my complexion that's lighter than Dad's, my thick, curly hair. Hers is in a braid that hangs past her shoulders. Her eyes, big and dark like mine, are filled with tears.

"Alexis is the name I gave you," she says thickly. "I'm your mother."

FIVE

THE UGLY TRUTH

My heart pounds in my ears. "You . . . my . . . but . . ."

She takes careful steps toward me. "I know this is a lot, but I need you to trust me. We have to get out of here. Now."

She might've killed my dad, my godfather, and my best friend, and she wants me to *trust* her? Because she *says* she's my mom? She could be lying! She doesn't even know my name! "I'm not going anywhere with you!"

"Then you leave me no choice," she says sadly.

She pretends to zip my lips, and they snap together tightly. Then she raises her hand, and I levitate off the floor.

I thrash and try to scream, but it's no good. My lips won't part, and my arms and legs won't budge. An unconscious Dad, Uncle Ty, and JP stand up straight as boards, and this woman, whoever she is, makes them march like soldiers.

She leads us outta the museum.

Cops, firefighters, and paramedics crowd the outside of the museum to check out the earthquake damage. A local news truck has already arrived.

"What do you mean the earthquake only happened here?" I overhear one of the curators say. "That's impossible!"

All these people and cameras, and yet nobody notices me levitating or Dad, JP, and Uncle Ty walking like stiff zombies.

Mystery Lady takes us behind the museum to some sort of vehicle that looks like an alien spaceship combined with an armored truck. The doors and the top half are tinted glass, and the bottom is matte black. Where the wheels should be, lights whirl in a circle.

The doors lift like wings. Inside, it looks like it has as much space as a minivan. With a wave of her hands, the Manifestor tosses Dad and Uncle Ty into a cargo hold in the back. She sets JP and me more gently into seats. Harnesses automatically wrap over us snugly and lock into place as screens across the dashboard light up.

The vehicle lifts off the ground, and I shriek behind my sealed lips. We rise higher and higher, above the museum, downtown, the Jackson streets, and glide through the sky. A few minutes later, we land in my driveway.

Mystery Lady gets us inside. She flicks her hand, and

Dad and Uncle Ty get tossed aside like they're bugs. They land in chairs in the dining room, and ropes of light wrap around them and tie them in place.

"The nerve," she says through her teeth.

I'm terrified and impressed.

She motions toward the sofa, and JP and I land on it softly. Her fingertips glow like light bulbs, and she reaches for JP. I try to scream for her to stop, but my lips are glued together. She presses her fingers to his forehead, and he wakes with a gasp.

"You had a normal visit to the museum," she says. "Nothing weird happened."

"I had a normal visit to the museum," he repeats robotically. "Nothing weird happened."

"Go home," she tells him.

JP stands at once and leaves.

Mystery Lady turns to me. "I'll free you, but you have to promise you won't scream and you won't run."

I bet if I tried, she'd bind me again. I nod.

She kneels in front of me and does the same zipping motion as before, but in reverse. My lips unstick. I can move my arms and legs again, but I'm so stunned I can't budge. Looking at her really is like looking at myself.

She covers her mouth as tears fall down her cheeks. "Hi. Hi, pumpkin."

There's an ache in my chest, but it doesn't hurt. It's like someone's hugging my heart. I know where I've heard her voice. It sang to me in my dreams. "M-Mom?"

She smiles through her tears. "Yeah, baby. I'm your momma."

I still can't move, and it's got nothing to do with a binding juju.

"Oh my God, look at you. You've gotten so big." She cups my cheek. "I can't tell you how much I've missed you. There wasn't a second that went by that you weren't on my mind."

A hurricane of feelings stirs up inside me. She *is* my mom, my heart knows it. Looking in her eyes feels like I'm in a home I never knew I had.

But one thing won't let me get comfortable in that home. "Why'd you leave me?"

Her tears stop. "What?"

"Dad said—he said adults make decisions that they think are for the best and really aren't. I thought that meant you left."

Anger flashes across her eyes. She marches over to Dad and Uncle Ty and snaps her fingers. "Wake up! Both of you!"

Their eyes flutter open. "Zoe?" Dad says.

Zoe? She's Chloe from the Stevie books?

"What happened?" Uncle Ty groans.

"I finally caught the criminal I call my ex, that's what," she says.

Dad looks over his shoulder. "Ty! You called her?"

"No! Calvin, I wouldn't do that to you!"

"Even though he *should've*," she says, with a glare that

makes *me* shiver. "I was at home when I got a G-pen message from our daughter."

"G-pen?" Dad says. "Where'd she get—"

Uncle Ty closes his eyes. "I gave her one for her birthday. I didn't think she'd use it to contact Zoe."

"Good thing she did," Zoe says. "I hacked into the G-messaging network to find out where it came from. Led me straight to the museum where I found the three of you."

"You always were the smartest of the three of us," Uncle Ty says.

"I know," Zoe says. She sets her hands on the arms of Dad's chair and looks him in the eyes. "I've waited for this day for ten years, and now I find out that you let Alexis believe that I walked out on her? When the truth is you kidnapped her?"

It's like a Boo Hag sucks the oxygen outta me. "What?"

Dad's shoulders slouch. Worse, he doesn't say anything.

"Dad," I plead. "None of this is true, right? My name is Nichole, isn't it?"

He bows his head. "Nichole is your middle name. Your first name is Alexis."

"But . . . but—"

"It was easier to hide if we went by different names," he says. "That's why people know me as Maxwell, not Calvin. Sometimes it didn't matter. Other exiles would figure out who we were and report us to LORE. I'd catch word about it and move us away."

My head spins. All the cities we've lived in, all the

70

times Dad said don't talk to other Remarkables, all the times he claimed an Unremarkable saw him do something weird and we had to leave. "We've been living on the run?"

"Yeah," he admits. "I've been a wanted man for ten years now for kidnapping you."

Tears build in my eyes. This can't be happening. "But . . . why?"

"Baby girl, you gotta trust me. I always tell you protecting you is my priority, and I mean every word of that. I never wanted to keep you from your mom, but I promise I had reasons for what I did."

"What reasons?"

"It's complicated."

"It's not that complicated! You've been lying to me!"

"He's still not being completely honest," Zoe says. "Are you going to tell her the other reason you were on the run, or will you mislead her on that too?"

Dad's eyebrows meet. "What are you talking about?"

"You know what I'm talking about. Where is the Msaidizi?"

"You think *I* have it?"

She scoffs. "Don't play innocent. One of the most powerful weapons in the world disappeared the same night you and Alexis did—"

"It's missing?" Uncle Ty says.

"—and I'm supposed to believe that's a coincidence?" Zoe says. "Where is it?"

"I don't know! I'm not a thief, Zoe!"

"Says the man who stole our child!"

Their yelling shrinks the room. I need to get outta here. I head for the stairs, only to walk smack-dab into something I don't see.

"Ow!" it says.

I scream as I fall on my butt.

The air in front of me shimmers. Curly black hair appears first, then a brown forehead and eyes closed tight behind a pair of holographic glasses.

The rest of the boy becomes visible. He peeks at us with one eye. "Surprise?"

"Alex!" Zoe says. She helps me up and makes sure I'm okay before whirling on him. "Baby, what are you doing here? You're supposed to be with your grandfather."

"I drank an invisibility tonic. I made it myself, but it shouldn't have worn off on contact. Do you know how I can fix it?"

Zoe's lips thin. "That doesn't answer my question."

"Okay, okay, I hid in your trunk," he says sheepishly. "I wanted to see if you found Alexis this time." He looks at me. "Wow, you really do look like Mom. Grandma said you probably would. I'd say nice to meet you, but 'remeet you' feels more appropriate."

He resembles Dad. I have this feeling that I know him, but I've never seen him before. "Do I know you?"

"I'm Alex," he says. When I don't react, he goes, "Your brother? Twin brother?"

My chest tightens. "My what?"

72

I whirl on Dad, but I can hardly see him for my tears.

"Baby girl, I can explain," he says.

I don't give him the chance. I race upstairs to my room. This can't be happening.

I lie in bed, staring at my ceiling, waiting for the moment I finally wake up. There's no way this is real life. My name is not Alexis, it's Nichole. Dad wouldn't kidnap me from my mom. He wouldn't keep it a secret that I have a twin brother. This has to be a nightmare.

Problem is, it doesn't feel like one. Those tears in Zoe's eyes as she stared into mine were real. That Alex kid I smacked into, real. This feeling like I'm gonna throw up, real. I don't think I'm waking up anytime soon.

There's a knock at my door. "Nic?" Uncle Ty says. "Can I come in?"

I mutter a "Yeah" as I sit up. Uncle Ty comes in and pulls out the chair from my desk. He's quiet at first, as if he doesn't know what to say. That's cool. I don't either.

He sighs. "I'm sorry you had to find out this way, kid."

I hug my pillow to my chest. "It can't be true, Uncle Ty. Dad wouldn't do this."

"I wish he hadn't—"

"He didn't! She's lying! My name is not Alexis, it's Nichole, and my dad isn't a kidnapper!"

Uncle Ty looks at me with pity I don't want. "Nic, I know you don't wanna think of Calvin this way, but he did it. I'm sorry."

My lips tremble. "Something must be wrong with her

73

then. She's an awful person, isn't she? I bet she didn't want me and treated me bad. Dad did say he was protecting me."

"Zoe would never treat you badly. She's one of the most caring and loving people I know. If by some tiny chance she did, why would Calvin leave Alex with her?"

"She probably loved him more than me."

"No, Nic," Uncle Ty says sadly. "I know that's what you wanna believe, but it's not true. Zoe loves you to death."

"Then why did Dad take me from her?"

"I don't know. I was as shocked as anybody when he ran off with you. Even more shocked that he walked out on Alex."

"My dad wouldn't do that to a kid! He wouldn't—" My voice cracks. "He wouldn't keep me from having a family."

Now I'm crying too hard to talk. It feels like my world was made of sand and I didn't know it, and a gigantic wave has crashed in, wiped it out, and left me with something that doesn't resemble my life. I don't know who Dad is anymore, or who I am. Even my name has been a lie.

Cocoa hops up on my bed and licks my cheeks. Uncle Ty smiles. "That's a good birthday gift you got there."

I sniffle. I think about how I wished for a mom and a brother when I blew out my birthday candles. Now I wish none of this was happening. No wonder people say be careful what you wish for. "What's she like?" I ask.

"Who? Your mom? Well, I've known her since I was a kid, and I'm not joking when I say she's one of the sweetest people I know. She's brilliant and strong. These past ten years were rough on her. She missed you so much."

It's weird hearing that. I figured since she didn't wanna be around, she was happy that she didn't have to be a mom. Guess that wasn't true either.

This twin brother stuff is the real trippy part. I knew I had a mom, but Dad never mentioned this kid. Now there's a whole person who looks like me and shares my birthday. I'm too shocked to be excited about it. "What's Alex like?"

"I haven't been around him much, but he's a lot like Zoe. Super smart, kind. I think you two will get along."

I stare at my socks. The hardest part about moving so much was that I was alone. I could've had a twin to go through that stuff with me had Dad taken him too.

Why *did* Dad take me and leave this other kid? He said it's complicated. What could be so complicated that he kept me from my mom? He had to have known he'd get caught one day.

A sinking feeling hits the pit of my stomach. There's no way Dad is gonna get away with taking me and that weapon Zoe mentioned. "What's gonna happen to Dad, Uncle Ty?"

He lets out a slow breath. "Hard to say. LORE doesn't believe in prisons, but who knows what they'll do, since they think he stole the Msaidizi?"

"Isn't that the Manifestor that might stop the destroyer person?"

"That's the Mshindi. I'm talking about the *Miss-a-dee-zee*." Uncle Ty sounds it out. "It's Swahili for 'helper.' It's a powerful weapon that changes form to be whatever the person it answers to needs it to be. You heard the story of John Henry?"

I nod. He was a half Giant who had once challenged a steam-powered drill to a rock-drilling contest and won using his sledgehammer.

"His sledgehammer was the Msaidizi," Uncle Ty says. "Then there's John de Conqueror."

High John, as some people called him, was a Shape-shifter who fell in love with the Devil's daughter. To get her dad's permission to marry her, he had to clear sixty acres of land in half a day, then plant and reap sixty acres of corn the other half. I guess the Devil wanted to make the world's biggest bowl of popcorn. High John used a special plow and ax to get the job done.

"Were his plow and ax the Msaidizi?" I ask.

"You got it," says Uncle Ty. "The half Giant Annie Christmas used it as a pole for her keelboat. Most recently, Roho wore it as a suit of armor."

"It helped *Roho*? He was evil!"

"The Msaidizi answers to who it is destined to answer to, regardless of their intentions," Uncle Ty says. "There's no common theme between any of the people it's answered to so far. The fact that it's been missing is a bit unnerving."

"You didn't know?" I ask.

"No. After Roho was defeated, LORE kept the Msaidizi in a secured facility. I assumed that's where it still was. I get why they didn't tell the public it was missing. People would panic. This would be like if the soul scythe went missing in the Stevie books."

Oh, geez. That's really, really bad. The soul scythe is this weapon Einan uses to steal people's souls. It makes him practically unstoppable. I almost don't wanna know the answer, but I ask anyway. "You think Dad stole the Msaidizi?"

"I don't. Calvin doesn't have any reason to take it, especially if the rumor is true."

"What rumor?"

"Some people believe that the Msaidizi will answer to the Chosen One next. Me. It would help me stop the real Manowari. Anyone who stole it would want to keep me from fulfilling my prophecy. Calvin is the exact opposite. He'd want me to have it."

"Then why does LORE think he took it?"

"It went missing the night he ran off with you. Plus, he was on the run. That doesn't exactly look innocent, Nic."

A knot swells in my throat. "Oh."

We don't say much else for a while.

"Who would steal it, though?" Uncle Ty mutters, and I don't think he's talking to me. "It couldn't be . . . could it?"

"Could it what?"

He hops up. "The time doesn't—but what if . . ." His eyes widen. "That . . . that could be it."

"Uncle Ty?" I say.

"Sorry, it's just I think I know what happened to the Msaidizi, Nic." He smiles. "More importantly, I think I can prove your dad is innocent."

"But he still kidnapped me, didn't he?"

The smile slips off his face. "Yeah."

"And he didn't tell me about my mom and my brother?"

"No, he didn't."

"And you don't know why he did it?"

"No," he admits.

"No offense, Uncle Ty, but that's what I care about. Not some weapon."

Outside my window, birds fly across the sky, and car engines hum on the street. It's not fair that everyone else's life is normal while mine's been turned upside down, inside out.

"I'm gonna get you some answers, kid," Uncle Ty says. "I don't know how, but I will."

He holds his fist out to me.

Tears blur everything around me again. I never wished for a godfather, but he may be one of the best birthday gifts I've ever gotten.

I bump his fist with mine, hoping it tells him the thank-you I can't.

SIX

TUG-OF-WAR

Last night, I dreamed my parents were playing tug-of-war, and I was the rope.

My dad had one of my arms, and Zoe had the other. They tried to pull me in opposite directions, and I was stuck in the middle, not sure which way to let myself go.

"Trust me, Nic Nac. Please!" Dad said.

"No, trust me, Alexis!" Zoe said.

I wanted to scream for them to stop, but my lips were sealed—I didn't have a voice. Worse, I didn't know who to trust. They kept pulling and pulling, and I knew if they tugged any harder, I was bound to break.

I woke up, panting. Couldn't sleep after that.

The sun is up when I start to drift off again, but my eyes haven't been closed long when I get the feeling someone's watching me. I peek out one eye and find Zoe at the foot of my bed.

"Hi?" I'm not sure what else to say to her.

She smiles like that was enough. "Hi. I didn't wake you, did I?"

I sit up. "No. I couldn't sleep anyway."

"Me either," she says, wringing her hands. "You hungry? I can make pancakes. You used to love them. I'm sorry, that was a long—I shouldn't expect you to—"

"I still like pancakes," I say.

"Oh, okay. Cool."

We're quiet as she stares at me again. I don't know if I'm supposed to stare back.

"Sorry for the awkward staring," she says. "The last time I saw you, you were asleep in a crib. A lot's changed since then."

"It's fine."

"I can imagine how you're feeling after yesterday, and here I am, making it weird with the staring." She smiles a little. "Social interactions aren't my strong suit."

"Like Chloe in the Stevie books," I say.

"Tyran and those books," she says with a slight head shake. "I still don't know how I feel about him writing about me without my permission."

"If it helps, Chloe's cool. She's my favorite, which I guess means you're my favorite. Dad and Uncle Ty wouldn't have survived without you."

"You got that right."

We both smile at that.

Zoe checks out my room. It's messy but she doesn't seem to mind. She looks at my video game collection, my sneaker collection (which nearly rivals Dad's), and my WNBA and NBA posters.

"I see somebody's a basketball fan," she says. "Who are your favorite teams?"

"In the WNBA, I like the Las Vegas Aces and the Washington Mystics. NBA, the Pelicans, but I like the Hawks too. It's kinda hard to have one favorite since—"

Since Dad and I moved from city to city 'cause we were on the run 'cause he kidnapped me. My dad kidnapped me.

My eyes prickle. My nightmare was easier to deal with than this.

Zoe sits beside me. I wait for her to tell me it's okay or encourage me to tell her how I'm feeling. Adults love talking about feelings. But she doesn't do either. Instead, she brushes her fingers through my hair. I don't know if it's the *scritch scritch* of her nails along my scalp or what, but I don't wanna cry anymore.

I look at her. "Are you using the Gift on me?"

"Not unless being a mom is part of the Gift. This always worked when you were a baby. You'd get upset, and I'd brush my fingers through your hair. Would soothe you every time."

"You remember that?"

"I remember everything. Memories were all I had."

I don't know what to say. It's weird being loved so much by somebody I don't know.

I kinda wanna know more about her. Before when I thought she didn't wanna be around, I didn't care whether we were alike or not. Now I'm thinking of things that I do that Dad doesn't, stuff I like that he doesn't, and I wonder if it came from her. "Can I ask you some questions?"

"Of course," she says, and turns all the way to me, like she wants me to have her full attention. "Ask away, pumpkin."

"For starters, why do you call me that?"

"That's an easy one," she says as a smile takes over her face. "You were a little butterball when you were a baby. You had these chubby cheeks that I swear I could've kissed all day. It only felt right to call you pumpkin."

I smile. It felt like she had hugged me without touching me. "Do you like basketball? Dad isn't as into it as I am. He's more a football guy."

"Do I? As a kid, I watched WNBA and NBA games religiously to see which players were Remarkable and didn't know it. I probably get into the games a little too much sometimes. Between you and me, I've almost gotten kicked out of a couple of RBA games."

"What's the RBA?"

"The Remarkable Basketball Association. Mostly Giants and half Giants play."

"What the what? What does the ball look like, then?"

"It's the size of a boulder. The entire arena shakes whenever someone dunks. I have courtside season tickets to the Vipers games. They're the favorites to win the title. We can go to some games after we get you settled in."

"Settled in where?"

"Oh," she says, somewhat surprised. "You didn't . . . Baby, you're coming to live with me and Alex. We're going to Uhuru tomorrow."

I sit up. "What?"

"I know this is sudden, but Uhuru is your home. You have an entire family there that loves you and misses you."

It's still a new place, and I'm gonna be the new kid. Again. "I don't wanna move."

"I know."

"I love Jackson. I need to stay here." It's a feeling deep down in my bones, as if Jackson is part of me. Leaving here would be like leaving a piece of myself behind.

"Alexis—"

"I'm not Alexis! My name's Nichole!"

She blinks fast. "I'm sorry. *Nichole*. You can't stay here, baby. Uhuru is where you belong. Remarkables shouldn't live around Unremarkables."

"Exiles do," I say, thinking of Ms. Lena and the folks in her juke joint.

"They do, but what kind of life is that, keeping who you truly are a secret? Not to mention the horror stories I've heard about Unremarkables. Killing kids in schools, killing women while they're sleeping in their beds, killing men by kneeling on them in the street. Knowing that Calvin brought you into this kinda place . . ." She closes her eyes, shakes her head. "You deserve better."

She acts like there's a world where that stuff doesn't happen, which seems impossible. "It's not like that in Uhuru?"

Zoe smiles sadly. "I hate that you have to ask that. Those situations shouldn't be seen as normal, baby. I don't care how many times it happens, how often it happens. It should *not* be normal." She cups my cheek. "In Uhuru, you'll be safe. You'll be free. You'll be loved. That's what you deserve. You, me, and Alex are gonna have a wonderful life together."

Me, her, and Alex. "What about Dad?" I ask.

"What about him?"

"What's gonna happen to him?"

"That's for LORE to decide."

"But Zoe—"

"*Mom*," she says.

Silence.

I guess neither of us knows what to call the other.

Cocoa hops up on my bed and nudges her nose against my legs. I think that's her way of telling me she needs to potty. Scooping up poop sounds way better than dealing with this. "I'm gonna take her on a walk."

"Okay."

More awkward silence. Zoe turns to leave, stops, and looks back at me. I think she's gonna say something, but she decides not to and goes on her way.

I'm feeling a lot of things, and I don't know which feeling is the right feeling or if there is a right feeling. I throw on a hoodie and some shorts, grab Cocoa and her leash, and go downstairs. . . .

Only to find my dad. Great.

He's still bound to a dining-room chair by ropes of light. A bowl and a spoon hover in front of him. The spoon tries to feed him, but Dad sees me and moves his head away from it.

"Nic Nac, hey," he says.

"Hi."

"You sleep okay?"

No, I was too busy dreaming you were playing tug-of-war with me. But I don't tell him that. "Not really."

"It was silly for me to ask. I'm so sorry, baby girl. I am."

Any time I apologize, Dad tells me to explain what I did or why I did it. He says it's an empty apology without it. That should go for him too. "Why'd you do it?"

"I can't say. You gotta trust me, Nic Nac. One day you'll understand—"

"I'll never understand why I was stolen from my mom!" I shout. Dad flinches like I hit him. "You let me think she didn't wanna be around for me."

"Baby girl, I'm sorry. I know that's not enough, but please—"

I storm outta the house with Cocoa, not wanting to hear another empty apology.

———

There's not a cloud in the sky this morning. Birds chirp happily and golden sunrays glisten on morning dewdrops. Such an awful day shouldn't be beautiful.

I let Cocoa lead the way. She zigzags from yard to yard, sniffing grass and marking her territory. Wish I only had to worry about whether some grass is worth peeing on or not.

Zoe wants me to call her Mom, but it would be weird to call a stranger Mom. Then Dad wants me to trust him, but how can I? Now I get why I dreamed they were playing tug-of-war with me.

"Wait up!" someone calls. I look back, and Alex jogs down the sidewalk toward me. Once he catches up, he says, "Mom sent me to join you. She doesn't want you to be alone."

All I wanna be is alone. "You don't have to come."

In other words, please leave, but Alex doesn't get the hint. "I'd like to come. I'm super interested in seeing Unremarkables up close."

I almost tell him they aren't that interesting—the closest thing they have to the Gift is fried fair food—but I won't ruin it for him. "If you say so."

We follow Cocoa down the sidewalk. I honestly don't know what to say to Alex. Twenty-four hours ago, I didn't know he existed. He's not just my brother but my *twin brother.*

What do I say? "Nice being outta the womb, huh?" Or "Do you still like milk these days?" I can be awkward, but not that awkward.

"So, what do I call you?" Alex asks. "My whole life I've known you as Alexis. You go by Nichole or Nic?"

"Just Nic is fine."

"Cool."

A car passes by, and Alex taps the side of his glasses. The lenses are holographic, and the glasses make a sound like a camera snapping a photo. G-glasses, another Giftech item I've heard of but never seen. They can be used like prescription glasses, or just as a fashionable tech item.

"Wow, the cars stay on the ground," Alex says. "Are all Unremarkable homes on the ground as well?"

"Where else are they supposed to be?"

"In the sky, underwater, in trees," Alex says, as if it's obvious. "Or underground like in N'okpuru. Though from the looks of their primitive nature, I doubt Unremarkables possess the advanced technology for diverse habitation. What kind of currency do they use? Is it physical or have they gone fully electronic yet?"

He sounds like a forty-year-old professor in a twelve-year-old's body. "They use both."

"Fascinating. LORE switched to electronic currency decades ago. I can only imagine the amount of bacteria and disease that physical currency carries."

Meanwhile I kiss a dollar when I find one. I've never felt more unlike a kid in my life. "Yeaaaah. Bacteria. Scary."

Alex taps the side of his G-glasses some more. "My teachers are going to love my report on Unremarkables."

"You're not on summer break?"

"I am, but it's never too early to begin preparing for the next school year. A report on Unremarkables in their natural habitats is guaranteed to get me an A-plus."

"You make them sound like animals in a zoo."

"Compared to grootslangs, Unremarkables are far more interesting."

"Groot-what?" I ask.

"Half elephant, half anaconda," he says, like I should know. "Unremarkables don't have them in their zoos?"

"No! They have regular elephants and snakes."

"Geez. What about dragons?"

My. Mouth. Drops. "You have dragons in your zoo?"

"Technically dragons aren't in zoos but on farms. In kindergarten, we'd visit the baby dragon farm and ride around on them."

You mean to tell me I was stuck feeding baby goats at the petting zoo when I could've been riding dragons? "I've always wanted a dragon," I say.

"Why? They're super destructive unless they're properly trained."

"I'd train it to attack my enemies."

"You have enemies?" he asks.

"Not yet, but in case I do—dragon."

"Interesting," he says, like that tells him everything he needs to know about me. Not sure I'm cool with that. "Don't you think we should head back? We've traveled too far without adult supervision."

"Bruh, we've only gone around the corner."

"That's too far without a bodyguard."

"You have a *bodyguard*?"

"Of course. Mom had one child kidnapped by that criminal," he says, and I flinch at "criminal." "She wasn't going to risk it happening to another. Plus with Grandma being the president—"

"The president of what?" I ask.

"Oh boy Du Bois! He didn't tell you? Mom's mom is the president of LORE".

What the what? "She is?"

"Yes! Why do you think your kidnapping was such a huge deal? Granted, anyone being kidnapped would be a huge deal, but yours was a huge, huge deal. You were kidnapped the night she was elected."

My ears hear him, but my brain is stuck. "Really?"

Alex taps his G-glasses a few times, and a miniature hologram of a Manifestor man at a news desk floats between us.

"What started as a celebration ended in tragedy," the man says. "Last night as President-Elect Natalie DuForte celebrated her victory with family and friends, it appears that her two-year-old granddaughter, Alexis Blake, was kidnapped by her father, Calvin Blake. LWTV's very own Donna Balzer has more."

The mini hologram becomes a Manifestor woman in front of a mansion.

"That's right, Adam," she says. "According to officials, Zoe DuForte returned home from her mother's celebration and found her babysitter unconscious from a knockout juju. Once she went to her twins' bedroom, she found her son, Alexander, unharmed, but her daughter, Alexis, was missing. Several witnesses saw Calvin Blake flee the home with the toddler. From what we've been told, the recently divorced Ms. DuForte and Mr. Blake have been going through a nasty custody battle that seems to have reached a fever pitch with tonight's kidnapping. Though the Guardian force went after Blake, he managed to escape Uhuru. I spoke with the distraught mother earlier."

The hologram becomes Zoe. She's obviously younger, but the bags under her wet, weary eyes make her look older than she is now.

"I just want my baby back," she cries. "Please, Calvin, bring her back."

A lump swells in my throat. This is a lot.

Alex taps his G-glasses again, and a poster floats between us. On one side of the poster there's a photo of a smiling baby girl. On the other, an age-progressed drawing that looks like me now. At the top it says, "Missing Child: Alexis Nichole Blake, Granddaughter of President Natalie DuForte. Reward: five million Ben-E's. If spotted, contact LORE immediately."

The image dissolves and changes into a wanted poster for Dad. He's younger, with a short haircut and a clean-shaven face, and he's wearing glasses. There's a five million Ben-E reward for his capture.

"Those are all over the G-net," Alex says. "There's also

an annual TV special to mark the anniversary of your disappearance."

I sit on the curb. A grandma for president, millions in reward money, TV specials. Seems like nothing about my life before was true.

Alex turns off the hologram and sits beside me. "Sorry if I overwhelmed you."

"You're not the first," I mumble as Cocoa rests her head in my lap. I scratch her back. "I didn't know anything until yesterday."

"Our father didn't even tell you about me?"

"No," I say, and I feel bad about it. Not that it's my fault, but it can't be easy hearing that your dad didn't talk about you.

"Oh," he says, and I feel worse. "I always knew about you. On holidays, Mom would have a plate for you at the dinner table, and on Christmas and our birthday, she'd have presents with your name on them. She tried to hide her sadness from me, but I always knew that when she disappeared into her room, she was crying over you."

"Did that happen a lot?"

"More often than I'd like. I only wanted her to be happy, but she never truly was . . . because you weren't there."

That's nothing like what I imagined. To be honest, part of me hated my mom for not being around. She didn't wanna be there for me? Fine, I didn't need her. She was the one missing out.

Now to find out she cried 'cause she wasn't there . . . it's like Alex tossed my feelings into a blender and turned it on high speed.

"I'm glad this is over now, for Mom's sake," he says. "I'm sure Grandma is already planning a big celebration for your return. A parade. A party. She may declare it a holiday." He rolls his eyes. "Meanwhile I get perfect test scores and only get a raise in my allowance."

It doesn't sound like he's happy I've been found. Maybe I should've wished for a brother who wanted a sister and not just for a brother. "Sorry? Trust me, I don't want the attention."

Something in the sky catches his attention. "You better get ready for it. Here comes LORE."

I look where he's staring. "Where? I don't see anything."

He lifts this thing off his ear that resembles the wireless earbuds, and his holographic glasses disappear. He hands it to me.

I slip it on. The G-glasses reappear in front of my eyes, and icons float around me. It's like I'm inside a phone. Some of the icons say normal stuff like Notes or Camera. Others say 1001 Mojos and Tonic Direct. One icon called X-ray mode flashes green. I look at the trees and houses, and I can see through them. Looking at Alex, I see his bones. Then I look up.

A gold V-shaped aircraft speeds across the sky. It could be a spaceship 'cause of how it looks, or a rocket as fast as it flies. I'm used to hearing a rumble from plane engines, but this thing is silent. There's a red, black, and green flag with a golden lion in the middle of it painted on its tail. On the underbelly it says "Guardian Force."

"What's the Guardian Force?" I ask Alex.

"The LORE police. They're here to arrest our father."

SEVEN
THE GUARDIAN FORCE

I can't run home fast enough.

Cocoa and I bound down the sidewalk. Without Alex's G-glasses, I can't see the LORE jet, but I bet it's at my house by now. They may be arresting Dad at this very moment.

Alex's footsteps aren't far behind mine. "What are you doing?"

I don't know, but I keep running.

I don't get far. A block away from my house, I see a dozen Manifestors wearing gold-plated tribal masks and white leather jumpsuits rush through my front door.

Alex comes up beside me. "See? There's nothing you can do."

He's probably right, but I can't just stand here. "I need to sneak in through the back."

"What?" Alex says as I run off with Cocoa.

I dart down Coach and Mrs. Green's driveway and through the gate to their backyard. The Greens are this really nice couple who give out cookies to everyone on the block for special occasions. They won't mind me running through their backyard and climbing their fence with my hellhound and my brother.

Mr. Ingram next door to them probably won't like that I run through his yard and get his old bulldog worked up. The bulldog growls and barks at Cocoa from a window. I pick Cocoa up and climb the fence into the McCollums' yard before Mr. Ingram can come see what the ruckus is about.

"This is trespassing!" Alex says as we cross the McCollums' backyard.

"Only if we get caught."

"That's not how the law works!"

It is today. We climb into JP's backyard. Since it's Sunday morning, he and his parents are still at church and won't be home for hours. Pastor Williams preaches long sermons. I cross their yard, then climb into mine.

Out-of-breath Alex climbs the fence and falls over onto the other side. "I did not plan to break a sweat this early. What now?"

"I need to see what's going on in there."

"I have a solution for that."

Alex crawls toward my house. I follow him and we end up under the kitchen window with our backs against the wall.

Alex taps the side of his G-glasses. "Shared mode," he says.

I yelp as my backyard disappears and Alex and I are suddenly on my kitchen floor.

"Four-dimensional holographic projection," he says. "Physically, we're outside, but this allows us to see what's happening inside the house. Don't worry, they can't see us."

"They" are a dozen Guardians, rummaging around my house. The onyx markings on their masks resemble various animals and creatures; each mask is unique. Two Guardians stand guard near Dad, Zoe, and Uncle Ty, who are bound to chairs by ropes of light.

Alex's forehead wrinkles. "Why is Mom tied up?"

Dad has more ropes around him than the other two. Part of me is like, "Yeah! Punish him!" But the part that loves the guy with the silly dance moves has a hard time seeing this.

A short, lean, brown-skinned woman in a gold jumpsuit slowly paces in front of him. Specks of gold flicker through her natural black bun.

"That's General Sharpe, the head Guardian," Alex whispers. "She used to go to school with our parents and Mr. Porter. I heard she was a tattletale back then. These days there aren't many Remarkables who *aren't* afraid of her."

"Althea," Zoe says, "would you please explain why your officers bound *me*?"

"It's General Sharpe, not Althea, and this isn't Douglass

Academy, *Ms. DuForte*. Having powerful parents doesn't put you above the law anymore." She sneers at Uncle Ty. "Neither does being the Not-So-Chosen One."

Uncle Ty's jaw hardens as some Guardians snicker. What does she mean by that?

"Tyran did more to stop Roho than any of us!" Zoe says.

"Keep telling yourself that," General Sharpe says as she steps up to Dad. She grabs his chin, and her long gold-painted nails dig into his skin. "Calvin Blake. I've waited years to say this. You're under arrest for kidnapping and for stealing—"

A Guardian clears their throat.

"On *suspicion* of stealing the Msaidizi," General Sharpe says. "You will be taken to Uhuru, where you will be tried by the Council of Elders. Do you have anything to say?"

I want him to apologize for what he's done, offer some kinda explanation, but he simply bows his head.

"I didn't think so," General Sharpe says smugly. She looks at Zoe and Uncle Ty. "As for you two, you failed to alert LORE of Calvin Blake's whereabouts the moment you found him. You will be tried by the council as well."

"What?" Alex squeaks.

General Sharpe's head whips toward the kitchen window. "What was that?"

I clamp my hand over Alex's mouth. Please don't let the Guardians look outside. . . .

But Dad looks this way, and his eyes get slightly wide. No way, can he see us?

He looks at General Sharpe. "Wow, Althea. Little noises got you nervous? Guess you're the scaredy-cat you always were."

Her nostrils flare. "Too bad you and your friends aren't the 'heroes' everyone thought you were. Well, everyone but me. I always knew you three were no good."

A Guardian in a tiger mask walks up to General Sharpe. "Ma'am? There's no sign of the Msaidizi or the twins. We searched the entire premises."

They must've searched before we got back.

General Sharpe raises an amused brow. "Oh? I should've known. I'm sure the infamous three here sent them off with it. Anything to get your way, right?"

"What? No!" Zoe says.

"Why would we do that?" Dad says. "Why would *I* take the Msaidizi?"

"Maybe you wanted it for yourself," Sharpe says. "Or maybe you planned to sell it. I'd bet these two were accomplices somehow. I've got several theories of my own, but the fact remains that it was taken from Uhuru the same night you left. That's far more than a coincidence."

"Look, Althea, Cal didn't take the Msaidizi," Uncle Ty says. "I think I know what happened. If you free me, I can search—"

"Ha! I would be the laughingstock of LORE if I let *you* search for the Msaidizi."

"You don't understand! Please—"

General Sharpe does a zipping motion, and Uncle Ty's

lips press together tightly. "Better. Let's go to the ship and assemble search teams. Those twins couldn't have gone far. Wherever they are, I bet that's where the Msaidizi is."

Zoe tries to break free. "Don't touch my babies!"

General Sharpe zips her mouth shut. Then the general raises her hand, and my parents and Uncle Ty levitate off their chairs.

The general marches toward the front door, and the three of them float behind her, with the Guardians following.

Dad looks back toward the kitchen window, and it's as if he's looking right at me and Alex. He mouths two words.

"Find it."

Less than two minutes after the Guardians leave with our parents and Uncle Ty, Alex loses it.

"We're fugitives!" he wails at my kitchen table.

I sit here in a daze. I never would've thought that my dad would be a wanted criminal or that the mom I just met would be arrested. It's hard to believe this is my life.

And it's all Dad's fault. Sorry—the stranger who calls himself my dad. The dad I knew wasn't real.

After five minutes, I snap out of my daze and tell Alex to call our grandma. She's the freaking president, there's gotta be something she can do. But Alex says the Guardians may intercept the call. I grab my G-pen and suggest using it.

"We can't. They could trace our location like Mom

99

traced yours," he tells me, which makes sense, but then this boy goes, "We should call the Unremarkable police."

I look at him like he grew a second head. "Why in the world would we do that?"

"We're minors without adult supervision. Can't they bring us meals and send someone to keep us entertained until Mom comes back? That's what the Guardian force would do if we weren't considered fugitives."

"No! Besides, you really wanna tell Unremarkables that a secret police force arrested our parents for stealing a powerful weapon and took them away in an invisible jet?"

"Valid," Alex admits. "We wait for Mom, then. They won't keep her long. She'll get us as soon as she's free."

Except thirty minutes pass, and there's no sign of Zoe.

Forty-five minutes, nothing.

An hour in, I get this scary thought—the Guardians could come back. I figure we need to get outta here, so I rush upstairs and throw some essentials into my backpack, including the Miss Peachy's bag I got on my birthday. You never know, it may come in handy. I tell Alex we should go, but he hyperventilates at the idea of going anywhere without an adult and says he'd rather get caught by the Guardians. This is not what I imagined when I wished for a brother.

It's been two hours now, and Alex and I still can't agree on what to do.

I sit on the floor and feed Cocoa some treats. Alex impatiently taps the kitchen table, his eyes trained on the front door. "Any minute now, Mom will come back," he says.

I stopped believing that an hour ago. "I don't think she's coming, Alex."

"Yes, she is! She's innocent! She doesn't deserve this!"

He looks away, but not quick enough. I see that his eyes are wet.

I hand him a napkin. I can't cry too. I may not stop.

Alex wipes his face. "Thanks."

We don't say anything for a while. This must be what having a twin is like. You get someone who automatically understands.

"Can't believe General Sharpe thinks Mom is in cahoots with that low-down, dirty—"

Aaaand the moment is over. "Hey, watch it."

"You're sticking up for him? He lied to you your whole life!"

I know that, but he's—I can't say a good guy, 'cause good guys don't kidnap one kid and abandon the other. But I still . . . love him? Do I even know him? I wanna say no, except . . .

Way deep down, this little voice in my head tells me Dad loves me, that I should trust him, and that he took me for a good reason. It's the same voice that told me we needed to move to Jackson. Right now, it keeps reminding me of what Dad did before the Guardians took him.

He told me to find it.

"When they were taking Dad, did it seem like he looked at us?" I ask Alex.

His face scrunches like he swallowed a lemon. "That's impossible and illogical. He can't see through walls."

"He somehow did, Alex, and he told us to find it. Did he mean the Ms—"

Cocoa's growling cuts me off. I follow her eyes, and the bag of treats falls from my hands.

Three men just appeared in my backyard.

Alex sees them too. "Hide!"

I snatch up my backpack, and we hurry into the pantry. Cocoa watches us and tilts her head. I hiss at her to come on. It's not until I show her another bag of treats that she joins us.

We close the pantry door just as glass shatters.

"Looks clear," a gruff voice says. Feet crunch over the broken glass. "You're sure the Guardians got Blake?"

"Positive, boss," says a high-pitched voice. "My connection said we'd find all kinds of goods here."

A smoother voice goes, "Who would've thought a Guardian would help scavengers?"

I've heard of scavengers. They're exiles who go around stealing Remarkable items and artifacts. They'll do whatever to get what they want, and the last thing you want is to cross their path . . . or be stuck in a house with them.

"Snoop, hit the basement," the gruff-voiced one says. "Rock, upstairs. I got dibs on the first floor."

I crack the door an inch. A hairy Black man with locs

and a goatee gives orders. His gray Glow tells me he's a Rougarou. So does the wet-dog odor coming from him, geez. A brown-skinned man with a red Glow goes into the basement—a Vampire. The other man is dark brown and thin, wears a do-rag, and has tattoos and an orange Glow. A Shapeshifter. He goes upstairs.

The Rougarou throws open our kitchen cabinets. He tosses out dishes and glasses, breaking them to bits. He chucks the mug I bought Dad for Father's Day. Sounds like his buddies are trashing the basement and upstairs.

"Nic, I'm sorry," Alex says softly.

I ball my fists at my sides. I wish I could run out there and jump these jerks. . . .

"Hey, boss!" the Shapeshifter calls out. "I found something interesting up here."

"It better be good," says the Rougarou. His footsteps thump up the stairs.

"We need to leave," I whisper to Alex. I put Cocoa in my backpack and let her head stick out the top. "We can't stay in the house as long as they're here."

"No!" Alex whisper-shouts. "We wait for them to leave. Mom—"

"She's not coming, Alex! These guys are dangerous. We need to go, now." When he doesn't respond, I say, "I know we're basically strangers, but you gotta trust me. Please?"

I can practically hear the back-and-forth in his head, and I can see the moment he decides to give me a shot.

Alex opens the pantry door.

I sling my backpack over my shoulder as we hurry out, but just as we do, JP strolls into my backyard, wearing a fanny pack and a red "Vacation Bible School" T-shirt.

"Hey, Nic!" he says loudly. He sees Alex. "Hi, kid I don't know! I wanted to say goodbye before I leave for my camping trip."

Shoot, shoot, shoot! Alex and I wildly wave our arms to get him to shut up.

"What?" JP calls out louder. "Are y'all okay?"

The Rougarou storms down the stairs. He spots us. "Hey!"

Alex and I rush out the back door. I grab JP's hand, and the three of us take off.

Unfortunately, Rougarous are fast. I'm talking track-star fast. We race down the sidewalk, and though we got a head start, the Rougarou snarls and snaps his teeth only feet away. His wet-dog odor makes my eyes water. His Shapeshifter friend tries to catch up, and strangely enough, he has his phone pointed at us. Cocoa barks smoke at them from my backpack.

We pass Unremarkables on the sidewalk. I don't know what they see, but none of them seem to care that three kids and a dog are being chased by a Rougarou and a Shapeshifter.

A busy intersection awaits us. We can't stop to cross. Just ten seconds is enough for the Rougarou to catch up.

"Which way do we go?" JP asks.

"Left!" I say, while Alex says, "Right!"

"Guys! Which way?"

"Left!" I repeat, and again Alex says, "Right!"

"Guys!" JP hollers.

The Rougarou closes in. He could pounce any moment. . . .

An old pink convertible screeches to a halt at the stop sign, driven by a familiar face.

"Get in!" Ms. Lena says.

Where—? How—? Forget it. I hop in the car, and Alex and JP follow my lead. Ms. Lena speeds off, and the Rougarou is a hairy dot in the distance.

EIGHT

JP CAN SEE

Ms. Lena takes us to her juke joint. Only a few customers and Ms. Sadie the Aziza sit around.

"Lock the doors," Ms. Lena orders. "If them scavengers show up, deal with them."

Ms. Sadie nods. A couple of folks stare at JP 'cause he doesn't have the Glow. JP stares back just as hard.

"That's a fairy!" he says, pointing at Ms. Sadie. She scowls. Don't *ever* call her a Fairy. "Is she talking to a were-wolf?"

Ms. Lena hurries him along. "The correct names are Aziza and Rougarou. Less talking, more walking, boy."

She takes us to her office, closes the door, and orders us to sit on her beat-up sofa as she goes over to her mini fridge.

We plop down, sweating and panting. Cocoa goes from lap to lap, licking our faces like, "Good job getting away from those scavengers."

I feel a pang in my chest. I won't ever see my house the way it used to be. The scavengers are gonna trash it.

JP looks around the office in awe. "What *is* this place?"

Tiny black-and-white lightning birds chirp in cages, and tonic vials glow in the sunlight. A demon no bigger than Cocoa snoozes in a cage in a corner, and blue-glass bottles of haints rattle on a shelf in the very back.

Ms. Lena brings us a couple of waters. "I'm Lena, this my juke joint. Since you saw Sadie's true form, you a Seer, an Unremarkable who can see the Remarkable."

Holy moly. That explains it.

"Heeey!" JP says. "I may not be the smartest guy, but you don't have to call me unremarkable!"

"*That's* what you're focused on?" Alex says.

JP tilts his head. "Who are you?"

Between finding out I was kidnapped, that my dad may be a criminal, and that I have a mom and a twin brother, I never got a chance to tell JP what's going on. "He's Alex, my twin brother. Long story. Alex, this is JP, my best friend."

"You're friends with an *Unremarkable*?" Alex says the word like it tastes bad. "Geez, Mom should've rescued you a long time ago."

JP narrows his eyes. "I don't know what that means, but I resent it."

"As you should," Ms. Lena says, with a sideways look

at Alex. "Unremarkable ain't a bad thing. You simply don't have Remarkable powers, and it's rare for Unremarkables to see the Remarkable without a wand. Bet you've seen strange things your whole life, haven't you?"

"Yeah!" JP says. "When I was five, I saw a fairy in my granddad's backyard. My dad said it was a cockroach. Super offensive to the fairy when you think about it. In third grade, I told everybody my teacher was a vampire, but nooo. 'JP has a wild imagination.' In fifth grade—"

"JP," I say. If I don't stop him, he'll tell his entire life story. "We get it."

"So all the stuff I've seen is real? I haven't been imagining it?"

"It's very real," Ms. Lena says. "You can also identify folks that are Remarkable too. We got a Glow 'bout us, don't we?"

"Yeah! I thought you just had good skin-care routines."

Ms. Lena chuckles. "Angel pee keeps my skin nice, but that's my Glow you see."

Ew, no thank you. I'd rather deal with pimples.

"Seers like you are rare," Ms. Lena goes on. "Most likely you descend from a Dud."

"Isn't that a firecracker that doesn't pop?" JP asks.

"It's also what we call somebody who should be Remarkable but ain't," Ms. Lena says. "An ancestor of yours probably should've been a Manifestor. That's a person similar to them wizards you see in books and movies, but more powerful. These two here are Manifestors."

JP gasps. "Nic, you're a wizard? Do you have a wand?"

Alex gasps louder than he did. "How dare—"

"Manifestors don't need wands," Ms. Lena cuts in. "Wizards and magic are a touchier subject we won't get into."

"We shouldn't be getting into any of this!" Alex says. "According to the statute of—"

Ms. Lena waves him off. "Statute my behind. The boy gotta know the truth. I've got a feeling y'all gon' need him to help you with this mess."

"You know what happened?" I ask.

"I had a vision of your daddy tied up. Didn't know what it meant. My vision didn't reveal everything, but they never do. What happened, li'l girl?"

I start at the beginning, with the "Dad kidnapped me" stuff, then the Msaidizi, the Guardians, and the scavengers. We give JP a quick lesson on LORE and the Msaidizi. He asks if it can change into a pair of underwear—someone could need clean undies as much as John Henry needed a hammer. I seriously wonder what goes on in that brain of his sometimes.

"Lord. I'd heard rumors that the Msaidizi was missing," Ms. Lena says. "Not real surprised they're true. I can't believe LORE thinks Calvin stole it. I knew he was bound to get caught for taking you, but accusing him of that is ridiculous."

"Hold up. You knew he kidnapped me? And you knew his name was really Calvin?"

"I figured it out eventually," Ms. Lena says. "Y'all were once a headline story. I remember seeing your momma crying on TV. 'Bout broke my heart. Then a few years ago, a shapeshifting friend in New Orleans asked me to hire an associate who was moving to Jackson. They said he was good at creature catching. Didn't tell me he was a fugitive, but us exiles don't get into that kinda talk. Each of us got our own issues with LORE. I can't lie to you—once I saw your daddy and realized who he was, I almost turned him in.

"But my gut told me not to, and it ain't failed me yet. He didn't seem like the man they portrayed, which led me to believe he must've had good reason for what he did. I hired him. He's not the first fugitive to come to Lena's. Plenty walk through that door. They know this is a safe place. It helps that a Manifestor friend of mine put a secret-keeping juju on the joint. You could come in here with a secret, tell it to every person in here, and not one of them could repeat it once they left. Nobody could leave here knowing who he was and rat him out."

"Basically, you help criminals," Alex says.

"I live in a glass house, so I never pick up stones," says Ms. Lena. "Now, I'd bet my life your daddy didn't steal the Msaidizi. As many times as that boy done had haints blow toilets up in his face, shoot nah. He would've used the Msaidizi to help him. Somebody else must've taken it."

I think back to Dad looking at us before he left and mouthing those words. "Why would he want us to find it?"

"What you mean, girl?" Ms. Lena says.

"Dad looked at us somehow as the Guardians were taking him—"

"She thinks he did," Alex says. "It's impossible."

"I know what I saw. He told us to find it," I say. "I think he meant the Msaidizi."

"He most likely did see you," Ms. Lena says. "He wears Giftech contacts. He can see through walls with 'em."

"He does?" Yet another thing I didn't know.

Ms. Lena nods. "Mmmhmm. They come in handy in his line of work. He probably wants y'all to find the Msaidizi 'cause it tells its own story. It can tell LORE how it went missing and clear his name. He needs you, chile."

He needs me.

He needs *me*?

I hop up and pace. There's no way. No freaking way.

"That probably ain't an easy thing to hear," Ms. Lena says.

I whirl on her. "You think? I just found out my life's a big fat lie 'cause of him, and now he wants me to *help* him? He won't even tell me why he took me!"

"He's still your dad, Nic," JP says.

I fold my arms tight. "So? I don't wanna help him."

"That makes two of us," says Alex. "He doesn't deserve our help."

"He don't," Ms. Lena agrees. "Y'all got every right to be mad at him. Downright ticked off, if you ask me. But this ain't just 'bout helping him. For one, it's 'bout helping your momma and Tyran."

111

"They're innocent," Alex says.

"Knowing Althea Sharpe, she gon' try to see that the hammer comes down on them. They need as much help as they can get. This is also 'bout helping yourselves."

There's this grimness about her voice that stops me in my tracks. "Why do you say that?"

"LORE might give Calvin the maximum punishment for stealing the Msaidizi. They may take the Gift outta him or . . . they might erase his memory."

I unfold my arms. "What?"

"LORE don't believe in prisons. With good reason. It's a form of modern-day slavery. Don't get me started on the Unremarkable prison system. LORE believes in rehabilitation instead. If the crime is bad enough, they remove that Remarkable's power until the person learns to be better. Sometimes they never give it back. For the real bad crimes, LORE erases a criminal's memories, so that person can start anew."

"But then he wouldn't remember me," I say.

"He also wouldn't be able to explain why he took you and left this one." She motions at Alex. "LORE won't wipe his memory for kidnapping you, but I wouldn't put it past them to do it over the Msaidizi to make an example outta him. You gotta clear his name to get some answers. Only way to do that is by finding the Msaidizi and the real thief."

I sit on the couch. I want Dad to get what he deserves. I don't wanna care about what happens to him, and yet . . .

ugh, I do care. Although he hurt me, I know he loves me and I love him too.

I hate having feelings, bleh.

I also gotta admit that Dad shouldn't be punished for something he didn't do. Ms. Lena and Uncle Ty don't think he took the Msaidizi, plus I've never seen him use a powerful weapon of any kind. It wouldn't be fair for him to lose his memory or the Gift over it.

The big problem? Dad's asking me to do something impossible. "How could we find the Msaidizi, Ms. Lena? LORE couldn't, and they're a government. We're kids."

"I'm gon' guess LORE focused more on looking for Calvin than for the Msaidizi itself. That allowed the real thief to get away with it. And so what, you kids? When your parents and Tyran were kids, they traveled in time, went to different realms—"

"Whoa! Out time!" JP says.

"Do you mean time out?" I ask.

"Not important!" JP says. "What did you mean that Nic's parents traveled in time and went to different realms? That sounds like what happens in the Stevie books."

I explain that Mr. Porter is the real Stevie and my parents are Kevin and Chloe.

"Holy baloney Tony!" he says. Only JP would say that.

"Uh-huh, and while the books ain't completely accurate, a lot of it is right on the money," Ms. Lena says. "Being kids didn't stop them. Why should it stop you?"

I could give her a long list, starting with the big one: they knew how to use the Gift, I don't. Besides . . . "We don't know where to start," I say.

"Or what to look for," Alex adds. "The Msaidizi changes form. It could be anything."

"Like underwear," JP says.

"Look for this." Ms. Lena pulls out a necklace from under her shirt and shows us the tree-shaped pendant hanging from it. Rubies glisten along the limbs. "We call this the Mark of Eden. It's an ancient symbol that'll be on the Msaidizi."

I've never seen that mark before, but just looking at the pendant makes the hairs on my arms rise. Everything about it screams *power*.

I bet the Msaidizi does the same. "Uh, Ms. Lena? The Msaidizi is pretty powerful, right? Wouldn't it be dangerous to look for someone who's stolen it?"

"Thank you!" Alex says. "They could use it on us."

"I ain't say take the thief down! Find it and let LORE know who has it and where it is. Goodness, girl, be smart, not brave!"

The smart thing to do is to say no to this. It's impossible. "I don't think I can find it."

"You can," Ms. Lena says. "Your daddy believes in you. You oughta."

I hate how hearing that makes me think I have a chance. Dad still has that effect on me. "Where would we even look, Ms. Lena?"

She sits back, folding her arms. "That's where things get interesting. I told y'all, I heard rumors the Msaidizi was missing. I also heard that it was spotted in my hometown."

"New Orleans?" I say.

She nods. "Wouldn't surprise me if the perp was down there. New Orleans is the most remarkable Unremarkable city in the world. The Msaidizi was used there by both High John and Annie Christmas. The Gift left its mark on that place."

"I'm not going to an unfamiliar city to help that thief," Alex says. "I don't care about getting answers that much."

"You sure?" Ms. Lena asks. "'Cause the Guardians are on their way here."

"You had a vision?" I ask.

"Nah. I'm listening in on their audio feed." She points to what I thought was a silver earring. "Gotta keep up with what they do since some 'questionable' folks spend time here. Just heard one of the commanders send out the order."

"We need to go to New Orleans," I say.

"Then what?" says Alex. "We search the entire city for a weapon that changes form?"

"I can send word to my shapeshifting friend down there who can help y'all look," Ms. Lena says. "A thing that powerful is bound to leave a trail."

Alex folds his arms. "I'm not traveling to a city I've never been to before. Mom would be worried sick if she found out! We can't do that to her."

"Alex, please?"

"No, Nic. You didn't hear her crying. I did. It messed her up bad, not having you around. I don't care about getting answers from him. Nothing he could tell me would make what he did to her any better."

I hear him, and trust me, I get it. I'm going back and forth between wanting to help Dad and letting him deal with whatever happens.

But I want answers. I deserve them. I find that Msaidizi and save Dad, he'll have no choice but to look me in the eye and tell me exactly why he kidnapped me and lied to me. That's the only reason I'm doing this.

I gotta change Alex's mind somehow. I bet he knows how to use the Gift. He probably only knows a few basic jujus like most Manifestor kids our age, but that's more than I can do. I've got no chance without him. "Alex, please? Obviously they haven't cleared Zoe, or she would've come and gotten us by now, right?"

He slowly unfolds his arms. "I suppose."

"Then Ms. Lena is right—we need to find the Msaidizi for her sake. It can tell LORE that Zoe didn't tell us to run off with it. She needs us."

That last part seems to do the trick. "As long as this is about helping Mom and not him, I'll go."

"I'll go too," JP says. "My parents think I'm on my camping trip. Plus I love beignets and po'boys and gumbo and pralines. Not crawfish though. I can't eat anything that has eyes."

116

I smile. I can always count on JP. I look to Ms. Lena. "How do we get to New Orleans?"

"We can take a rideshare," JP says.

Ms. Lena sets her hand on her hip. "You got rideshare money?"

That's a no from me. I only have my birthday money, and it's not enough for a three-hour ride to New Orleans. "How else do we get there then?"

Ms. Lena wears a knowing smile. "I have a way."

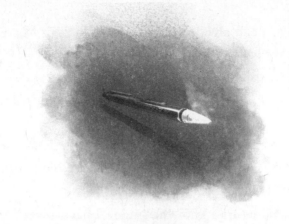

NINE

THE (LITERAL) UNDERGROUND RAILROAD

Ms. Lena goes over to the shelf where the lightning bird-cages are. The birds squawk and beat their wings, making small bolts of lightning flash around them.

"Open up," she says.

The shelf swings open like a door, revealing a set of stairs that go downward. Ms. Lena hums as she goes down a couple of the steps. She stops and looks back at us. "Well? Y'all waiting for the Guardians to come knocking or what?"

Uh, okay. I put Cocoa in my backpack, slip it on, and we follow Ms. Lena.

The wooden stairs creak under our weight, and I wave cobwebs outta my face. A thick blanket of dust covers the stairs, and it gets stuffier the farther down we go.

"Ain't gonna let no-body turn me around," Ms. Lena

sings. "Turn me around, turn me around. Ain't gonna let no-body turn me around. . . ."

At the civil rights museum, I saw videos of marches where folks were singing that song. But as Ms. Lena sings, lights flicker on, and a new step appears with each word. Seriously, one second there's nothing and the next, a stair.

"I'm gonna keep on walking, keep on talking, marching into free-dom land."

Her voice echoes off the stone walls. It sounds as if other voices are joining in. Rich yet whispery voices. The lights brighten. The chill leaves the air. I think Ms. Lena's song is bringing this place to life.

A faint boom rattles the ceiling, sending dirt raining onto us.

"What was that?" Alex squeaks.

"Ah, sounds like the Guardians showed up," Ms. Lena says. "My girl Sadie must've used that Aziza strength on them. Probably tossed one clean across the juke joint. Folks always underestimate Azizas."

"Won't she be in trouble?" I ask.

"Nothing new. Sadie got a record longer than a Giant's arm. That's my fly or die right there."

Well, geez.

Ms. Lena steps onto a landing, and several lights come on at once. We're in a vast stone room. There are several tunnels with train tracks coming out of them. Where the tracks meet in the center, an odd vehicle awaits. It's shiny silver and resembles an RV—has a door and wide windows on the sides—but it also has a smokestack and big wheels with pistons like a locomotive.

"Welcome," Ms. Lena says, "to the Underground Railroad."

My mouth falls open. "I thought this got shut down!"

"It was!" Alex whirls on Ms. Lena. "LORE shut it down during the war on Roho. Nobody is supposed to be able to access it!"

Ms. Lena sizes him up. "Since when do exiles answer to LORE? They only closed routes that led to Remarkable cities. Some of us exiles use the tunnels to travel to Unremarkable cities. Me and ol' Bertha here used to take plenty of trips."

"The Underground Railroad is an actual railroad?" JP asks. "In school they said it was routes and safe houses."

"The Unremarkable one was, but it was named after this one," Ms. Lena says. "And this one was used to help enslaved peoples too. You see, way back in the day, the main purpose of LORE was to find enslaved Remarkables and get them to freedom. They'd send spies to plantations to find folks with the Glow, and the spies would speak the ancient words to reactivate their Gift. But it was impossible to leave nonGifted people behind, so they'd help them escape as well. Once slavery ended, Black folks were still terrorized and treated less than human. My granddaddy used to say LORE had plans to form an army to liberate them."

"What stopped that?" I ask.

"Your guess is as good as mine. Anyway, many folks found themselves here. You're in a sacred place, chile."

I can almost see families huddled around, scared yet excited. Hopeful but weary. I don't wanna think about what they went through to get here, but I'm glad they did.

We follow Ms. Lena onto the train, and the inside is much bigger than it looks. The front is set up like a living-room area with a couch, a recliner, and a television. Behind that is the kitchen with a booth under a window. Ms. Lena leads us toward the back, where there are four curtained bunk beds, two on each side.

"Bathroom's through there." She points at the door at the very back. "Should be some toiletries and some food in the kitchen from my last trip. Keep this place clean now. Bring Bertha back looking a mess and we'll have a problem. Any questions?"

Alex raises his hand. "Not only am I uncomfortable at the idea of traveling without an adult, but I don't know how to operate a train. Nic and JP most likely don't either."

JP and I shake our heads. Not unless driving a train on a video game counts, and even then we killed a ton of NPCs.

"Y'all ain't gotta drive," Ms. Lena says. "You tell Bertha where you need to go, and she'll get you there. The more specific, the better. Too vague and she may take you somewhere random."

"That's it?" I say.

Ms. Lena tosses me a brass key. "That's it. Oh, and

keep the door locked. All sorts of creatures lurk the Underground."

"Creatures?" Alex says, wide-eyed.

"Oooh, what kind?" JP adds.

"The kind you don't wanna cross," Ms. Lena warns darkly. "Good luck! Once you get to New Orleans, follow the exit signs out the Underground. I'll tell my friend to meet y'all at the door. Hope y'all come back in one piece, and if you don't, I hope you can be put back together."

Talk about a disturbing send-off.

As she leaves the train, I think about the last time I saw Ms. Lena; how she grabbed my hands, how I saw her vision, how she freaked out and her aura flickered.

I set Cocoa down and go after Ms. Lena. She's halfway up the staircase when I reach out—

"No, girl, I can't explain what you did that day," she says.

I didn't even touch her! "You had a vision that I was coming after you?"

"Who needs a vision when you heavy-footed?" She turns around with a judgy glare. "Learn to pick your feet up!"

"Sorry."

"Uh-huh. It don't take a vision to know you'd wanna talk 'bout what happened on your birthday."

Whatever that was. "I'm sorry for what I did. I didn't mean it."

"I know. You saw my vision, didn't you?"

I grip my backpack straps as I glance back at the train. I don't want JP and Alex to know about this, but they're too far to hear. "Yes, ma'am."

Ms. Lena goes, "Uh-huh." The weight of her gaze is heavier than a boulder. "Like I said, I can't explain it. The vision or how you saw it. I've never had anybody touch me and see one before."

"You haven't?"

"No, but I do know one thing." Ms. Lena leans in closer to me. "You're way more powerful than you think, Nichole Blake. Way more powerful."

With a wink, she leaves.

I'm rooted in place. Me, powerful? That seems as impossible as a Vampire who hates blood. Besides, this has only happened twice. Like Uncle Ty said, it's probably a puberty thing.

Yeah.

I tell myself that the whole way back to the train.

Alex, JP, and I look at each other. It's just us, Cocoa, and Bertha the train.

I clear my throat. "Ms. Bertha?" I guess it's Ms. and not Mrs. I don't think trains can get married. "Can you take us to New Orleans?"

At first, silence.

The train's lights glow, and the engine growls to life. Bertha spins and lurches forward, knocking me, Alex, and JP off our feet.

New Orleans, here we come.

The tunnels of the Underground zip past the windows. Alex calculated Bertha's speed to be over two hundred miles per hour, which is "well below the Uhuruan average for public transportation." I don't know about that, I just know I almost fall on my butt a few times.

I make some sandwiches for me, Alex, and JP. Ms. Lena told us there should be some food from her last trip, and I find lunch meat, bread, beef jerky, ramen noodles, oatmeal, canned soup, and dried fruits. Old-people foods, but my stomach doesn't care. It's a feast at the moment.

JP's at the booth in the kitchen. "Yeah, Mom. I'm on the vacation Bible school bus. I—" He crumples a piece of paper into his phone. "Sorry I didn't say good . . . no signal in woods . . ." He crumples it some more. "See you when I get back!" He hangs up. "I think she bought it."

I set the plate of sandwiches on the table and sit beside him. "Wow. You lied to your mom."

"I was bound to give in to my sinful human nature at some point. Breaking two of the Ten Commandments at once is kinda extreme." He tilts his head. "Does this mean I've entered my rebellious phase?"

"Nah, it means you're an awesome friend. I hope this trip is worth lying to your mom."

"Why do you say that?" JP says between bites of a sandwich.

"My dad's a criminal, JP. He lied to me. My real name isn't even Nichole!"

"It's not?" JP says.

"No, it's Alexis. What if my dad is lying again? What if he did steal the Msaidizi, hid it in New Orleans, and needs me to retrieve it so he can pull off an evil plot that will lead to him taking over the world and I'm an accomplice and can never live with myself 'cause I helped him become an overlord?"

"Uh, Nic? You watch too many movies."

"It's possible! How can I trust him?"

"You can't," JP says. "You can trust your gut, though. What's it saying?"

I practically inhale a sandwich 'cause the loudest thing my gut is saying is, "Feed me!" But it's also saying that Dad is innocent as far as the Msaidizi goes, that he loves me, and that I need to trust him. But my gut also tells me that I can eat an entire caramel cake, so it's not exactly the most reliable source. "I don't know about this. I doubt we can pull it off."

"Yes, you will. If anyone can find it, Nic, you can."

JP always sees the good stuff. Dad once said he's an eternal optimist. I asked him what that meant. "It could be pitch-black outside, and JP would find the one star in the sky. You're lucky to have him as a friend, baby girl."

That's one thing he didn't lie about. "I hope you're right," I tell JP.

"I know I am. We're a real-life Stevie, Kevin, and Chloe, and it always works out for them, even when it gets grim like it does in book three." He raises his eyebrows. "You have read book three, haven't you?"

"Bruh. I been a li'l busy."

"No excuses, Nic! The fandom is waiting for us to update the wiki! I'm working on the summary of the new book and hope to get it up next week. How will people feel if character bios aren't updated as well? That's your job!"

"What are they gonna do if we don't update it, JP? Troll us?"

"Worse. Boycott the site and make us fall to the second page on search engines. Nobody clicks on the second page." He snaps his fingers. "Hey! You think the books could help us with our search for the Msaidizi?"

Alex comes up the aisle. "What kind of helpful information would be in books about a wannabe Chosen One who clams up when it's time to stop the bad guy?"

JP gasps. "You spoiled the series!"

I shoot Alex a glare. "That's probably not how the books will go."

He sits across from us. "If they're based on Mr. Porter's life, they will."

"What are you talking about? Uncle Ty defeated Roho."

"Is that what he told you?"

Now that I think about it, Uncle Ty never said he defeated Roho. "I figured since he's the Chosen One—"

"He *thinks* he's the Chosen One, but that's impossible. The real Chosen One already fulfilled the Manifestor Prophecy."

He taps his G-glasses, and a holographic newspaper

floats above the table. There's a photo of a thin-faced Black boy with twists in his hair. He looks around sixteen and has a wide-eyed, surprised expression, like he wasn't expecting his picture to be taken. Above him, the headline reads, "Chosen One? Not So! Tyran Porter Fails to Fulfill the Manifestor Prophecy."

Under his photo is a picture of an older Black man in his fifties or so. He's dressed casually—jeans, a button-down plaid shirt. A baseball cap sits on top of his head. Below him it says, "The Real Chosen One! How Dr. Blake Took Down the Most Powerful Manifestor in the World."

"Dr. Blake?" I say. "Who is that?"

"Oh boy Du Bois! You don't know Grandpa Doc? He's our father's father, and he's one of the most brilliant Manifestors in the world."

Weird, Dad never mentioned him. "He sounds like Dr. Lake in the books. He's this wizard who mentors Stevie."

"Dr. Lake, Dr. Blake. Wow, creativity is not Mr. Porter's strong suit," Alex says. "I don't know how he wrote Roho in the books, but the real one nearly destroyed LORE completely, just as the Manifestor Prophecy said."

"What's that?" JP asks.

I explain the prophecy like Uncle Ty told me, that a Manifestor will destroy the Remarkable world as we know it and only one person can stop them—the Chosen One.

"Mr. Porter thinks the Manifestor Prophecy hasn't been fulfilled, but it was," Alex says. "Roho was the Manowari. He did destroy the Remarkable world as we know it. Used to be twelve LORE cities, now there are only six, thanks to him. He wiped out the rest."

"That's horrible!" I say.

"Mom says it was a terrifying time. Once Roho got the Msaidizi, it seemed like he was unstoppable. Mr. Porter was supposed to defeat him. He was trained by some of the best Manifestors in the world to do it. It was the moment he'd prepared for most of his life."

"But?" JP says, on the edge of his seat. I don't think he cares anymore that Alex is spoiling the books.

"When he and Roho were finally face-to-face, Mr. Porter froze."

"No way," I say.

"Way. Grandpa Doc came to the rescue. He battled Roho and won. After that, everyone realized Grandpa was the Chosen One and Mr. Porter wasn't. Mr. Porter's in major denial, though. It's no secret that he's convinced that the 'real' Manowari will show up one day and he'll defeat them." Alex snorts. "Not happening. General Sharpe called him the Not-So-Chosen One for a reason."

Geez, poor Uncle Ty. I can't imagine thinking a prophecy was about me, then seeing someone else fulfill it. "He told me the Msaidizi is supposed to answer to him next and it'll help him stop the Manowari."

"That's a conspiracy theory," says Alex. "On the G-net, there are holographic chat rooms full of Remarkables who think the real Manowari is coming soon. It's sad Mr. Porter fell for that."

"I hope Stevie doesn't turn out like that," JP says. "The online fandom would be in shambles. The wiki may crash."

Alex grabs a sandwich, and Cocoa hops up into his lap. It couldn't be more obvious she wants some of his food. He smiles and gives her a small piece of lunch meat. "What's a wiki?"

"It's an online encyclopedia. JP and I run an unofficial one for the Stevie James series."

"We've only been up for a year, but we're already the top Stevie James source," JP says proudly. "Nic and I put a lot of hours into it."

"Interesting way to spend your time," Alex says.

I shrink. It's like he called us silly.

"It's cool to us. That's what matters," JP says, and I smile a little. He never lets shady comments get to him. "What do you and your best friend do for fun?"

"I don't have one. Not unless you count Mom," Alex says. "When your grandma is the president, kids wanna be your friend for the wrong reasons."

"That stinks," JP says.

Alex focuses on his sandwich. "It's fine. I don't need friends."

I know a lie when I hear it.

Bertha slows down. We pass an old wooden sign, caked in dust, but I can make out the words.

WELCOME TO NEW ORLEANS: THE MOST
REMARKABLE UNREMARKABLE CITY IN THE WORLD

I put Cocoa in my backpack. JP throws on his fanny pack. Alex is fine with just his G-glasses. We lock up Bertha and set off.

The faint sounds of New Orleans play above us: rumbling and honking from cars, horns from jazz bands, random slurred shouts. We must be under a tourist area.

Alex taps his G-glasses, and bright light beams out of them. "Aw, man, I'm gonna miss Sunday dinner. Aunt Alice is bringing her pineapple upside-down cake too."

"Who's that?" I ask.

"Grandma's aunt," Alex says. "She's in her nineties but bakes the best cakes. She comes to Grandma's house every Sunday for dinner, along with Grandma's siblings and their kids and grandkids. Everyone brings a dish. Mom does the mac and cheese, it's her specialty. She makes sure I get the corner piece. That's my favorite part. Everyone's there all day, watching movies and playing games. It's like a weekly family reunion."

While I was blowing out birthday candles and wishing for a family, I had one that sounds better than anything I dreamed of.

This hurts. Alex got the stuff I wished for. Why was I the one living on the run without a family or a home?

Wanting answers to those questions is the only reason I don't hop on the train, go back to Jackson, and say forget this. Dad owes me.

"My family does Sunday dinners too," JP says. "Everyone

piles up at my grandparents' house. After my sister died, my parents and I stopped going for a while. We just started back."

"I'm sorry about your sister," Alex says.

JP stuffs his hands in his pockets. "Thanks. I don't get as sad about it anymore. I used to cry every day. Kids in the neighborhood called me crybaby. Till Nic moved in and threatened them with knuckle sandwiches."

"All day, every day if I have to," I say.

"It's fine if you do cry, you know?" Alex says. "Back home, the Elders say that tears of grief water the flowers of heaven. I think that means it's beautiful to our loved ones when we cry over them. It reminds them we love them."

JP manages a smile. "I like that."

Alex smiles back.

My brother is cooler with my best friend than he is with me. But I'm not jealous. Nope. "Where is this friend Ms. Lena told us about?" I ask.

"She said to follow the exit signs, and they'd meet us once we're outta here," JP says.

Except we follow the signs, and they lead us to a dead end. An exit sign on the wall hangs above solid stone. No door in sight.

"What now?" I ask.

Alex taps his G-glasses, and a green light scans the wall. "No illusion or hidden doorway detected. We have to find another way out."

"Nah now," a twangy voice behind us says. "You perfectly fine where you at."

The three of us turn around.

The pale man picks his teeth as he eyes us. His stomach hangs over his jeans, and sharp fangs hang over his lips. Shaggy blond hair hangs over his eyes, which are red, just like his Glow.

The Vampire inhales deeply. "Mmm, mmm, mmm! Manifestors. One of my favorite delicacies." He's got a thick Cajun accent like he's straight outta the bayou. "That Gift inside y'all blood is real tasty. Then I got myself an Unremarkable and a li'l bitty hellhound too? Oooh-wee! Ol' Mack love himself a good meal, I s'holl do."

"Isn't—isn't seafood better?" I stammer. "I know some good spots around the city."

"Girl, why waste my time? A meal wandered into my humble abode." He smiles menacingly. "And the scareder, the tastier."

"Scareder isn't a word," Alex mumbles. I jab my elbow into his ribs.

Mack lets out a belly-shaking laugh. "Y'all funny. I love me some funny blood. Now, which one should I help myself to first?"

Cocoa growls in my backpack, filling the tunnel with smoke.

"Think I'll have the hellhound as my appetizer. Shut up that yapping," Mack says. "Then the Manifestors can be my entrées. The Unremarkable will make a fine dessert."

"No, I won't!" JP says. "My blood tastes awful. I've licked enough cuts to know!"

I'm all for time-saving techniques, but ew.

"Mack!" someone shouts. "Where you at?"

The Vampire stomps his foot. "Dang it, woman! Leave me to my meal!"

She rounds the corner into the tunnel. I first notice her garlic-bulb necklace. Then, her Glow. It's the color of charcoal. I've never seen a Remarkable with a Glow like that. She's dressed in black from head to toe—black jeans, black blouse, black high heels. There isn't a wrinkle on her brown skin or gray in her dark hair, yet her eyes look older than she seems.

"You leave these kids alone, Mack. I'm only gonna tell you one time."

Mack pouts. "Aw, Dee Dee! C'mon now. It's been weeks since I got fresh blood."

"I don't care. Don't make me call my daddy on you."

Mack stiffens like a board. "No, ma'am, you ain't gotta do that. I'm gone!"

He scampers off, his feet smacking the concrete until they're barely a thump.

I sag against the wall. "Thank you."

She beckons us. "Come."

"Wait!" I call out. She disappears into another tunnel. Cocoa jumps outta my backpack and is right on her tail. We jog to catch up with them. "Are you Ms. Lena's friend?"

She affectionately scratches Cocoa. "The name's Dee

Dee, and I can help you find the Msaidizi."

She didn't answer my question, which makes me think she's not Ms. Lena's friend. "How do you know that's what we're here for?"

Dee Dee keeps walking. "For somebody who almost became an entrée, you sure ask a lot of questions. Now unless you wanna be stuck here with Mack, I suggest you keep up. Your call."

She disappears into another tunnel.

It's probably not smart to follow a strange lady with an even stranger Glow, but as her footsteps get farther away, so does our chance of getting out of here on our own.

We run after Dee Dee.

TEN

THE HAIRY MAN . . . JUNIOR

We climb out of a manhole cover between the Superdome and the Smoothie King Center. Usually on game days and nights, this street is packed with Saints and Pelicans fans. Today, there's an occasional car or two. Nobody cares that three kids, a hellhound, and a lady have emerged from a manhole cover in the middle of the street.

We get in Dee Dee's pickup truck, and she drives us to the French Quarter.

She parks at a two-story house with an iron balcony and tall windows. While the other houses around it have bright shutters and colorful front doors, this one is all black. Just a wild guess here, but it's probably Dee Dee's.

We go up the walkway, and the front door swings open on its own. It's not until we're inside that I see the smoky outline of a man holding the door.

Alex jumps a foot. "Haint!"

Dee Dee slips off her garlic-bulb necklace. Another smoky outline appears and takes it. "He prefers to be called by his name. Walter. This one here is Darcy. Do you want Eileen to get you something to drink?"

Yet another smoky outline appears, of a haint woman dressed in an old-timey maid's outfit and bonnet.

I've seen haints while working with Dad, but they'll never not be creepy. You can make out faces and features, but they have empty sockets for eyes, and they keep the same blank expression. It's like staring into nothingness and having the feeling that it's staring back.

JP gulps. "You have haints as servants?"

Dee Dee snaps her fingers, and Eileen vanishes. "Technically, they work for my daddy. Have a seat."

Three chairs zoom across the floor and hit the backs of our legs, forcing us to sit.

Alex whimpers. "Who . . . what . . . how—"

"Neither answer is important," Dee Dee says. Another chair scrapes the floor and gently taps her legs. Why couldn't ours be that nice? Dee Dee sits, and Cocoa curls into a ball on her lap. You know, a pet dragon wouldn't betray me like this.

I glance around. The walls, the furniture, and the flowers are black. I wonder if Dee Dee knows other colors exist. The brightest thing in the house is the steel door under the staircase, where a reddish light glows from beneath it.

"The basement," Dee Dee explains, although I didn't ask. "You don't wanna go down there unless you don't wanna come back."

That's inviting. "Not to be rude, but what kinda Remarkable are you?"

Eileen the haint reappears, holding a frosted bottle of root beer. Well, not holding-holding, since haints can't hold stuff. It's floating where her hand would be.

Dee Dee sips it. "I'm powerful, that's all you need to know."

A cold feeling washes over me. JP and Alex must feel it too, 'cause they jump. Another haint, this one a teenage boy in overalls and a paperboy hat, passed through us.

"Jesus!" JP squeals.

Dee Dee goes stiff mid-sip. The boy and the other haints gape at JP.

"Don't you know," Dee Dee snarls, "that you shouldn't throw certain names around?"

JP gulps again. "My daddy told me you aren't supposed to use the Lord's name in vain, but I think that was a good time to use it."

"My daddy would tell you it wasn't," Dee Dee snips. She sits back, and the boy haint carefully removes her high heels. He begins to shine them. "Now, on to business. You wanna find the Msaidizi to clear your names of wrongdoing, correct?"

"Who told you that?" I ask.

"It's on the news."

A TV powers to life across the room, and a Manifestor man in a shirt and tie appears on screen. Behind him there's a glass-domed building that's bigger than both the stadiums in New Orleans combined.

"The news that the Msaidizi has been missing for ten years has led to fear, outrage, and panic in Remarkable cities around the world," he says. "Alleged Msaidizi thief and kidnapper Calvin Blake was brought into custody a short while ago. LWTV has that footage."

I scoot to the edge of my seat. Dad's surrounded by Guardians as tiny drones fly around him. Voices from the drones bombard him with questions as the Guardians lead him forward.

"Where did you hide the Msaidizi?" a reporter asks from one.

"What were your plans for it?" says another reporter.

"Did you take it because of a conspiracy theory?" another asks.

Dad keeps his head down. He's the same size he's always been, yet he seems so small. Seeing that hurts more than I thought it would.

"First Daughter Zoe DuForte and alleged Chosen One Tyran Porter were also brought in, accused of aiding Mr. Blake," the original reporter says.

Alex sits forward as the video shows Zoe and Uncle Tyran getting escorted behind Dad. Zoe holds her chin up high. Uncle Ty looks ready to blow a fuse.

"Mr. Porter, did you have your friend steal the

Msaidizi?" a reporter asks.

"We're innocent! The real thief is still out there," Uncle Ty says. "They don't want me to get the Msaidizi and stop the real Manowari!"

Alex snorts, but man, I feel bad for Uncle Ty. This doesn't look good.

"Ms. DuForte, why did you aid Calvin Blake with the theft?" a reporter asks.

"It's ridiculous that anyone would think that about me," Zoe says. "I only wanna get back to my babies. I lost my daughter once, and now, because of Althea Sharpe, I'm separated from her again—along with my son." She looks straight at a camera. "Alex and Alexis, wherever you are, I love you. We will be together again, I promise."

I bite the inside of my cheek. I'm still getting used to having a mom who loves me.

"Ms. DuForte and Mr. Porter are being held in Guardian custody for questioning," the LWTV reporter says. "Our very own Mary Pender spoke with General Althea Sharpe regarding the situation."

The video cuts to a smug Althea Sharpe in front of the same building.

"I'm proud to say that the ten-year manhunt for Calvin Blake has finally come to an end. However, our search for the Msaidizi continues. We received footage from three Good Samaritans that confirms that the Blake twins have it in their possession."

"What Good Samaritans?" Alex says.

The news then shows a reporter and the three scavengers who looted my house, standing outside it. The Rougarou of the bunch smiles and waves at the camera, and his two buddies excitedly wave behind him and throw up what look like gang signs.

"My law-abiding friends and I were on a lovely morning stroll," the Rougarou says. "We heard strange noises coming from inside the house, and like the brave men we are, we checked it out. We found two kids ransacking the place. It was unbelievable! They ran off and grabbed this poor Unremarkable kid as a hostage."

"That's not what happened!" I say.

"I can see why they'd think that. I'm very kidnappable," JP says. "That's what my great-uncle Benjamin Lee says." He deepens his voice, "'Boy, you so naive, somebody could snatch you up and you'd let them.'"

You know, I think I agree with his uncle on that.

"Did the twins have the Msaidizi?" reporter Mary Pender asks.

"They sure did," the Rougarou says. "I saw the Mark of Eden on it, that's how I knew. I couldn't make out what form it took on, but it looked dangerous. My friend here . . ." He motions to the Shapeshifter, who waves. "Recorded them with his phone. We happily gave the footage to the Guardians and were so grateful for the large sum of money they paid us for it."

A video plays of Alex, JP, and me running down the

sidewalk in Jackson, and there's a bright burst of light coming from my backpack.

"That's not the Msaidizi, that's Cocoa!" I say. "They edited the video!"

"The Blake twins, Alexander and Alexis, who now goes by Nichole, are officially considered to be on the run," the original reporter says. "The Guardians are asking anyone with information to contact them immediately."

The age-progressed photo of me from the missing poster appears alongside Alex's school photo, with the word WANTED above us.

Dee Dee turns the TV off. "Still want my help?"

I clench the sides of my chair. There's not much that I hate more than being accused of something I didn't do. "You know who really took the Msaidizi?"

She crosses her legs as the haint boy massages her feet. "No, I don't know. However, a friend might. You call him High John."

"Isn't he dead?" JP asks. The haint boy turns toward him. "Oh. Right. He's a haint."

"John ain't a haint. Haints haven't crossed over. John, on the other hand . . ." Dee Dee sighs wistfully. "He wanted to see what was on the other side. He went to the light and became a ghost, but he had a connection to the Msaidizi."

"What kinda connection?" I ask.

"Haven't you heard that you shouldn't keep a dead person's belongings? Once people die, they can still have an attachment to an object. That's how houses get haunted, 'cause haints stay around their stuff. Ghosts can have an attachment too, but they don't stick around like haints do. They may come see about their stuff, then return to the other side. John could find the Msaidizi, but for you to talk to his ghost, I'd have to conjure him. I'll need my conjure root to do it, and it was stolen by Hairy Man Junior."

"The Hairy Man," I say, trying to place the name. "That's a Rougarou who got tricked by some kid, right?" In the story, this boy named Wiley went looking for poles to build a hen roost, and the Hairy Man attacked him, but Wiley's hounds scared him off.

"That's the daddy. I'm talking about his son, Junior. They're half Rougarou, half Shapeshifter, and a whole mess. Senior passed a few years ago, but he was never the same after crossing paths with that Wiley boy and his hounds out in the swamps." Dee Dee scratches Cocoa. "Junior's as scared of dogs as his daddy was. Your hellhound should do the trick."

"I thought the Hairy Man was just a story," JP says.

"You Unremarkables and your disbelief," Dee Dee mocks. "Surprised y'all think oxygen is real since you can't see it. The Hairy Man was real, and so is his son, and that dirty dog stole my root. I need y'all to get it back."

"Why can't you get it yourself?" Alex asks.

Dee Dee rubs the back of her neck. "Junior put up certain . . . *barriers* that keep me off his property. You three and the hellhound should be fine."

"Should be," not "will be." I didn't miss that part.

Alex raises his hand. "Can we have a moment to discuss this? Alone?"

Dee Dee waves her hand, and our chairs zip to the other side of the room . . . with us still in them. A warning would've been nice. Or a seat belt.

Alex grips the sides of his chair tightly. "I don't like this."

JP hugs himself. "Me either. This house is creepier than my uncle Willie's funeral home. Lucrative business, always in demand, but creepy."

"It's the haints," I say, hoping that'll get rid of the goose bumps. Ah, nope. Li'l Haint Boy walked through us again. "Dee Dee really may be able to help us."

"We don't even know what kind of Remarkable she is," Alex whisper-shouts. He eyes Dee Dee as she files her nails. Of course they're painted black. "I have a bad feeling about this."

"I had a worse feeling hearing the scavengers lie on us. Didn't you? We need the Msaidizi to prove we're innocent now. High John can help us find it."

Alex watches Dee Dee, and I can tell he knows I'm right. He sighs. "Let's do it."

So haints can operate boats.

The sun is beginning to set when Dee Dee drives us, Cocoa, and Walter the haint out to a dock in the swamplands. It's hard to keep an eye on Walter in daylight. His smoky form goes in and out of view like a spiderweb.

We get on the boat after him. Walter stares at the life jackets and doesn't budge until we put them on. I never knew the dead cared about safety. The airboat's fan spins to life, and we propel forward, gliding along the murky waters.

The Louisiana air is thicker and stickier than Mississippi's. Spanish moss hangs low from the trees, and we have to hold it back like curtains. A couple of alligators keep watch from the surface of the water. I keep Cocoa from the edge of the boat. When Dad and I lived in New Orleans, we'd come out to the swamps to fish. The gators didn't give us a lot of trouble, but sometimes if they smelled the minnows we used as bait, they'd come near the boat and try and see if they could get a meal. I don't want them thinking Cocoa is dinner.

Those fishing days were some of my favorites. Dad would pack sandwiches that he claimed he made himself, but I know Subway when I see it. He'd make up silly raps as we waited for a bite on our lines, and as the sun went down we'd go deeper into the swamps to listen to the Swampfolk put on jazz concerts. I'd fall asleep with my head in Dad's lap as he hummed to the beat.

I wipe my eyes. When you find out somebody's lied to you your whole life, everything feels like a lie, down to your memories. I hate this.

"You okay?" Alex asks.

"Yeah," I lie. "Thinking 'bout stuff."

"I get it. I've been thinking about Mom myself. I

hope she somehow knows we're okay. She's been through enough."

"Yeah," I mumble. Here I am missing the good times with Dad when I had a mom who was crying over me. This is so complicated.

JP wipes the fog off his glasses. Alex doesn't have that problem with his holographic ones. "So, Walter, how long have you been dead?" JP asks.

Oh my God, he's talking to a haint. "JP, I don't think haints can—"

Walter holds up one finger, then makes two zeroes. Never mind.

"Wow, a hundred years," JP says. "The world's changed a lot since then. You like it?"

Walter does a "so-so" motion.

"I get it. A hundred years ago is a different planet from today, and here you are, unable to enjoy any of the advancements society has made. Tough."

Wow, he's got me feeling bad for a haint.

"So, how'd you die?" JP asks, the same way he'd ask what Walter had for dinner.

"Don't you think that's a personal question?" Alex says, then goes, "I can't believe I'm speaking up for a haint."

But Walter points at a tree, hangs his head, and holds his hand up as if it's a rope.

"Oh," JP murmurs. "You were lynched."

I've heard about lynching. Dad said it happened a lot to Black people back in the day. If they did something illegal, like drink from the wrong fountain, an angry mob might hang them from a tree.

"I'm sorry," JP tells Walter. "Did they get in trouble for hurting you?"

Walter shakes his head.

"They killed you!" Alex says. "How could anyone get away with that?"

"That's how it was for Black people then," I say. "Sometimes people get away with stuff like that now. Unremarkables march and protest when it happens, but . . ."

"March and—wait." Alex shakes his head as if he's in a fog. "Why did that stuff happen to Black people? Why *does* it happen? Can't somebody stop it?"

"Remarkables could. Manifestors could've helped Walter if they were allowed to."

"I—like LORE says, we have to—the Gift has to be kept a secret," Alex says. "We can't use it to help Unremarkables."

"Why not?" JP asks.

Alex doesn't have an answer.

I don't either. I would've used the Gift to help Walter. I would've saved Emmett Till. I would've protected that kid with the water gun in the park with a mojo. Same goes for that lady who was asleep in bed. I would've used an invisibility tonic to help that kid with the tea get home safe, and the man who was jogging. I would've used a knockout juju on that jerk with the gun who went in the school. Once I know how to use the Gift, I'm gonna help Unremarkables with it. Forget what LORE says.

We glide deeper into the swamps. Trees block the glare of the sun, cooling things off a teeny bit. JP gasps when a school of Swampfolk swim past. Swampfolk have tails that resemble alligator scales, but they're not as wide as Merfolk tails. This group looks to be an actual school, too. The older swamp man has a book in his hands, and several swamp kids try to keep up with him. They wave at us.

JP hesitantly waves back. "Being a Seer is amazing."

"Wait until you see Merfolk," says Alex. "Their tails have jewels in them. Most of them live on the outskirts of New Atlantis."

JP's mouth falls open. "There's a new Atlantis?"

"Yeah, in the Bermuda Triangle," Alex says. "They have a water park with the world's biggest underwater roller coaster. Once I pop a motion sickness pill, I can ride it for hours."

"I take motion sickness pills and love roller coasters too!" JP says. "You should come with us to Florida. My dad gets all-access passes for the parks down there. We could ride roller coasters all day if we wanted. Between eating nachos, I mean."

"Long as there are jalapeños, count me in," says Alex.

"Dude, is there any other way to eat a nacho?" JP asks. "Otherwise, it's not yos."

Alex cracks up. Wow. JP finally found someone to laugh at the "not yo" joke.

"So, JP, maybe when this is over, we could interview Uncle Ty for the wiki," I say. Is it a random conversation to start? Yes. Am I feeling some kinda way about Alex and

JP? Of course not. I only want JP to remember that we have our thing, you know? Yeah.

"An interview would be awesome!" he says, then looks at Alex. "You should give the Stevie books a chance. I'll read them with you if you want. We could read a chapter, talk about it, then read another one."

Alex smiles. "That would be cool."

What the what? Read-alongs are *our* thing.

"I'm telling you, you'll like them," JP says. "The third book is my favorite so far. Stevie and his friends set out to steal the soul scythe that Einan uses to take people's souls. Super intense, but man oh man, it's worth it."

Alex pinches his bottom lip. "In the book, they want to steal a powerful weapon, and in real life, our father's been accused of stealing a powerful weapon."

"What are you trying to get at?" I ask.

"It's interesting, that's all."

The look on his face says it's more than just interesting. Part of me wonders if there's something to it too.

In the distance, a shabby shack on stilts comes into view. The cross painted on the side of the shack makes me think it's a church, but Walter points to it.

"That's where Hairy Junior lives?" I ask. He nods.

"We're really doing this, aren't we?" Alex says.

"Yep. Like Dee Dee said, Hairy Junior is afraid of dogs. A hellhound should make him pee his pants."

"*That* hellhound?" Alex points at Cocoa as she snoozes in my lap. JP snickers.

"She's getting her rest before she attacks."

"Suuuure," he and JP say, then point at each other and go, "Jinx!" They crack up again.

I don't know if I'm cool with this new bond they have.

Walter turns off the propeller fan, and we float the rest of the way. More crosses hang from the porch railing and are painted on the windows in different sizes and colors. Never would've thought of the Hairy Man as religious. The stilts that the shack is on are rotting, and I don't know how they're holding it up.

Walter gets us to the stairwell. I slip off my life jacket and put Cocoa in my backpack. I steady myself as the water gently rocks the boat, but I manage to get off. JP follows me.

"Breaking and entering," Alex mutters. "How did my life come to this?"

He climbs out, complaints and all, and we creep up the staircase. I start for the door, but Alex grabs my arm to stop me. He taps his glasses. A green light beams out and scans the house, showing outlines of the furniture inside.

"I don't see Hairy Junior," Alex says. He taps his glasses a few more times. The X-ray zooms in on what looks like a jar on a table. "The conjure root is in the kitchen."

Giftech for the win. I jiggle the handle of the front door, but it's locked. I try opening a window, and what do you know, it lifts right up.

I climb through, and holy moly this place is holy. More crosses hang on the walls, and statues of angels guard every corner. It's outchurching every church I've seen.

JP, then Alex, climbs through behind me. "What's with the decor?" Alex asks.

I shrug. "He found Jesus, I dunno."

"Jesus found him," JP corrects. We look at him. "What? My daddy says Jesus isn't lost. Everybody else is."

"Okay, Pastor JP. Let's get this root," I say.

We pass photos on the hallway wall of a short boy covered in hair from head to toe, smiling with a man who's much taller and hairier than he is. In one they're at a lake, and Hairy Junior proudly holds up a fish he caught. His dad has on a silk shirt with black-and-gold sunglasses. Not quite fishing attire, but nice. In another, they're at a fancy event, and Hairy Senior wears a glittery two-piece suit. Next to that photo, they roast marshmallows in the woods, and Hairy Senior rocks a purple linen shirt and pants with a matching brimmed hat. When I think of the Hairy Man, I don't think of a fashionista. Go figure.

Next to the photos, there's a large map pinned to the wall. I almost pay it no mind till I see what's printed at the top of it: Jackson, Mississippi. Weird.

We go to the kitchen and wade through garbage that's up to our ankles. A mouse squeaks somewhere in the trash, and large bones are scattered around.

"Are those human bones?" JP says.

I hope not, but there's a large burlap sack on the kitchen counter. Word is, Hairy Senior used to capture people and throw them in his sack, and they'd never be seen again. That's what happened to that Wiley kid's dad.

Good thing we don't have to look long for the con-jure root. The jar is on the table. The roots inside resemble shriveled-up potatoes, and they float in some sort of amber-colored liquid.

I don't know much about roots and conjuring, just that you're not supposed to disturb the dead. I don't wanna think on that much. I need Dee Dee's help.

I stuff the jar inside my backpack. "Easy," I say.

Cocoa leaps outta my backpack, her fur standing on end. She growls and prowls toward a corner where a little rat squeaks wildly.

"Guys?" JP says. "Is it me, or is that rat glowing?"

Uh-oh. Dee Dee said the Hairy Man and his son are half Shapeshifter, half Rougarou, and the rat has a golden-brown Glow, like the orange of a Shapeshifter mixed with the gray of a Rougarou. It stands on two feet, squealing as it stretches taller and wider.

Hairy Man Junior stands before us. He's shorter than I expected, with red eyes, cow hooves for feet, and coarse black hair all over his body like his dad had in the story. He has on the orange silk shirt his dad wore in one of the photos, but it's a few sizes too big for him. The sleeves hang past his hands. His lips quiver as he stares at Cocoa.

"Why you in my home?" he says.

Alex mouths wordlessly, and JP's frozen. My heart pounds. Hairy Junior's terrified of Cocoa, but that doesn't make him any less scary looking.

"Oh wow! This is your house?" I say. "We got lost and

just wandered in here—"

"You lying! I saw you take my root. Dee Dee sent you, didn't she? You can tell her that root is mine! I've used it for years now to talk to my daddy. It belongs to me!"

"That's not how ownership works," Alex manages.

Junior bares his teeth. "It does in my book."

Cocoa lunges, and Junior yelps, but I snatch her leash, keeping her away by inches.

I smirk. "You were saying?"

"Look, look, look, it don't gotta be like this," he says. "What did Dee Dee promise you to make you come looking for me? I bet I can give you something better. You want money? I got plenty. You want valuables? I got them."

JP eyes the trash. "*You* have valuables?"

"I do! You want some clothes? I inherited my daddy's wardrobe. . . ." He holds out his arms to give us a better view of the oversized silk shirt. "He had some of the finest threads you'll find in the swampland. I can give you suits worth more than that root."

I doubt his dad's tacky wardrobe is that valuable. "No thanks, we want the root." I look at JP and Alex. "C'mon."

"Wait!" Hairy Junior shouts after us. "What 'bout the Gift?"

I stop. Turn around. "What about it?"

"I can teach you to use it in some cool ways."

"Impossible," Alex says. "In order to do that, you've gotta be a—"

"Manifestor?" Hairy Junior says. "My daddy's momma was a Manifestor. Don't you see that my Glow got a li'l gold in it? My daddy learned the Gift, then he taught me. Young as y'all are, you probably don't know much. You wanna learn some stuff?"

"No," I say.

"You lying, girl. I see it in your eyes. I can teach you some good stuff them Manifestor schools won't. What you wanna know?"

I grip my backpack straps. I mean . . . if there was a way to bring the Msaidizi to us, we wouldn't need High John. "You know how to use the Gift to find things that are lost?"

"Nic," Alex hisses.

"Hold on, now. The girl posed a good question," Hairy Junior says. "I do know a mojo to find lost things. It's complicated, but I can do it."

"I doubt he could! That mojo is too complicated even for an advanced Manifestor," Alex says. "There are Elders who can't do it! Besides, I bet LORE tried it already."

Hairy Junior raises his bushy eyebrows. "LORE? Y'all looking for something mighty important then. I tell you what, give me my root, and I'll help you get whatever you looking for."

Alex doesn't give me the chance to consider it. He turns me toward the door. "No, thank you. Have a nice day!" he tells Junior, then whispers to me. "We need to go. Now!"

The kitchen door slams shut at once.

"Would you look at that?" Junior says. "I lock doors without touching 'em."

"Let us out," I say, "or I'll put my dog on you."

"That's a baby hellhound. She ain't gon' do much. And I been working with my therapist on my dog phobia. Them relaxation techniques paying off."

Therapy is cool, but uhh . . . "*You're* in therapy?" I ask.

"Sure am! I'm breaking generational traumas. My daddy was terrified of dogs. I refuse to have the same fate."

"Good for you . . . I think?" JP says.

"But bad for you," Junior says. "We were supposed to address my obsession with eating folks last week, but my dog phobia took up our time. And boy oh boy, am I starving."

He grabs his burlap sack, and I don't know what he's gonna do with it, but I don't wanna find out.

Think, Nic, think! Wiley didn't just use his dogs to scare Hairy Man off. He tricked him. Wiley convinced the Hairy Man to turn himself into three animals—a big one, a not-so-big one, and a small one, a possum. The Hairy Man loved to show off what he could do. But turning into those animals took a lot of energy. Once he turned into the possum, he was tired enough that Wiley could throw him in a bag, then toss him in the river. Could that work on Junior?

"Prove it," I say.

"Prove what?" he asks.

"Prove that you know the Gift."

"I locked the door, ain't that proof?"

"It could be a Giftech door," I say. "Show us something better."

He waves his hand, and the lock on the kitchen door clicks again. "There! I unlocked it."

"Still could be a Giftech door. I don't think you're really part Manifestor. Or much of a Shapeshifter."

"What?" he shouts. "I turned into a rat, didn't I?"

"Yeah, but that's easy. Rats are small. Basic. I heard your daddy could turn himself into way more impressive animals."

Alex looks confused, but then I practically hear the silent "ohhhh" as he gets it. "Y-yeah. Rat? Big deal. Nobody's scared of a rat. I've never cried and ran from one. No, not ever."

I'm gonna guess that he did.

"Couldn't your dad turn into a possum?" I ask Hairy Junior. "Those are way scarier."

"Oh yeah," JP adds. "Trust me, my uncle Troy had a nasty run-in with a possum on a two-lane highway. He hasn't been the same since."

That's oddly specific, but okay. "Your dad turned himself into a giraffe, an alligator. He turned himself into the wind! And you're bragging about being a rat? C'mon, dude."

He angrily knocks a plate off the table. "I'm sick of being in his shadow! 'Junior ain't as big and tall as his daddy. Junior ain't as scary as his daddy. Junior don't dress as nice as his daddy.' I'm more powerful than he was! Tell me something to turn myself into, bet I can do it!"

155

"Nope, I don't believe you," I say.

"Tell me right now! Go on! I can turn into anything, anyone, down to their Glow if they're a Remarkable. Watch this!"

He shuts his eyes, and he shrinks about a foot. The coarse hair disappears, and his skin gets a little lighter. Curly hair appears on his head, G-glasses appear over his eyes, and he takes on a golden Glow. He's Alex.

Alex frowns. "My head is shaped that oddly?"

"Yep," JP says with a nod.

I snicker as Alex shoots him a glare. "Cool, but not impressive," I say to Junior. "Can you turn into a bear?"

"That's nothing!" he says. He shuts his eyes, and his hair becomes thicker and browner. His nose and mouth become a snout, and his eyes turn beady and brown. He's a full-grown bear in just a few seconds.

"Not bad," I say, trying not to be scared 'cause there's a freaking bear right in front of me. "I'd be way more impressed if you could turn into something smaller. Like maybe a sheep?"

"You ain't said nothing but a word," he says.

He shrinks to half the size of the bear, and tightly curled white wool replaces the hair. The space between his eyes widens, and his ears shrink and stick out at the sides. He's a sheep.

"Baaaa!" he bleats. "Told you!"

I tap my chin. "I guess that's cool. But bears and sheep

are mammals. Alex is too. And you're a mammal. It's not that impressive."

"Then tell me something different," Junior says. "A bird! A reptile! A fish!"

"A fish would definitely be more impressive."

"Baaa! What kind you want then? Catfish, trout, bass? Name it, I can do it!"

"How about something super tiny? Like . . ." I tap my chin, pretending to think it over, then snap my fingers. "A minnow?"

Hairy Junior closes his eyes tight, and his arms shrink away at once. His hair disappears and gray scales pop up all over him. Then, in the blink of an eye, it's as if he disappears, leaving a pile of clothes behind.

I dig through the silk shirt and pants and find a tiny minnow thrashing around on the hardwood floor.

I scoop it into my hand. "Geez, Junior. Bet you need water, don't you?" I'm gonna take that thrashing as a yes.

"Okay, I know the Wiley story," JP says. "My grandma told it to me. But why did you tell Junior to turn into a fish?"

"One of Dad's friends is a Shapeshifter," I say. "She gets tired if she shapeshifts a lot, and she also needs her strength to turn back into her normal form. Junior should be tired from changing into those animals, plus a fish out of water isn't strong. He can't do much of anything."

"And the smaller the creature is, the more strength it

takes to return to normal," Alex adds. "Smart."

"Thanks," I say. I think that's the first nice thing he's said to me.

JP picks up Cocoa, and we hurry outta the shack. The minnow version of Junior jumps around in my cupped hands, and I keep ahold of him until we're in the boat with Walter. Walter turns on the propeller fan, and we glide away from the shack.

I lower my hands toward the water. "Nice meeting you, Junior. Thanks for the root."

As soon as I open my hands, he leaps into the water, and it ripples as he swims toward his shack. But not far away, three large alligator heads poke just above the surface of the swamp.

The water splashes as they zip through the murky waters after Minnow Junior. He reaches his shack before they reach him. He jumps outta the water and onto the staircase, and he's his normal size again, but his body is covered in gray scales.

"I'm gon' get y'all!" he yells between gasps for air. "You messed with the wrong—ahh!"

One of the gators lunges for him on the stairs. The other two ram their heads against the rotting stilts of his shack. He probably smells like a giant minnow to them, and they wanna feast.

"Go on now!" he hollers at them, but the alligators keep ramming. The one near the stairs starts to crawl up them. "Get!"

Crack!

Alex, JP, and I jump at the sound.

One of the stilts splits across the middle, and one side of the shack lowers. That's all it takes for the other stilts to give way. And then, with a loud rumble and a gigantic splash, the shabby house drops into the water, taking Hairy Man Junior with it.

ELEVEN

HIGH JOHN DE CONQUEROR

"You think he's okay?" JP asks.

The boat's a ways away from the shack now, and that's the first thing any of us has said since Junior disappeared into the water.

I feel awful. On one hand, the guy wanted to turn us into dinner. On the other, now he could be alligator dinner. But I can't worry about him. I can't. "We gotta focus on finding the Msaidizi," I say.

"He could be hurt," says Alex, and JP nods. "Shouldn't we go back and look?"

"He wanted to eat us! Guys, we have a mission, remember?"

They share a look that makes me feel like I'm the odd one out, but neither of them says another word.

I try not to let it get to me. Once I find the Msaidizi, everything will be better again.

Dee Dee picks us up at the dock. I wait until we're at her house to hand over the root.

Her eyes glimmer at the sight of it. "You really got it."

"Yeah," I mumble, and try not to think about what it took. "The root is yours, but you gotta conjure High John for us first thing."

It's a wonder she hears a word I say as hard as she stares at the root. "I'll conjure my John. Now give me the root."

I hold it toward her, and Dee Dee lifts it outta my hands as fire dances in her eyes.

Fire.

Dances.

In her eyes.

"My John, my John," she says. "The time has finally come."

Alex backs up. "How do you know High John again?"

The black Glow around Dee Dee darkens. She licks her lips, and a forked tongue darts out of her mouth. She did *not* have a forked tongue before.

"We go way back. Isn't that how people say it nowadays?" she asks. "I can't keep up with the phrases you humans use throughout the centuries."

You humans?

JP and I back up with Alex. "Answer my brother's question," I say.

Dee Dee's lips curl up. They're leathery now, like a

lizard's skin. "I've been trying to figure out if you're brave or flat-out ignorant. I'll give you points for bravery, but you've also proved your ignorance by questioning who I am when the answer should be obvious."

She snaps her fingers. The steel door under the staircase flies open and flames pour out. Countless voices wail as a cackle echoes in the distance, sounding as evil as the Devil himself.

That's because it *is* the Devil himself.

Her name isn't Dee Dee.

It's *DD*.

"You're the Devil's daughter," I say. "The one High John fell in love with."

DD snaps her fingers again, and the doorway to hell shuts. "Took you long enough. Usually, hell in my basement makes it obvious. Don't worry, Manifestor. You retrieved my beloved root. I'll keep my end of the deal and let you speak to my John before the ceremony."

JP trembles down to his toes. "What kind of ceremony?"

The flames in DD's eyes dance wildly. "You'll see."

A table floats over with candles on it. In the center, there's a framed black-and-white photo of a Black man in a jeweled crown.

In the story Dad taught me, High John was an African prince who was kidnapped and sold into slavery in America. Using his powers as a Shapeshifter and a Prophet, he'd give other enslaved people hope with his prophecies about freedom and his stories about the legendary tricks he'd pull

162

on slave masters. Tales of his antics spread from plantation to plantation. His most legendary trick was the time he outsmarted the Devil so that he could marry his daughter.

Now folks are gonna tell stories about the time the Devil's daughter got us to steal her conjure root so she could talk to High John. DD pulls the root outta the jar. I can't see what she does with her back to us, but she begins to chant in a language I've never heard before. The floorboards rattle, and lights flicker throughout the house. A coldness fills the room, as if a hundred haints walked in.

DD chants louder. A cyclone of white smoke whirls above the table. Dark brown arms form, then legs and a torso, a chest, a neck, and a head of curly hair.

Unlike haints, ghosts have eyes, and High John opens his. It would be easy to think he's a living person, except I can see through him. "Where am I?" he asks. His voice is faint as if he's speaking from a faraway place. "Who conjured me?"

DD steps forward. "Baby, it was me!"

"DD!" He reaches for her cheek, but his hand goes right through. "Why you ain't been conjuring me, sweetheart?"

"That rascal Hairy Junior stole my root! These kids retrieved it for me."

High John eyes us. "Them kids right there faced Hairy Junior?"

With how we're trembling and whimpering, I can see why he'd doubt it.

"Yes, sir. It was us," I say.

High John chuckles. "Boy oh boy, I ain't been called sir in ages. Over in these parts, there's no respecter of persons. I'm High John de Conqueror. Who might you be?"

"We . . . ," Alex says, and that's it. No other words come outta him.

"Nice to meet you, We," says High John. "Y'all are mighty brave to face Hairy Junior. How can I repay you for helping my lady?"

I force myself to look at John. Ghosts are as creepy as haints. "We need your help, sir. We're looking for the Msaidizi."

"Ah, the Helper itself. What you kids need it for?"

"My parents and their best friend are accused of stealing it, and we need to find it so it can clear their names," I say. "We were told it was spotted here in New Orleans. DD said you have a connection to it and could locate it."

"I'm sorry, child, I don't know where it is. My connection is broken. It's somewhere I can't find and can't get to."

"How is that?" Alex says. "You're a ghost. Can't you go where you want?"

"Usually, yeah. That's one of my favorite parts 'bout being a ghost. I particularly like going to Coachella. Y'all sure have some good entertainers these days. That Beyoncé? Ooowee! That lady can put on a show! I went when she headlined some years ago, and I was singing and dancing along—"

"So, the Msaidizi?" I say, steering back to the topic.

"My apologies, li'l lady. The last time I saw it was about

ten years ago, if memory serves me right. It was with a person who was boarding a bus here in New Orleans. They gave me the impression they were running and in hiding."

"The thief." Now a hundred questions buzz around in my head. "What did they look like?"

"They were short, plump, had a tree tattooed on their hand. That Mark of Eden, I think that's what it's called."

"That's the symbol that's on the Msaidizi, isn't it?" I ask.

"Yes, ma'am, it sure is. They had it on the back of their hand. I didn't see their face 'cause they were wearing a mask."

"Did they . . ." I'm almost afraid to ask. "Did they have a baby with them?"

"Nah, no baby. I'd remember a baby. They were alone."

Relief floods through me. It wasn't Dad. For one, he's tall and lanky, not short and plump. Two, he doesn't have the Mark of Eden tattooed on his hand. Three, he would've had me with him as he left New Orleans. That little voice in my head that's been telling me he isn't the thief is right.

This also means the real thief is out there somewhere, and my dad's taking the fall for what they did. "Did the thief talk to you?" I ask High John. "Did they tell you why they had it?"

"They said they were ordered to hide it for 'the time to come.' It was after they left town that I lost my connection to it. Wherever they put the Msaidizi, it's protected by a juju powerful enough to keep spirits away."

"Who ordered them to hide it?" I ask. "And what's the time to come?"

"Unfortunately," DD says, stepping forward, "those are all the questions you'll be asking today. We have more important matters to deal with."

The eager look in her eyes makes me step back. "What are you talking about?"

She advances. "I kept my end of the deal and allowed you to speak to my John, but that's where my loyalty to you ends. You see, I wanna bring my baby back to life, and I need a young soul to do it. Lucky for me, I have three to choose from. But I'm a fair woman." She smiles. "I'll kill all three of you."

JP pulls a cross necklace from under his Vacation Bible School T-shirt. "Stay back!"

DD jumps backward. "You brat! How dare you bring that in my house!"

"My daddy told me to take Jesus with me wherever I go! I'm glad I listened!"

DD winces. "You won't be when I'm done!"

The rest of her skin becomes leathery and bloodred. Talons rip out of her shoes, horns sprout from her hair, black wings tear through her blouse. She flaps them and lifts off the ground.

JP's cross falls from between his fingers. "Holy—"

"Baby!" the ghost of High John calls. "Calm down!"

"No!" DD says. "I've wasted enough time!"

166

She starts for us. Cocoa protectively jumps in front of us, but with one look from DD, she collapses with a squeal.

"Cocoa!" I holler.

"You runt!" DD bellows. "Your ancestors were born in my father's kingdom. In this house, you answer to me alone!"

She waves her hand, and Cocoa rolls away like a tumbleweed.

Taking my soul is one thing, but nobody, and I mean *nobody*, hurts my dog. I grab the first thing I see—an unlit candle—and I chuck it at DD.

She dodges it, and the fire in her eyes burns angrily. "That's how you want to play, Nichole? Okay. Let's have a little fun."

She opens her mouth wide and a pillar of flame blasts out, heading straight for me, Alex, and JP. I dive one way, and Alex and JP dive the other.

I land next to Cocoa. She happily jumps around me and licks my face.

I grab her as I sit up. Thick black fog fills the room. It's impossible to see anything. No sign of Alex, JP, or DD.

"Guys!" I shout.

"Nic!" Alex calls, and it sounds like he's upstairs.

"Where are you guys?" JP shouts. His voice seems to come from upstairs too. How'd they get up there so fast?

I don't have time to figure it out. I manage to get Cocoa into my backpack. Through the darkness, I can see the steel door, and that helps me make my way to the stairs. I gotta find JP and Alex.

The smoke hasn't reached the second floor, but the walls and floor of the hallway look like molten lava, with a fiery glow that pulses underneath. The hall stretches for miles. Flames pour out from under hundreds of steel doors.

It's impossible this house is that big. "This is an illusion," I mutter.

I take one step, and the ground explodes in front of me. I stumble back.

DD cackles. "You're in *my* home. I make the rules. There is no escaping, little one. You, your brother, and your friend belong to me. But maybe . . ."

"But maybe what?" I snap.

She makes a *tsk-tsk* sound. "You're not in a position to make demands, Nichole. You should be nice to someone who knows your destiny."

I lose my grip on the backpack straps. "W-what?"

DD appears with a smile. "Now I have your attention. Your parents have kept a secret from you, Nichole. They've failed to tell you who you truly are."

"You're lying!"

DD twiddles her fingers. "Am I? Don't you wonder why your father ran off with you? The answer lies in the prophecy, my dear."

"There's a prophecy about . . . about me?"

"Yes, and it's no ordinary prophecy, just like you're no ordinary child."

"You're not!" a voice says.

"Listen to her!" says another.

They're not in my head, not loud as they are. This is demon trickery. I cover my ears. "I don't believe you."

DD gently lifts my hands off my ears. "Sweet girl, you and Tyran Porter are very similar. Some may say you're two sides of the same coin. His failure will be your success."

Wait, what does she . . . "What are you saying?"

"Allow me to have your brother's and your friend's souls, and I will answer every question you have."

"Say yes!" the loud voice tells me.

"Do it!" the other adds.

DD's flame-filled eyes look at me with pity. "Don't you want the truth? You've been lied to so much. Let me give you the answers you seek. Just say yes."

Nothing else matters beyond the flames in her eyes. They're so warm and inviting. This nice lady wants to help me, I should let her.

"Yes, that's it," DD says. "Say yes, Nichole."

I don't know what I'm saying yes to, but it must be good, coming from her. "Ye—oww!"

Sharp hellhound fangs pierce my neck. The haze lifts, and the illusion disappears.

Hellhound venom. Remarkables call it truth serum, 'cause it's one of the few things that breaks through illusions. I can now see that the hallway is normal sized and has only four doorways, and DD is a shriveled, gray-haired woman with paper-thin wings and rotting horns. She was an illusion too. I don't blame her, looking like that.

"Hellhound, I warned you!" she says.

She makes a grab for Cocoa, and I do something that would get me grounded for life if this was a regular old woman: I shove DD so hard, she falls on her butt. Nothing special, but it gives me a chance to run.

I dart into a room. The walls flicker between the molten lava illusion and black wallpaper. Since Cocoa's a puppy, her venom probably isn't that strong. "Alex! JP!"

"Nic!" JP hollers back from down the hall.

"JP! Where are you?"

"Ahh!" Alex screams. He runs smack-dab into me and Cocoa.

He grabs my shoulders. "Nic! There was smoke, and I heard you and JP up here, so I ran up this staircase that appeared and now I can't find my way out! We're not getting out! There are too many doors! We—"

I grab his hand and put it near Cocoa's mouth. She sinks her teeth into him.

He yelps, looks around. "Oh boy Du Bois! It's an illusion."

"Yeah, and we gotta find JP and get outta here!"

"That's almost impossible! She's the Devil's daughter. I've heard she's just as powerful as Manifestors. We'd have to neutralize her to break any curse keeping us inside."

"You wanna *kill* her?"

"Impossible. We should restrain her with a binding juju and make a run for it."

A laugh pierces the air. "Cute plan," DD says. "Too bad it won't work."

The door bursts open, and she flies in, flames where her eyes should be.

"Enough of your games," she growls. "It's time for one of you to be sacrificed for John!"

She swoops in on us, but Alex sends a rope of light around one of her ankles. DD yanks her leg back, which pulls Alex with her, and she drags him across the room.

"Nic, help!" he says.

"Sweet, innocent boy," DD purrs. "Look in my eyes."

He meets her gaze, and his eyes turn blank, as if the light in them has switched off.

"Don't you want to stay here with me?" DD says. "Why go out in that dangerous Unremarkable world? You don't want to be in it, do you?"

"I don't," he says robotically.

"Alex!" I shout. "Snap out of it!"

DD waves her hand, and an invisible force knocks me to the floor. Cocoa tumbles outta my backpack. I try to get up, but skeletal hands burst through the wooden planks and hold me and Cocoa down.

"Meet some of my friends, Nichole," DD says. "They wanna take you to meet Daddy. He loves guests. So much so that he never lets them leave!"

Cocoa barks at the hands. I attempt to pry one off my ankle, but two more break through the floor and grab my feet. They pull me away from Alex and DD, toward a gaping, flaming hole. The Devil cackles inside it.

"Alex!" I call. A long skeletal arm flies across my waist. One goes around Cocoa's mouth. "Alex, bind her!"

"Why would he do that when he's going to be my sacrifice?"

"Sacrifice," Alex repeats.

"Yes, dear. You're gonna love it. You won't be in the afterlife long. You'll come back as a life source for my John. Doesn't that sound lovely?"

I grab the hand that's across my waist and try to pry it off me, but another hand breaks through the floor and grabs my wrist. "Alex! Don't listen to her!"

"No, Alex, don't listen to that awful girl," says DD. "She doesn't care about you or your mother. She only cares about saving that deadbeat father."

"That's not true!" I shout.

"Poor boy. That horrible man abandoned you, hurt your mother, and your long-lost sister expects you to help him. She doesn't give two pennies about your feelings."

"Alex, I do care about you!"

His head whips around, and I jump. There are flames where his eyes should be. "Liar!"

DD smiles. "You tell her, sweetheart."

"I'm not lying!"

"Then why isn't she using the Gift to save you, Alex? Hmm? Oh, I forgot." DD eyes me. "She doesn't know how. She's not a real Manifestor."

I stop fighting the hands. "Yes, I am."

"Then use the Gift to stop me! Go ahead, use it!"

"Shut up!" I shout, my voice shaking.

"You're not good enough! You'll never be good enough! You'll never be a real—"

Somewhere in the hall, JP screams, "Jeeee-suuuus!"

He bursts through the door, holding a cross made of forks, spoons, and rubber bands like a shield. He points it in DD's direction. "Jeee-suuus!"

The skeletal hands explode into dust, freeing me and Cocoa as DD shrieks and shudders. She drops to the floor, her hands over her ears, her eyes shut tight.

"Stop it!" she says.

With all of her focus on JP, it seems like DD loses her mind control over Alex—he snaps out of his daze. He looks around, seems to quickly remember where he is, and whips a new rope of light into his hand. He lassos it around DD's legs, tying them together.

JP closes in on her with the cross. "Jesus!"

"Stop!" she hollers.

She reaches for JP, but Alex draws another rope, and it wraps around her arms.

"Nic, do something!" Alex says. "Help me tie her up! It may be the only way we can get out of here!"

I . . . I don't know how to draw rope. Is it a mojo or a juju? Do I imagine light and it appears? Are there words I think or an image I imagine or—

173

"Nic! Help us!" Alex says.

I have to do something. I flick my wrist like Alex did. Nothing.

No, no, no, no. Please, please let me be able to help.

I flick it again and again and again. Alex shouts for my help, and DD laughs gleefully.

"She's not a real Manifestor! She's useless!"

"No!" I shout. Hot tears roll down my cheeks, and I flick my wrists over and over. Not even a glimmer of light appears.

Alex lets out a frustrated huff that tells me how useless I am. He draws a rope and hog-ties DD's arms and legs together while JP keeps shouting "Jesus!" with the cross. I can only stand there and watch.

DD thrashes, but there are too many ropes for her to do much. Walter and the other haints drift into the room, their eyeless faces watching what's becoming of their mistress. She must not be a good one—none of them try to help her.

"You've sealed your fate and your father's," DD growls. "My daddy is gonna make you pay for what you've done to me!"

It's the last thing she says before rope wraps around her mouth and she's a mummified version of herself, twitching on the floor.

Alex tries to catch his breath. He holds his palm out to JP. "Nice work."

JP slaps it back. "Right back at you."

It's like I don't exist. Considering how I couldn't help,

I may as well be invisible.

A rage-filled scream erupts, and my heart drops into my gut.

DD's daddy.

The house shakes furiously, as if he's ready to destroy it just to get rid of us. My brain says, Run! The literal Devil is out to get you! But my feet are frozen in place.

Pictures fall off the walls and crash violently, and finally my instincts take over. I snatch up Cocoa, and Alex, JP, and I race outta the room. Walter and the haints circle us in a frenzy. They're celebrating.

"Binding her broke her hold on them," Alex explains. "They're free."

The young haint boy and Eileen hook arms and dance. Darcy's mouth moves like he's saying, "Thank you," over and over. Walter's focused on getting us out of here. He leads us downstairs.

We jump off the last step just in time. The steel door under the stairwell flies open and flames burst out as we sprint through the front door.

It's completely dark outside now. Walter and the other haints disappear into the night. Alex, JP, and I run through the French Quarter as the Devil's daughter's house goes up in flames.

TWELVE
SOMEPLACE SAFE

JP's the one who sees it.

We're running past the Smoothie King Center when he stops dead. "What *is* that?"

He points at the sky, but I only see stars and clouds. Alex taps his G-glasses and gasps. It's not until he hands them to me in X-ray mode that I see it too: a gold V-shaped aircraft hovering in the night sky. Lasers beam from it and scan the streets below.

The Guardians are in New Orleans, and they're looking for us.

We climb down the manhole cover that DD led us through and run back to Bertha. I tell the train to get us someplace safe.

Alex lies across the lumpy living-room sofa, chomping

on beef jerky. JP's slumped in the recliner with a couple of pieces of dried fruit. I'm on the floor with Cocoa in my lap. I nibble on beef jerky and break off pieces for her between bites.

I know I shouldn't let anything DD said get to me—she's the Devil's daughter, for goodness' sake—but I'm scared that she was right, that I'm not a real Manifestor. When Alex and JP needed me the most, I couldn't do anything. Just stood there like a rock. Nah, scratch that. A rock could at least knock DD out. I couldn't do that.

I wanna ball up and disappear. I shouldn't even be called a Manifestor.

Alex bolts straight up. "Wait a second." He turns to JP. "How did you see the Guardians' aircraft without X-ray vision? It's invisible."

"It wasn't invisible. It was right there."

Alex throws his legs over the side of the couch. "What about when we were at DD's? How did the hallway look to you?"

"Like a normal hallway?" JP asks more than says. "How was it supposed to look?"

"Hold up," I say. Now *I'm* confused. "You didn't see the lava? Or the fire coming from under the doors? Or the hundreds of doors?"

"No?"

"How did DD look to you?" Alex adds. "Like a young woman or an old lady?"

"She resembled a raisin, to be honest, but I didn't

177

wanna say that. You guys didn't see her that way?"

"The blessing of the Seer," Alex mutters. "It's real."

"The what?" I ask.

"I once did some light reading about ancient Remarkable history—"

That's what he calls light reading?

"In Africa, our ancestors believed that Seers were blessed," he says. "Not only because they see the Remarkable, but because they thought illusions and invisibility didn't work on them. Looks like they were right. JP's more powerful than we thought."

JP points at himself. "I'm powerful? Nic, I'm powerful!"

"That's awesome." I try to smile, but it's hard. My Unremarkable best friend is more powerful than me.

"What's wrong?" JP asks.

"Nothing. I just wish we got more outta High John about the real thief."

"Well, now we know it wasn't Mr. Blake," JP says.

"Definitely seems less likely," Alex says. As much as he hates Dad, I'm surprised he's admitting that. "But who *did* take it?"

"Uncle Ty thinks someone wants to keep it from him," I say.

Alex scoffs. "Nic, don't fall for that conspiracy theory."

"Just consider it for a moment, all right? And even if it isn't true, there may be someone out there who thinks it is and stole the Msaidizi to keep it away from Uncle Ty."

"Einan would do that to Stevie," JP says. "Could it have been the real-life Einan?"

"Impossible," says Alex. "LORE wiped his memory and took the Gift from Roho years before the Msaidizi went missing. He lives in the Unremarkable world and doesn't remember his past life."

JP looks horrified. "He lives in the Unremarkable world?"

"He's not a threat anymore," says Alex. "LORE gave him a new identity. Last I heard, he's something called a telemarketer now."

He spams people's phones for a living? That's nightmare material. "Then who could be the thief?" I ask.

Alex is about to say something when his G-glasses flash red. "Uh-oh."

"What's wrong?" JP asks.

"I set my glasses to receive media alerts about us. We must've made the news again."

He taps the side of the glasses, and a mini hologram of a Manifestor man at a news desk appears. It's the reporter we saw on TV at DD's. Behind him, DD's house is ablaze.

"The infamous New Orleans abode belonging to the Devil's daughter went up in flames earlier, in what Unremarkable officials think was a gas leak," he says. "However, Guardians, under the guise of firefighters, found the centuries-old Nephilim bound in an upstairs room. Once rescued, she claimed that the inferno was set by Alexander and Alexis Nichole Blake, the grandchildren of President Natalie DuForte, who are on the run with the Msaidizi."

I blink. Nope, not dreaming. "She attacked us! Then her dad set the fire! What the what?"

"LWTV spoke exclusively with President DuForte regarding these developments," the reporter says.

He disappears, and a hologram of an older Black woman appears. If Zoe is me but older, then this woman is the next evolution of us. Her face is just like ours, with an added wrinkle or two and specks of gray in her tightly coiled natural curls. She's my grandma, President DuForte.

"We are all aware that the Devil's daughter has a history of lying," she says. "Besides that, she's been under Guardian surveillance since 1921, when she conspired with terrorists to destroy the original Black Wall Street. I would personally like to know how this encounter with the children happened in the first place since she's supposedly being watched, and I look forward to discussing this with General Sharpe myself."

My grandmother disappears, and Althea Sharpe takes her place.

"We're investigating the lapse in surveillance," General Sharpe says. "However, that does not take away from what occurred in New Orleans. These misguided children are clearly working under the orders of their parents and godfather. I'm not surprised. I've always known that—"

A Guardian comes up to General Sharpe and whispers in her ear.

"Released?" she barks.

The hologram quickly switches back to the reporter. "This just in! We've been told that Zoe DuForte and Tyran Porter have been released from Guardian custody."

"Thank God," Alex breathes.

"The charges against Ms. DuForte have been dropped; however, Mr. Porter is still being investigated. Calvin Blake remains in Guardian custody," the reporter says. "Moments ago, we spoke with Elder Aloysius Evergreen regarding the alleged thief and kidnapper."

The hologram of an older, balding Black man with a whiskery chin appears.

"We're monitoring the situation in New Orleans closely," he says. He has a raspy voice. "As for Calvin Blake—" He stops. His forehead crumples in confusion. "Blake absolutely stole the Msaidizi. It's plain as day! We're gonna remove the Gift from him and wipe his memory. The children are guilty too. They must be apprehended immediately!"

"What?" Alex and I shout.

"Guys, guys, wait," JP says. "Did you see that? Alex, rewind the hologram thingy."

Alex motions as if he's turning a page, and Elder Evergreen goes in reverse.

"Right there!" JP says, and Alex taps the hologram.

"We're monitoring the situation in New Orleans closely," Evergreen says again. "As for Calvin Blake—"

"There!" JP says. "On his shoulder. Don't you see it?"

I squint, but there's nothing there. "What are we supposed to be seeing?"

"That tiny red creature!"

"X-ray mode," Alex says to his G-glasses.

Elder Evergreen becomes see-through, and on his shoulder a small, red-skinned creature with yellow slitted eyes becomes visible. It wears a toothless grin as it whispers in his ear.

"A demon," I murmur. "Why would a demon—"

DD's voice rings in my ears. *"You've sealed your fate and your father's. My daddy is gonna make you pay for what you've done to me!"*

Alex and I look at each other. "DD," we say together. We're not only up against the Guardians. We're up against the Devil himself.

Alex sinks onto the sofa. "We're doomed. Absolutely, positively doomed. Our lives are over. Our futures are ruined. We'll only ever be able to get tier-one jobs in Uhuru."

I don't know what that even means. "Our lives aren't over," I say. "We just have to find the Msaidizi and the real thief."

Alex motions at the hologram. "Nic, *the literal Devil* is out to get us! We don't stand a chance!"

I look at the grinning demon on Elder Evergreen's shoulder and clench my fists. I should be scared, looking at that thing, but I wanna smack that grin off its ugly face.

"We're not going out like this," I vow. "I don't care what we have to do. We're saving Dad and ourselves."

Bertha's brakes whine, and she slows down. I glance out the window. The tunnel walls are now white brick, and candles light up as we pass them. A wooden sign welcomes us to—

"'Someplace Safe?'" I read aloud.

JP and Alex yelp, and I turn around.

A flickering hologram of a Black woman has appeared. She has short locs and wears a plain black dress with a small LORE flag stitched on the chest. I can't put my finger on it, but she's different from other holograms. Every other one I've seen looks so much like a real person that it's hard to believe it's a hologram. This one is more like a hologram of a mannequin.

"Welcome, traveler," she says. "You've arrived Someplace Safe, one of the original safe havens of the Underground Railroad. Here you will find a plethora of history commemorating this wondrous place where many Remarkables and Unremarkables found themselves as they sought freedom and safety. As you make your way to Uhuru or another Remarkable city, we invite you to take the time to explore this just-as-Remarkable place."

"This is like a roadside attraction," I say.

Alex checks out the hologram. "LORE uses the term self-sufficient museum. They have several of these. This is an older version of a virtual assistant. She uses a projection processor, as opposed to an integrated processor."

"Meaning?" I ask.

"She appears as a hologram. We have a virtual assistant

at home, and it's simply part of the house. You tell the house to do things, and it does them. LORE hasn't used this type of Giftech in its museums for over a decade. I'm assuming they abandoned this attraction when they shut down the Underground."

"It's safe to spend the night here?" JP asks.

"I think so. I'll run a scan with my G-glasses to make sure we're alone."

My stomach growls loud, and Cocoa growls right back. Guess that beef jerky wasn't enough. Alex goes to run his scan while JP and I decide to fix some dinner. JP loves cooking, so he offers to handle it. I sit at the booth, and Cocoa curls up beside me. JP chops the rest of the beef jerky into smaller pieces and seasons it with packets from the noodles. He says it's his own take on beef ramen.

"I'm glad you're here," I tell him. "I couldn't do this without you."

"Yeah, you could. So, what, you're being targeted by the Devil and you're a wanted criminal? You've got this."

In JP-ish, that was helpful. "How do you do that?"

"Do what?"

"Stay positive?"

JP bends to look at the bowl of ramen turning in the microwave. "My sister, Leah, had leukemia. Some days she couldn't get out of bed. But she never stopped believing that she'd get better." In the reflection on the microwave, his eyes drift down. "I didn't believe it even though I should've, for her sake."

"You can't beat yourself up about that."

"I don't. But right before Leah died, the doctors told us she didn't have long, and I got super mad. It wasn't fair. She believed, and it didn't work. But she told me, 'Things don't always go the way we hope, li'l bro, but they've got a way of working out.' I think she's in a better place now, just like she believed she'd be. Knowing that, I can't give up when it comes to much else."

My problems feel silly compared to JP seeing his sister die. "Leah sounds like an awesome sister."

"Your brother isn't so bad."

"Glad you think that," I say as Cocoa sleepily turns over on her back. I rub her belly. "He doesn't like me, JP."

There, I said it. But honestly it couldn't be more obvious. Alex acts as if it's my fault everyone talked about me so much.

"He doesn't know you, Nic," JP says. "How can he not like you?"

"I don't know, but he doesn't! He likes you way more."

"Are you jealous?" JP says, sounding surprised.

"No! Of course not. It just stinks that I wanted a brother and I ended up with one who can't stand my guts."

"Well," JP says cautiously, "you may not be what he wished for either."

"Excuse you? I'm awesome!"

"That's an opinion, not a fact—an opinion I agree

with!" he quickly adds as I glare at him. "But an opinion. He may have hoped for a sister who is patient, thinks things through, likes chocolate like a normal human being—"

"Anyone with sense knows caramel is the superior confection. And how is this shade supposed to help me feel better?"

"Didn't say it would. You know, you guys remind me of me and Porkchop."

"Your mom's wonky-eyed cat?"

"He's technically my cat. I begged my parents for one. I thought they were gonna get me a cute kitten that would snuggle up and watch movies with me. Nooooo. They went to the shelter and brought home my nemesis."

JP and Porkchop's beef runs deep. "The cat isn't out to get you, JP."

"He tore up my Stevie James costume. That is pure hatred, Nic!" he huffs. "Anyway, Mom claims the reason I don't like Porkchop is that he's not what I wanted him to be and that's not fair. She says nobody has to live up to my expectations, but it's up to me to decide if I love them as they are or not."

"You love Porkchop now?"

"I will never love that demonic beast. You guys remind me of us, that's all."

I watch JP take the bowl of noodles from the microwave and put the beef jerky pieces in it. More and more, I get why Dad said he could find the one star in a pitch-black sky.

"JP?"

"Yeah?"

"You make too much sense sometimes."

He smiles without showing his teeth. "I love you too, Nic."

THIRTEEN

THE LEGACY OF LORE

Last night I dreamed that Dad was tied to a chair in a darkened room, surrounded by Manifestors in hoods. Somehow, I knew they were with LORE.

"You stole the Msaidizi, Calvin Blake," one of them said. "Now you must pay."

They placed their hands on Dad's head. Slowly his Glow began to dim. They were taking his Gift. His eyes rolled to the back of his head as they took his memories too.

I woke up with a sweaty forehead and tear-stained cheeks.

This morning, my nightmare lingers in my head like fog. Alex's scan showed that there's nobody else here at Someplace Safe, and he and JP want to check things out.

They both love museums, and it's basically two against one. I have no choice but to go along.

It's totally fine that my best friend has a lot in common with my brother. Yep.

I hold Cocoa's leash and follow them off the train. A set of tracks are lined up along a long-abandoned platform. A thick layer of dust has taken over the place. Cocoa barks at a couple of rats that run around. A stained-glass ceiling looms above us and depicts a dozen different Black people. Some of them fly, some of them have orbs of light in their hands, some make water shoot outta the ground. Manifestors.

Alex gasps softly. "It's the Twelve."

"Who?" I ask.

"The twelve original Guardians. That one there"—he points out a large, smiling man—"is General Wesley Blake, our great-great-great-grandfather. That's Sarah on his left, our great-great-great-grandmother on Mom's side. She was the first Manifestor in America to fly to freedom."

I remember her from the story. She was working in the fields with her baby on her back, and her baby wouldn't stop crying. The cruel overseer whipped her and the baby, and she begged the old man Toby to set her free. He spoke the ancient words that activated the Gift inside her, and she flew off to freedom.

"I didn't know she was a Guardian," I say.

"Not just any Guardian. She and the other eleven established Uhuru and freed hundreds of Remarkables and

Unremarkables from slavery. She's a legend."

I bite my lip. Famous parents, famous grandparents, and now Sarah and General Blake. I come from brilliant, powerful Manifestors. Compared to them . . . I can't compare.

I try to shake it off as we move along. Someplace Safe reminds me of an art museum. Off the train station are three vast marble halls of exhibits. I see why LORE wouldn't call it a roadside attraction. Even with the layer of dust, it's nicer than any of the ones Dad and I would visit. He always found the weirdest attractions, like the Bigfoot museum in Georgia.

I think that's the hard part about this. It never felt like Dad and I were on the run or like I'd been kidnapped. I was just hanging with my sneaker-loving, off-key-singing goofball dad.

Now I gotta convince everyone that's who he is, including Alex. Out of the three of us, he's the most interested in the exhibits. We find cots that, according to a sign, Remarkable and Unremarkable runaways slept on. The sign explains that the Unremarkables had their memories wiped after they left here. We see photos of Guardians guiding runaways through woods.

We go to another hall with several statues, including one of a woman holding a shotgun and a lamp. Her hair is covered by a bonnet, and a satchel hangs from her shoulder. The sign tells us she's "the famous Seer Harriet Tubman."

"Harriet Tubman was a Seer?" JP says excitedly.

"Yeah," says Alex. "There's a Remarkable school named after her."

Nearby, one statue depicts the Manifestor Nat Turner, who used the Gift to lead a rebellion of enslaved folks, and another depicts Booker Bailey, a Manifestor who stopped a hundred lynchings in a year with jujus. Alex says there's a school named after Nat Turner too, and a library named for Booker Bailey.

This is the stuff we oughta use the Gift to do. Obviously LORE thought so—they built statues and named places after these people. Why'd they later decide it was better to do nothing?

"Guys, look," JP says.

He points out a bronze statue of a muscular man holding a sledgehammer—John Henry. If it's an accurate depiction of him, he was short for a half Giant. He doesn't look like he could break a tree in half like some of his relatives, but he could snap a big branch.

I eye a bronze version of the very thing we've been searching for, the Msaidizi. Even as a statue it looks special. On the bottom of the statue, there's an inscription. I bend to look.

"'The half Giant John Henry made a name for himself by challenging steam-powered, rock-drilling machines on the railroads in various towns across the United States with the help of the Msaidizi,'" I read aloud. "He did it more than once?"

"At least ten times," Alex says. "It was his way of giving Unremarkables hope."

JP bends and reads the rest. "'John Henry forged a special connection with the weapon. It stayed with him until his dying day.'"

I fold my hands on top of my head. High John said he lost his connection to the Msaidizi, but maybe it wasn't strong enough to begin with. "What if the spirit of John Henry knows—"

Large sparkly letters appear in front of me. I shriek.

"Nic! What's wrong?" JP says.

I catch my breath and read the words.

NIC! IT'S ME, TYRAN.

I DON'T HAVE MUCH TIME.

THE GUARDIANS ARE MONITORING MY EVERY MOVE.

The messages fade away, then three huge words appear.

DON'T WRITE BACK.

"It's Uncle Ty," I tell Alex and JP. "He sent me a G-pen message, but he says not to write back?"

"G-pens are traceable the moment you write with them," Alex explains. "You send him a message, and the Guardians can locate us in seconds."

The rest of the message begins to appear in front of me. "'I hope you guys are okay.'" I read it aloud. "'Zoe is worried sick.'"

Alex frowns. "Poor Mom."

More of Uncle Ty's handwriting materializes. "'Calvin doesn't have much time. They're going to—'" My heart plummets. "'They're going to sentence him in two days.' What?"

"That's so soon!" says JP.

"Too soon," I say. "What about a trial?"

More sparkly words appear.

"'I don't know what's going on,'" I read, "'but the Elders are convinced he's guilty without any proof. It's unlike anything I've ever seen.'"

"That's what happens when literal demons are involved," Alex says.

My stomach twists into a gigantic knot. "What do we do?" I ask.

As if Uncle Ty hears me, the answer appears immediately. "You must find the Msaidizi in the next two days. It's the only way to save him."

Two days.

I waited for Uncle Ty to send me more messages, maybe a hint about where to look for the Msaidizi, but nothing else came through. He said the Guardians were monitoring him; maybe he was afraid to say more. Maybe they took his G-pen.

We came back to Bertha, and I've been sitting on the living-room sofa ever since. Uncle Ty's warning bounces around in my head like a Ping-Pong ball.

We have two days to find the Msaidizi, or Dad and Uncle Ty are done for.

I could puke.

JP sits next to me. He drapes his arm around my shoulders in a sort of hug. Half of a JP hug would usually help me feel better, but I'm numb. Couldn't feel a meteor if it dropped from the sky and landed on me.

"Whenever I was discouraged, Leah always told me her motto," he says. "Nothing is impossible. Even the word 'impossible' says, 'I'm possible.' We have to believe it'll work out."

I shrug away. "Your sister's saying isn't gonna save my dad and my godfather, JP." His face falls, and I immediately wanna take it back. "Sorry."

"It's cool," he says softly. "You're dealing with a lot."

Understatement. Sometimes Dad used to do handyman work at a nursing home in Jackson. I liked going 'cause the nurses always gave me free chocolate pudding cups. I didn't like seeing the patients, though. A lot of them didn't remember their names or their families. This one time, an old man's daughter came to visit him, and he thought she was a stranger. She kept a brave face inside the nursing home, but later I heard her sobbing in the parking lot.

I get teary-eyed. That might be me and Dad once LORE wipes his memory. I'd be a stranger to the person I love the most. "Where do we search for this thing?"

JP doesn't answer. Alex quietly studies his G-glasses.

I look out the train window, and I think about the statues of Harriet, Nat, and the others, and the photos of Guardians helping runaways. I think of General Blake and Sarah getting hundreds of people to freedom. Once upon a time, LORE helped those who needed it and celebrated people who did the same. I can't stand by and let them punish Dad for a crime he didn't commit. Old LORE wouldn't.

It must be like Dad says: "You can't wait for other people to tell you what's right, Nic Nac. You gotta figure that out for yourself."

That's the man I need to save. Scratch that. That's the man I *will* save.

I hop up and pace. "Okay, John Henry may be our best bet. We need to talk to his spirit. We either look for his haint or conjure his ghost."

"Whoa, whoa, time out," Alex says. "You're not supposed to disturb the dead."

"I don't care."

"Do you hear yourself? Look, I was willing to search for the Msaidizi before, but now I think we should call Mom. She can come get us, and Grandma Natalie can get us out of this mess."

"No! What about Dad?"

"He should pay for what he's done."

"By losing the Gift and his memory?"

Alex folds his arms. "Yesterday you didn't care what happened to him. What changed?"

I shake my head. "You don't understand."

"What's there to understand?"

"He's my dad! I can't turn off my love for him!"

Silence.

"You're right, I don't understand," Alex says tightly. "He was never a dad to me."

It's like he knocked the wind outta me. "Alex—"

"I don't need a demon to tell me that that lowlife scum deserves whatever punishment comes his way."

I step toward him. "Hey! Don't call him that!"

JP gets between us. "Whoa, whoa, Nic. Chill."

Alex hops up, holding his G-glasses high. "Come one step closer and I'll send the Guardians our location right now!"

"You do that, and I swear I'll—"

"You'll what? Use a juju on me?" Alex taunts. "Yeah, right. You'll fail like you did at DD's!"

No.

He.

Didn't.

"Arrrrrrghhhh!" I scream as I charge.

Alex squeals.

JP holds me back. "Nic, no!"

"Let me at him!"

"I'm telling Mom!" says Alex.

"Tell her, I don't care! I wish she'd never found me!"

The words escape before I can get ahold of them, but you know what? Why keep them to myself? They're true. My life was fine before Zoe and Alex came along. Dad wasn't a criminal, I wasn't on a most-wanted list, and I didn't care about finding a stupid weapon. Alex and Zoe scrambled everything into a big ol' mess.

"C'mon, Nic. You don't mean that," JP says.

"Yeah, I do! I wish she and your new best friend had never showed up!"

"My what?"

I snatch away from JP and ignore how hurt he looks by that. "Nothing. Forget it."

He starts to argue, but Cocoa trots into the living room, her face covered in crumbs. She licks her lips, then hops up on the sofa and licks her paws too.

JP glances toward the kitchen area where she came from. "Uh, we have a problem."

Alex and I go check things out, but we don't have to go far. Wrappers and empty containers litter the kitchen floor. Our food is gone.

"Thanks, Cocoa," I mumble.

"I know you wanna figure out our next move, but we need to get some food, Nic," JP says. "I've seen you hangry, and it's not pretty, no offense."

"She can be worse?" Alex says. I side-eye him. "There's no point getting food. I'm calling Mom. She'll be here in no time."

"Fine!" I stomp over to the door and throw it open for him. "Hope the demons haven't turned her against us too. DD did say she was gonna make us pay. I'm sure she definitely has it in for the kid who tied her up."

Alex noticeably gulps. "Mom wouldn't fall for demon trickery."

"I'd think having the freaking Devil out to get you is a

couple of steps above regular ol' demon trickery, but that's just me. Good luck!"

Alex stares at the door, nervously tapping his foot and chewing on his lip. I already know his answer before he says it.

"Let's go get some food," he says.

Alex's G-glasses tell us that there's a store a few minutes away. I grab some cash outta my backpack but I leave the bag itself on the train. It's not smart for kids like me to go in stores with backpacks. Some adults think I wanna steal. We leash up Cocoa and set off for the exit. It lets us out through the column of a bridge on a two-lane highway. Once we close the door, it blends in with the rest of the column.

Stone-colored clouds hang overhead as thunder rumbles in the distance. The tiniest raindrops tickle my arms. It's late afternoon, and from what I can tell, we're in the middle of nowhere, surrounded by grassy fields. Oh, and cows. Lots of cows.

Alex uses his glasses to lead the way along the shoulder of the highway. An eighteen-wheeler drives past, and that seems to be the only vehicle in either direction. Good. We don't have time to deal with some concerned adult who wants to know why we're alone on the side of the highway.

JP falls in step beside me. "I'm not dropping this, Nic," he says, low enough so Alex doesn't hear a few feet ahead of us. "What did you mean on the train?"

I hoped he wouldn't bring that up. "It's nothing, JP. Forget it."

"Just 'cause I'm cool with Alex doesn't mean you're not my best friend. You know that, right?"

No, I don't know how this friend stuff works. I do know that I don't ever get to keep the good stuff for long. Whether it's a house I love or a city I wanna call my home, every time I have something great, I lose it. Meanwhile, Alex gets everything I wish I had. I'd be silly to think it's any different with JP.

"It's whatever. I'm fine," I say.

"No, you're not. You're jealous, which on one hand shows me how much you care about me, but on the other, not a good look, Nic." He pats my shoulder. "Not a good look."

I wish I was just jealous. I hate being scared.

A gas station comes into view up ahead, the kind that people pass by because it's small, shabby, and they're not sure it's open. A neon sign lets us know it's called The Nearest Store.

We cross the parking lot. Alex puts his glasses in invisible mode and heads straight for the door, but I reach out and stop him.

"Take your hands outta your pockets," I say.

"Why?"

"Kids like us shouldn't go into stores with our hands in our pockets. Some people might think we're stealing. Also, don't pick anything up unless you're gonna buy it."

"And be polite," JP adds. "It helps."

"What's so different about us that we have to do that?"

"Just do it, okay?" I say.

He raises his hands. "Fine. Is it that big of a deal?"

He has no clue. We go inside and the bell dings to let the clerk know we're here. She glances up from her phone at the counter.

"Welcome," she says, but that's not what her face says.

"Thank you," I say as I pick up Cocoa. I'd like to think the clerk doesn't like dogs, but I've seen that look before. It says we don't belong. I hate how small that makes me feel.

We go up an aisle and grab off-brand snacks I've never heard of: Sour Patch Adults, Chocolate Sandwich Cookies with Cream, Rainbow-Colored Chews, and my favorite, A Chocolate Bar with Peanuts and Caramel. I get beef jerky for Cocoa. I feel someone staring, and I glance up front. The clerk stretches her neck to keep an eye on us.

"Why is she watching us so closely?" Alex asks under his breath.

I toss a jumbo bag of Doritos—I'm sorry, Cheesy Tortilla Triangles—to JP. "I told you, some people think kids like us steal."

"Kids like us as in—?"

"Black kids," JP says.

"Because we're Black, some Unremarkables act like . . ." Alex nods toward the clerk.

"Yep," I say. "Some, not all. Dad calls them ignorant

Iggys. Don't ask me who Iggy is, I don't know. I'm sure you don't have to deal with that in Uhuru, Mr. President's Grandson."

"*Nobody* deals with it in Uhuru. It would be like assuming the worst about your family."

I just stare at him. "You assume the worst about Dad!"

"Different. Why would you want to live in the Unremarkable world and deal with that?"

"I don't know. Why are you cool with LORE standing by and letting it happen?"

Like I thought, he can't say anything to that.

"Whatever." I walk off toward the checkout counter. I'm over him and LORE.

He and JP bring their goodies. The clerk glances at us constantly as she rings us up.

"The Nearest Store is a fascinating name," JP says in his friendly JP way. "Is there a story behind it?"

"Folks ask GPS for the nearest store, it brings 'em here," the clerk grunts.

"Smart! How long have you—"

"Total's thirty-five seventy-three," she cuts him off. Someone's in a mood.

Alex's eyes widen. "I don't have Unremarkable money."

I elbow him and hiss, "Quiet, Smart Alex!"

The clerk's eyebrows raise high. "What was that?"

"Nothing," I say, and dig in my pocket for my money. JP gets some cash from his fanny pack. Between the two of us there's enough to cover the bill.

The clerk bags us up. I don't really breathe good until we're outta the store.

Thunder cracks. The clouds resemble wet stone now, darker and heavier. I hurry down the side of the highway, peeling open a stick of jerky. I blame Ms. Lena for my new love of this stuff.

Alex jumps in front of me, blocking my path. "Hey! I don't appreciate that nickname."

"I think it's funny. Smart aleck, Smart Alex."

He moves in closer. "I said I don't appreciate it."

"Guys, stop," JP begs. "Nic, apologize."

"You're on his side now?" I shout.

"I'm not on anyone's side, but it was a mean thing to say!"

"You're right, I shouldn't call him Smart Alex," I say, and glare at Alex. "Mentioning Unremarkable money to an Unremarkable is the least smart thing he could do!"

Whoop whoop!

Red and blue lights flash on top of a black SUV. I freeze.

Dad gave me a talk on what to do if I'm ever stopped by a cop. He said not all cops are bad, just like not all people are bad, and I don't need to be afraid. I just need to be smart and respectful. He said keep my hands visible. I stick the jerky in my pocket and drop my bags.

The Giles County sheriff's SUV parks, and the deputy gets out. I can see my reflection in his sunglasses. He's short and super round at the waist. His face and arms are tanned, but his neck is pale, with splotchy red spots. It's like he went to the beach wearing a turtleneck.

Cocoa growls. Every hair on her body stands at attention.

"May we help you?" Alex asks.

"I got a call from Lula at the store saying three kids came in, unsupervised," the sheriff says. His Southern accent is thick as maple syrup. "What y'all doing out here by yourselves?"

"We were buying food," Alex says, with a bit of an attitude.

"Sir," JP adds.

The sheriff chuckles a little. "Y'all ain't from here, are you?"

"No . . . sir," Alex says.

"It's obvious." He spits something black and gooey into the field and wipes his mouth. "What's this Lula heard y'all say 'bout unremarkable money?"

I close my eyes. Alex's big mouth. "It was nothing, sir."

"Nah now, it was something, all right."

He reaches for his holster, and I swear I stop breathing, but he whips out a wooden wand, a wizard's weapon of choice.

The sheriff points it at us. "Get in the truck. Now."

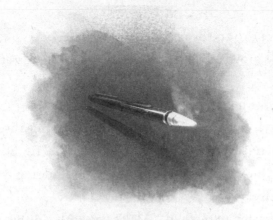

FOURTEEN

THE GRAND WIZARDS OF GILES COUNTY

The wizard drives down a dirt road into a forest.

JP, Alex, and I are huddled on the back seat. Cocoa growls in my lap. The sheriff drives with one hand and keeps his wand pointed at us with the other.

I can't stop trembling. He makes one wrong move with that wand, and it could be over for us. Wands produce magic, and not only is magic a corrupt form of the Gift, but it's also harder to control, especially for Unremarkables. Wizards and witches are Unremarkables. When they use a wand, they could accidentally zap off someone's limbs or create a hurricane.

"Where are you taking us?" I ask.

"To meet some friends of mine," the sheriff says. "They'll be really happy to see y'all."

"It's illegal to possess a wand!" Alex says. "What kind of officer of the law are you?"

The sheriff chuckles. "LORE's laws don't apply around here, boy. You in wizard country now."

The trees open to a large clearing, dotted with log cabins that look like some sort of camp. The sheriff parks near a bonfire burning in the middle. He opens the back door with his wand pointed at us.

"Get out. No funny business or I'll be forced to use this thing."

We climb out, watching the wand. Thunder rumbles in the distance as Unremarkables in camouflage come over. I notice wands on most of their waists. I stay close to JP—and Alex, I guess—and clutch Cocoa to my chest.

"Coming through!" a thick Southern accent hollers, and the crowd parts for a freckle-faced, red-haired man in camouflage. He has a long wand tucked into the side of his cargo shorts. His trucker hat says "Grand Wizards, est. 1855."

JP gasps. "Grand Wizards? My granddaddy said that's what they called the Kla—"

The man groans loudly. "Dagnabbit! We ain't them grand wizards! See, I keep telling y'all we need to change the doggone name. I'm sick of being associated with them fools."

"Aw, hush, Ralphie," says the sheriff. "It's only a name."

"It's bad for marketing, Bobby! Don'tcha think Grand Wanders sounds better?"

"Wanders?" I ask.

"Yeah. Can't you picture that on T-shirts and mugs? I

can't move a lick of our current product line."

"Ralphie!" Sheriff Bobby says. "Forget that! We got more important matters. I think these them kids the Guardians looking for."

He's got Ralphie's full attention now. "What make you think that?"

"Lula heard them mention Unremarkable money. Them exiles told us it was three kids. Two Manifestors and an Unremarkable. I think this them."

Chatter buzzes through the crowd.

Ralphie steps forward, taking his wand from his waist. "Reveal the truth," he tells it.

Light beams out the tip of the wand, and I remember what Dad taught me—that wands can allow Unremarkables to see the Glow. Ralphie points his wand at JP, and nothing happens. Then he points the wand at me and at Alex, and the light brightens. The crowd gasps.

"They glow!" somebody says.

"That's that Gift in them," says Ralphie with a knowing smile. "We got a couple of Manifestors on our hands."

You'd think he said they've got fugitives on their hands (okay, technically we are fugitives, but not the point). Every wand in the camp points in our direction.

I clutch Cocoa tighter. "We're just kids."

"Just kids nothing!" Bobby the sheriff says. "You set the Devil's daughter's house on fire in New Orleans!"

"Who told you that?" I say.

"A couple of exiles," says Ralphie. "Word is, the

Guardians are willing to pay big money for y'all. Plenty of exiles wanna turn y'all over for the reward."

"They should be turning *you* over to LORE!" Alex says. "Wandcraft is illegal!"

Ralphie rolls his eyes. "You Manifestors and your rules. What make y'all think you the authority on who should have magic? You ask me, everybody oughta have a gift of some sort."

A couple of "Tell 'em, Ralphie!" and "That's right!" shouts come from the crowd.

They puff Ralphie up. "I come from a long line of wizards who've been studying magic and wands for over a hundred years. We believe it's a blessing that wands allow us Unremarkables to see Remarkable things. We don't need to be in the dark!"

"S'holl don't!" a lady shouts. "Reveal the truth!"

"Reveal the truth!" the crowd echoes.

"You got that right!" says Ralphie. "We Grand Wizards believe everybody need to see the Remarkable. We've made it our duty to spread the word 'bout magic and the Gift. Most folks think we full of nonsense till we get 'em a wand, and it show 'em things they never seen. Then they start believing, and we get 'em here to teach 'em to control magic. Our goal is to get wands into as many Unremarkable hands as possible, 'cause you mark my words: there's gon' come a day when we gon' need magic to protect us from you Manifestors."

"That's right!" a gummy-mouthed man says as the others clap and cheer.

"You don't need protection from us," I say. "Manifestors haven't done anything to you!"

"Ha! One name: Roho," says Ralphie. "He messed with Unremarkables too. We'd be foolish to think another Manifestor like him won't pop up. In fact, some Manifestors believe the worst one is yet to come, and I'm inclined to agree with 'em. We better use magic to protect ourselves! So, what, we still learning to control it?"

"You literally just said you can't fully control it," Alex says. "This is dangerous!"

"Who cares? We do what we wanna," says Ralphie. "That right there is true freedom."

He flicks his wand. I don't know what he expects to happen, but I don't think it's the sparks and the smoke that come from the wand.

"Dagnabbit!" Ralphie shouts as he drops it. "My wand ran outta magic!"

"But freedom," I mumble under my breath.

Ralphie shoots me a dirty look. "RJ!" he hollers. "Bring my other wand out here!"

A teenage boy who resembles Ralphie comes out of a cabin, holding a wand and the chain of a gigantic hellhound. The horns, though cracked and caked in dirt, mean she's a girl. Cocoa smells like perfume compared to the odor coming off her.

Cocoa wiggles in my arms. The bigger hellhound looks up. She practically drags the boy over. Cocoa leaps outta my arms and jumps around her with excited squeals. The older hellhound nuzzles her affectionately.

I realize who she is. "That's Cocoa's mom."

"Aw, look at that. A li'l family reunion," says Ralphie. "I thought your dog looked like my Cleo."

"Why do her horns look that way?" JP asks.

"Something wrong with 'em? Shoot, I be forgetting she got horns," Ralphie says. "I can't see 'em till I scan her with my wand."

"You have a beast from hell as a pet, and you can't see her true form unless you use a wand," I say. "Do you realize how messed up that is?"

Ralphie shrugs. "It don't matter. A dog is a dog."

Bobby smacks Ralphie's arm repeatedly. "Hold on. Your wand didn't reveal that that one there got the Glow. How he see that Cleo got horns without a wand of his own?"

The other wizards murmur.

"I—I don't see," JP stutters. "I see nothing."

Ralphie steps toward JP. "That smells like a lie."

I jump in front of him. "Leave him alone."

"Aht, aht, aht." Ralphie wiggles his finger. "One move, girl, and every wand in this camp will light you up."

The crowd of wizards lifts their wands higher to make his point.

"I don't care. I said leave him—hey!"

A muscular woman grabs my arms, forcing them behind me, and moves me outta the way. I squirm, but her

209

grip is too tight. Also, she smells like a giant armpit. Ugh.

Ralphie closes in on JP. He takes his replacement wand from the boy and points it between JP's eyes.

"Can he see?" he asks.

The tip of the wand glows green. Some of the wizards drop their wands in shock.

Ralphie gets an excited glint in his eyes. "Slap me silly and call me Billy, we finally got a Seer, y'all."

The crowd cheers. Wands and trucker hats get tossed into the air.

Sheriff Bobby lifts his sunglasses as he stares at JP. "Never thought I'd see the day."

"I knew we would!" says Ralphie. "Boy, we been waiting on you for over twenty years."

"Me?" JP points at himself. "I'm nobody."

"You a Seer! Y'all Seers can find wand wood real easy," Ralphie says. "We can only find it by scanning trees individually to see if they got the Gift in 'em. That takes time in a big ol' forest. Not to mention our wands run outta magic after a while, then we can't scan nothing. Last Seer we caught found enough wand wood to last a few years."

"Last Seer you *caught*?" I ask.

Ralphie gets a wicked grin. "Grab 'em."

It happens so fast. Two wizards grab Alex and JP like the muscular woman grabbed me.

"You're manhandling President DuForte's grandchildren!" Alex says. "She'll personally see that you're punished!"

"Ah-ha!" Sheriff Bobby points at Alex. "It *is* y'all! Them exiles told us you were the president's grandkids!"

"Alex!" I hiss.

"Thank you for solving the mystery, boy." Ralphie picks up Cocoa and makes a kissy face at her. She snaps her fangs at him. Ralphie laughs. "Stow them Manifestors and the mutts in my office." He tosses Cocoa to a wizard. "As for the Seer . . ." The excited glint in his eyes brightens. "We got some wand wood to search for."

Thunderclaps sound close by. The wizard holding JP lifts him off his feet.

"No!" JP shouts. "Nic, Alex! Help!"

"JP!" I holler as Alex and I get lifted as well. We scream and thrash as we're carried away, and JP is hauled off into the woods.

The wizards toss me, Alex, and the hellhounds into a small, windowless office. There's a unicorn horn and a Merperson tail on display on a wall, like a hunter would display a deer's antlers. A huge freezer hums over in a corner. Stacks of papers crowd the desk, and boxes scattered around the room overflow with Grand Wizard™ branded mugs, hats, and T-shirts.

An old wizard in camouflage with a dirty beard and unkempt hair takes out a wand. He looks like the backwoods version of a wise wizard from the movies. He points his wand at me.

A jet of red light hits my neck, sending a burning

sensation through me like flames are licking my skin. I scream and drop to my knees. Alex hollers as red light hits him, and I notice a red X appears on his neck, branded into his skin.

"What did you do to us?" I shout.

Two more wizards sit us up and tie our hands behind us with black ropes. One says they oughta tie our legs, too, but the other tells him there's not enough rope.

The old wizard comes and removes Alex's G-glasses.

"Give those back!" Alex says.

"Nah, I think we gon' keep these for ourselves in case you get it in your li'l head to call for some help," says the old wizard. "Woowee! That reward money gon' be real nice."

He and his buddies crack up as they leave. Keys jingle, and the two locks on the door click into place.

I clench my teeth through the pain as the burning sensation on my neck worsens, but then it starts to die down. "What did he do to us?"

"It's the anti-Gift curse, like the slave catchers used," Alex says. "It keeps us from using the Gift to escape."

My head pounds. The same curse that was used to hurt my ancestors was just placed on me.

I frantically wiggle my hands, but the ropes tighten around my wrists. "We gotta get outta here!"

"Stop fighting it!" Alex says. "These ropes are made from Giants' hair. They tighten when you resist."

Oh no. I remember from my homeschool lessons that

Giant's hair is one of the strongest materials there is. "What do we do then?"

Alex opens his mouth and closes it. "I . . . I don't know, Nic. It doesn't look like there's much we can do. If I could use the Gift, I might be able to get us outta here, but without it . . . we may have to just wait for the Guardians to come get us."

"No! If they capture us, then we can't search for the Msaidizi anymore and Dad doesn't stand a chance! Ugh!" I kick the wall like I wanna kick the wizards—ow, bad idea.

Cocoa comes and licks my face, then runs over to play with her momma. It would be cute if we weren't imprisoned.

Rain pounds the roof like the sky burst open. JP's out in a storm with a bunch of evil wizards who could easily hurt him, and I can't do anything to help him.

"JP will be okay," Alex says.

"How'd you know I'm thinking about him?"

"Twin intuition, I guess. But I'm worried about him too. I doubt they'll hurt him, though. They need him to find wand wood."

Wand wood comes from sacred trees that have the Gift in them, and it's forbidden to cut one. That's why magic is corrupt.

"Long as they're using magic, they're dangerous," I say as Cleo and Cocoa trot over. Cleo sniffs at my pocket, and I notice a small red X branded on her fur. They put a curse on Cleo too. No wonder she hasn't burned down the camp. She can't.

"Evil, wand-carrying jerks," I grumble as Cleo finds the beef jerky that's sticking outta my pocket. She sets it on the floor, and she and Cocoa share it. "I should've made JP stay in Jackson. Actually, I shouldn't have gone on this trip in the first place."

"You said it, not me," says Alex. "All of this drama isn't worth it."

In other words, Dad isn't worth it. I sigh. "You hate Dad. I get it, okay? You don't have to keep making it so obvious. What I don't get is why you hate me."

"I never said I hate you. You're the one who hates me. You're mad I'm becoming friends with JP."

"'Cause you already got everything else! A home and a family. You—" my throat tightens. "You have everything I wished for. The perfect life."

"Yeah, my life is so perfect," Alex says sarcastically. "Bodyguards follow me everywhere I go 'cause Mom's afraid of losing me. Not having friends is great too. And being abandoned by my dad, wonderful. Can't forget being stuck in your shadow."

"Bruh, you act like that's my fault! You think I wanted to be kidnapped and live on the run? No! Okay, yeah, it's crummy of me to be jealous of you and JP, but I don't have much else. I don't wanna lose him too."

"You mean like how I'm gonna lose Mom to you?" he asks quietly.

"What?"

His eyes glisten. "I've always dreaded you coming back. It's gonna be as if I don't exist. You think I had everything? You had our dad and you're about to have our mom. I never had a dad. You're the lucky one, if you ask me."

Oh.

I hadn't thought about it like that.

"Wanna know what's messed up?" he says. "This would be easier if he was an awful dad, but the way you wanna save him, he must've been pretty good. For some reason, he chose you over me and didn't tell you I existed. You know how that makes me feel?"

I stare at the blanket of dust covering the floor. I kinda know. I thought Zoe had abandoned me for the longest time, and I wondered why I wasn't good enough for her. Had I known I had a twin and that she kept him instead of me, I would've been mad. Then I probably would've treated him like Alex has treated me.

"I get it," I say. "Well, sorta. For a long time I thought our mom abandoned me."

Alex looks surprised. "Really?"

"Yeah. I hated her. I would've hated you if I'd known you existed, like you hate me."

"For the record, I don't hate you," Alex says. "I hated how sad Mom was over you. Losing you devastated her. She couldn't celebrate my birthday without getting upset."

I watch Cocoa snuggle up with her momma. Although I don't remember being like that with Zoe, I still missed it.

It's like the feelings were traced in my heart, waiting to be filled, or like big pieces were missing from the puzzle that makes me *me*.

"I figured she didn't care about my birthday," I murmur.

"No, but our father didn't care that it was mine. Bet he didn't buy me presents like Mom did for you every year."

"No, but—" It hits me. "The cakes! Alex, Dad would buy two cakes on our birthday. One for me, one for you. And our birthday! He has it tattooed on his arm twice. I thought it was part of the design, but no, one of them is for you."

"That's supposed to make me feel better?"

"No, but he was always down on our birthday too. I'd ask him what was wrong, and he'd say he was reminiscing or some cheesy mumbo jumbo. I think—no, I *know* he was missing you."

Alex watches Cocoa and her mom. For a while the only sound is the rain drumming against the log cabin with the random rumbles and cracks of thunder and lightning.

I sigh. "I'm sorry for calling you Smart Alex."

"I'm sorry for blowing up about it," he says. "It's just . . . that's what some kids in Uhuru call me, and not in a good way. President's grandkids can get bullied too."

"Oh. I'm sorry."

"It's okay. I'm sorry for what I said about you not knowing how to use the Gift at DD's. That was foul."

"That doesn't make it any less true. At this rate I'll probably never learn to use it."

"Doubtful. You'll learn once you get to Uhuru. There's Manifestor school and Gift tutors. If you have a really hard time using it, Mom can take you to the Gift Research Center, and they can figure out how to make it easier for you."

"There's a Gift Research Center?" I say.

"Of course! Uhuru isn't considered the Gift capital of the world for nothing. Everything you need to learn to use it is there."

I've heard about Uhuru my whole life, and I've always tried to imagine it, but I've never known if what I see in my head is close to the real deal or not. "What's it like there?" I ask.

Alex's face lights up in a way a person only would when talking about something they love. "It's hard to describe it, since each district is different. There are five of them. Mom and I live in the tech district. It's made up mostly of glass high-rises. Grandma lives in the governing district. Those are the busiest parts of the city, along with the trade district, which has shops galore. Things are much quieter in the farming district, which you'd expect in a place that's mostly fields. Grandpa Blake lives on the family estate in the garden district. Mom wants to get a summer home there, though the flowers bloom year-round."

Now the pictures in my head are clearer. "Does everyone drive flying cars?"

"Mostly. Some Manifestors, Azizas, and Vampires fly themselves, but most prefer cars because self-flying can be exhausting. There's also the New Underground Railroad, or N-UR. It's free to use and can get you to other Remarkable cities in minutes. Once a month Mom and I take the N-UR to New Eden to visit our favorite candy shop and bakery. She calls it 'getting sugar wasted.' Bet the three of us will take a trip soon."

I smile a little. "Will there be caramel?"

"Trust me, Mom and I wouldn't go if there wasn't. We love caramel. The shop in New Eden has caramel fountains and—"

"Whoa! You can't say that like it's nothing. Caramel fountains?"

Alex nods with a grin. "Caramel, chocolate, vanilla, and peanut butter fountains. Mom rented the place out for my seventh birthday, and they let me stick my head in the caramel fountain. I think I saw the ancestors. It was amazing."

Now I'm imagining dunking caramel cake in the caramel fountain, and my brain might explode. "That must be what heaven feels like."

"Okay, quiz time," Alex says. I raise my eyebrows. "We don't have anything else to do. May as well get to know each other. Tacos or pizza?"

"Pizza tacos. It's not taco toppings on pizza but pizza toppings in—"

"A taco shell! I do that too!" he says.

"No way. Grape juice or orange juice?"

"Grape and orange together," he says. "Mom calls it—"

"Grorange!" I say, with him. "That's how I like it too!

It's gotta be seventy percent grape with—"

"A hint of orange just to add some tartness," Alex finishes.

"Right." I smile. This twin stuff isn't so bad. "What's your favorite ice cream flavor?"

"Trick question. Ice cream is okay, but I prefer—"

"Snowballs," we say together, "with sweet cream drizzled on top!"

"Did we just finish—"

"Each other's sentence, yeah," I say. "I think this is what they mean by—"

"Twin intuition," Alex says.

"Amazing," we both say with smiles.

"We gotta get you to New Orleans again once DD isn't a problem," I tell him. "It's the snowball capital of the world. Dad loves them too. He gets extra cream on his."

"I do too," Alex says. He's quiet for a moment. "What's he like?"

I'm kinda surprised he wants to know, but I guess it's like Dad says: "To hate someone, you gotta feel something for them." He said it about Sean Cole, the kid down the street from us who likes to knock over trash cans, but the only thing I feel for Sean is disgust, so I don't know what Dad was getting at.

"Dad loves dropping wisdom," I tell Alex. "He homeschools me and acts like everything is an opportunity for some sort of lesson. He's a total goofball who thinks he's much cooler than he is. Don't get me wrong, his sneaker collection is top tier, but that's where his coolness ends. He can't sing or dance for the life of him, but he tries, especially if he thinks it'll make me laugh." I blink fast. "He loves to make me laugh."

I am not gonna cry, I am not gonna cry.. . .

"What's homeschooling with him like?" Alex asks.

Twin intuition must've told him I need a distraction. "It's cool. I get to learn stuff I wouldn't learn in an Unremarkable school. Like we just finished a unit on hellhounds. I didn't realize he was getting me ready for Cocoa. He taught me what they eat, what kinda environments they thrive in, how to catch—" I stop as Dad's lesson comes back to me. "Hellhounds . . . Giant's hair. Holy moly, Giant's hair! Dad taught me about it in my hellhound lesson. It's one of the few things strong enough to catch them. He also said you shouldn't try to catch a hellhound in cold climates because Giant's hair weakens in the cold."

"Oh boy Du Bois! You're right!"

I look at the freezer humming in the corner of the office, and Dad's mantra comes to mind.

"Your brain's the only gift you need. You're the only gift you need."

"I have an idea," I tell Alex.

FIFTEEN

WANDS GONE WILD

I do not recommend trying to stand up when your hands are tied behind you. Nope, don't recommend it at all.

I rock from side to side and try to use an elbow to prop myself up. Pretty sure I look like a fish outta water, flopping on dry land. The Giant's hair digs into my wrists.

Alex lies on his back, puts his legs up, and throws them forward, trying to use the momentum to get to his feet. No luck. "The ropes are tightening!" he says.

I stop. Take a deep breath. Have I ever had to stand with my hands behind me? No. Have I ever seen someone do it? No—wait, yes, I have. In one of those silly online challenges JP likes to do. If I remember right, JP started out on his stomach, so I lie on mine. Then I bring one of my legs forward like he did and put all my weight on it as I use it to get on both knees. From there, I stand.

"How did you do that so easily?" Alex says.

"Thank JP," I say.

I go over to the deep freezer. Opening the lid without my hands is not easy. I use my chin to lift it, but it falls back down a couple of times before I finally get it up and open. I nearly wanna close it once I see what's inside: ziplock bags that say Unicorn Meat and Dragon Ears. There's even a frozen unicorn's head.

"Evil, nature-hating jerks," I mumble. I turn my back to the freezer so cold air blows on my hands and wrists. Almost immediately I feel the Giant's hair loosen. In a matter of minutes, I'm able to free myself.

I help Alex up and get him over to the freezer. The cold air weakens his ropes, and I easily free his hands. He rubs his wrists. "Good thinking. But now what?"

"We pick the locks," I say as I go over to the desk and snatch open a drawer.

"You know how?"

"Yeah. At our house in Atlanta—wait, maybe it was Memphis? Or DC? Anyway, it was an old house. I always locked myself outta my bathroom. Dad refused to teach me a mojo to unlock it, but he taught me how to pick a lock using hairpins or paper—yes!" I find a stash of paper clips.

I grab them, then bend and twist a few like Dad taught me. Then I go stick one in the keyhole on the top lock, but my shaky hands cause the thin metal to snap.

I hiss, then take a second to settle myself and carefully

slide another paper clip into the lock. Dad would call this one the tension wrench. It acts as a key would and provides leverage.

"You've lived a lot of places?" Alex asks.

I get my second paper clip, the lock pick, as Dad would say, and stick it into the keyhole above the tension-wrench paper clip. I've gotta use it to lift the little cylinders that lock the lock. "Seven cities, ten neighborhoods."

"That sounds overwhelming."

"I was with Dad. He made everything better than it should've been." I pull the lock-pick paper clip back a little, push it forward again. Back and forth, back and forth until . . .

Click.

Alex's mouth drops. "You did it."

"One down, one to go."

The second lock takes a little more effort than the first. It doesn't help that my hands shake. I end up breaking two paper clips. With the third paper clip, the lock clicks. I turn the knob, and the door opens.

I peek out first. Thank God, the cabin looks clear. "Let's go," I tell Alex.

I whistle for Cleo and Cocoa, and they follow us out into a large area that's a kitchen, living room, and dining room in one. Several closed doors lead to other rooms. The back door is off the kitchen.

I glance out the window at the top. Behind the cabin, a lake reflects storm clouds.

"It's clear back here," I say. "We can go in the woods and—"

Keys jingle toward the front of the house. Alex and I whirl around. The knob on the front door twists and the door swings open. . . .

It's the old grizzly-bearded wizard who cursed us.

"What in the—" He spots Cleo and Cocoa. "Hell-hounds! Where y'all think y'all going?"

I forget how to breathe.

The wizard whips out his wand and marches across the great room, pointing the wand back and forth from Alex to me. "I said, where y'all think y'all going?"

Eyes on the wand, I swallow down my fear. "Nowhere."

He gets in my face and presses the tip of his wand to my forehead. "You sure 'bout that?"

My eyes cross as I stare at the wand. He makes one wrong move, and I might be done for.

The wizard flashes a gummy smile. There isn't a tooth in his mouth. "You scared, li'l Manifestor? You should b-*eeeeow*!"

Cocoa has sunk her fangs into one of his ankles.

The wizard hops around on one foot and tries to shake her off the other one, but my dog acts like this is tug-of-war and refuses to let go. With a forceful kick, the wizard flings her off.

"You li'l runt!" he snarls. He points his wand at her.

I do the first thing that comes to mind—I grab the wand.

A strong surge shoots through my palms and up my wrists, sending heat through me. In a flash, I see the wizard using the wand to curse the room. In another flash, he swishes it, and gigantic warts grow on an old man's face. Another flash, he waves it around, and cars explode in a grocery-store parking lot. Flash after flash after flash, I see every awful way this thing has been used, and the warm sensation in my body gets hotter.

A loud crack, and the flashes stop. I'm back in the cabin.

The wizard gapes at me. The wand smokes beside his feet.

Alex stares at me slack-jawed. "Nic! Your Glow!"

I look at my hands and catch a glimpse of the green aura before it changes to Manifestor gold. Then I look at Alex as the red X fades off his neck. His eyes get big as he stares at my neck.

"You broke the curse," he says in awe.

"What'd you do to my wand?" the wizard demands. "Answer me, you li'l freak!"

Alex thrusts his hand, sending a burst of light shooting outta his palm. It hits the wizard upside his head. The wizard flies across the room, smacks the wall, and crumples in an unconscious heap.

I stare at my hands again. Dad told me that breaking a wand destroys the curse it creates. Now if only I knew how I broke it.

Cocoa happily jumps around me as if she's saying,

"Good job!" Her yaps become a yelp. A jet of red light zips into the cabin and misses her by inches.

The wizard lady who grabbed me earlier stands in the doorway, holding a wand and grinning. "I won't miss the mutt next time."

Cleo jumps in front of Cocoa and roars loud enough that I bet people three states away hear her. Her body glows like embers are burning underneath, and her fur shimmers into black smoke. She's now a dark cloud shaped like a dog with smoldering red eyes.

The wizard lady goes sheet white. "You took the curse off her."

Sure enough, the red X that was branded on Cleo has disappeared. She prowls toward the wizard lady. Thick black drool oozes from her lips.

"Good girl," the lady coos. "You wouldn't hurt me, would you?"

Cleo shoots across the room, straight through the woman, who falls backward, shrieking. She rolls around, holding her ears. "Birds! Birds everywhere!"

There aren't any birds in here.

So, hellhounds. Once they're fully grown, they can torture souls. I heard that's how DD's daddy uses them. They make people see their phobias.

A scream pierces the air outside as Spirit Cleo attacks a new victim. Feet thud against the mud and someone yells, "Them Manifestors freed Cleo!"

I look for something, anything, that could help us. The only thing I see is the wizard lady's wand.

Magic is corrupt and vile, I know that. Dad would blow a gasket if he knew I was considering using it, but I'm outta options here. I can only hope this is one of those instances that he would call "getting messy for the greater good."

I snatch the wand off the floor. Warmth surges up my wrist again, and for a terrifying moment I think I'm about to break it. All I can think is please, please, please don't break.

As if the wand hears my thoughts, the surge stops. Just in time too. Three wizards appear in the doorway. They lift their wands.

I quickly flick mine.

An invisible force lifts them off their feet at once. They shout, and that same force tosses them halfway across the camp.

Alex blinks in shock. "Magic can do that?"

"Looks like it."

We bound outta the cabin with Cocoa.

Outside is pure chaos. Raindrops pound the ground, lightning flashes across the night sky, and Cleo zips around in a blur. Several Grand Wizards scream and run from things that aren't there.

"Get these clowns away from me!" a gray-haired one hollers.

Another stands stiff as a board on the bottom step of a cabin. "Help! I'm too high up! I'm gon' fall!"

"Snakes!" a heavyset lady calls, sloshing through mud past us. "They gon' eat me!"

Those who haven't been attacked by Cleo try to stop her with their wands. A tree gets transformed into stone, and a rock into a bush. Cotton balls fall from the sky along with the rain. Large sinkholes open in the ground and swallow some wizards up, then spit them right back out.

This is what happens when Unremarkables use magic they can't fully control.

One of the wizards spots Alex and me. "That Manifestor's got a wand!"

Zzzzip! The red light of a curse whizzes past my ear. Alex and I duck right before another jet of red light zips over our heads. I flick the wand, and the ground in front of the wizards explodes, sending them flying into the air.

The commotion only alerts more of them, and about a dozen wizards come bounding outta the cabins and the woods, swishing their wands. I grab Cocoa, and Alex and I take cover behind the sheriff's truck.

A balding wizard runs at us from our left. Alex makes a whipping motion with his hand, and a rope of light wraps around the man and ties him up.

"We've gotta get out of here!" Alex shouts. There's a scream as Cleo gets another victim. "We need a distraction."

I grip the wand tight. This thing seems to listen to my thoughts, and I give it one more request. Help us escape.

I point it in the direction of the wizards and give it a big swish.

There's a loud crackling sound like fire makes, and a whistling of wind. The wizards yell and scream.

"Run!" one of them shouts.

I peek out from behind the truck, and I blink a few times to make sure I'm seeing right.

A tall, wide column of fire rips through the camp like a tornado, engulfing everything in its path in flames. Cabins, cars, picnic tables. Some of the wizards scatter about, screaming, while others try to use their wands on it. Flames shaped like arms sprout out from the sides of the cyclone and swat the wizards away.

"How'd you do that?" Alex asks in awe.

"I don't know."

Cleo zips over and nuzzles against me. It feels like standing in front of a fireplace.

"Can you help us find our friend?" I ask her.

She does a little shake, and just like that she's back to normal hellhound mode. Then she lowers her head, and I take it as her way of saying, "Hop aboard!"

She picks Cocoa up with her teeth, and Alex and I climb on her back. Cleo races us across the camp. The wizards are too busy fleeing the fire tornado to pay us any mind.

Cleo gets us into the woods. The forest resembles a war zone. In every direction, trees have been chopped down to short stumps, or gigantic holes have been dug out. All this destruction to try and find wand wood.

"JP!" I call out from Cleo's back.

Thump . . . thump . . . thump.

Cleo glances around. The sound is like a heartbeat, deep and steady, but it's too loud to be mine.

"You hear that?" Alex asks.

"Can't miss it." It's as if the forest has a pulse.

Cleo runs in the direction of the sound, and it vibrates the ground beneath us. I feel it as much as I hear it.

Then . . . there's light.

A bright glow pulses at the same rhythm as the thumps. In the clearing ahead, I make out the outline of a thick tree, wrapped in a rainbow of light. The thumping sound comes from it.

Cleo stops at its trunk, and Alex and I hop down. We can't take our eyes off the tree. It's not the biggest one in the forest or the tallest, but it's perfect. The trunk is perfectly round, the branches are all the same length, and every leaf looks like it was painted by an artist.

"It's beautiful," Alex says.

That's an understatement. "It's a wand-wood tree."

I don't know how anyone could want to cut it for wands, but that explains why magic is corrupt—making wands requires damaging something rare and powerful.

Cleo and Cocoa sniff out the area. There's no sign of Ralphie and the wizards who took JP, but they must be nearby since Cleo brought us here.

"JP?" I call out. "JP?"

"I don't think they've been here, Nic," Alex says. "The wand-wood tree is untouched."

I look at Cleo. "Why'd you bring us here, girl?"

She huffs impatiently, then forcefully nudges her nose against the back of my leg. I stumble forward, and something crunches under my feet.

My stomach bottoms out. It's a phone with a Stevie James case on it.

I bend and pick it up. "JP."

Cleo and Cocoa growl as their fur rises to attention.

I slip JP's phone into my pocket. "What is it, girls?"

The air around us bends and shimmers, and Guardians in white and gold appear. JP floats beside them, wrapped in ropes of light up to his neck. Ralphie and a few Grand Wizards float nearby, tied and bound as well.

JP lets out a muffled scream behind his sealed lips.

With no warning, the Guardians send ropes of light flying at us. I duck lower to the ground and they miss me, but they tie my brother's ankles and wrists. He falls at once.

"Nic, help!" he says, right before a juju forces his mouth shut.

The Guardians raise their palms to send more jujus at me. I flick the wand.

A wall of fire erupts outta the ground, and the force pushes me back a few feet. The wall separates me from the Guardians, Alex, and JP. Through the flickering flames, I see my brother's and my best friend's terrified faces. I don't know what to do except swish the wand again but before I can—

White-hot light hits my head from behind and knocks

me face forward. The wand falls from my grasp. Alex and JP let out muffled screams.

My body feels like it's engulfed in flames. My eyes are swelling shut, the right a little faster than the left. I can't cry out—my throat is on fire too—and I can't move.

Feet crunch against the leaves, and someone turns me over on my back. Through my left eye, I see Althea Sharpe standing over me with a wand in her hand and a cruel smile on her lips. The wall of flames flickers furiously and separates us from the others. She came at me from behind.

"I've heard magical curses are cruel," she says. "I may have to rethink my stance on wandcraft." She bends closer to me, a triumphant glint in her eyes. "It wouldn't go over well if LORE knew I used a wand on you, so I'm gonna tell them you accidentally used that little wand you stole on yourself."

"Liar!" I croak.

"Your word against mine, and who's gonna believe an out-of-control delinquent over—"

A jet of black smoke goes through General Sharpe and tackles her to the ground.

Spirit Cleo.

I manage to sit up. General Sharpe is on her knees, sobbing like a baby in pain.

"Please," she begs, "please give me another chance!"

I crawl back, but it doesn't matter. It's like General Sharpe doesn't realize I'm here anymore. She reaches out to some invisible person.

"You're the only one who's ever believed in me! Please don't give up on me!"

Cleo in normal hellhound mode comes over to me with Cocoa draped across her back. She lowers her head.

I look at Alex and JP, and I feel so powerless. I'm too weak to help them, and if I get caught too, this is all over. Dad will be punished, and so will we.

I'm gonna figure out how to save them. I am. For now, I gotta get outta here. I'm the only chance we have.

I use my last bit of strength to climb onto Cleo's back, and I hate what I'm about to say. "Take me to . . . Underground. Someplace Safe." I just hope Cleo knows where that is.

She takes off. The woods blur past us one second, and in another, everything goes dark. I grasp Cleo's fur as tight as I can, but my fingers can barely hold on.

I black out again. The next time I open my good eye, we're in Someplace Safe, and Bertha the train sits a few feet away.

I roll off Cleo's back. My head is too heavy to hold up. I somehow manage to stand and start to stagger toward the train.

That's when I notice the trail of hoofprints in the dirt.

"Long time no see," a voice says.

I turn around, and my good eye meets the gleaming red ones of Hairy Man Junior.

He throws his burlap sack over my head.

SIXTEEN

BOSS MAN

I dream that I'm running through a vast cave.

At least I think it's a cave. Large stalactites hang from the rock ceiling above me, but I'm running along a brick road. I pass what looks like a park with rusted playground equipment and boarded-up storefronts. An abandoned town . . . in a cave?

Dust kicks up around me, and a huge shadow looms overhead.

"Find me, Nichole," a voice says. "Find me!"

I jolt awake.

It takes me a second to catch my breath, but I quickly realize three things: one, I'm not dead. Yay. Two, I can see outta both my eyes now. Three, I'm lying on the couch on Bertha the train. A fuzzy blanket is draped over my legs, and out the window I see the abandoned train station of Someplace Safe.

I kick back the blanket. My clothes are glued to my skin with sweat. A strong aroma of fried potatoes and spices fills the room, and my stomach grumbles. It feels like I haven't eaten in days.

Cleo and Cocoa bound into the room. Cocoa leaps into my lap, and Cleo rubs up against my leg. I give them both scratches.

"Hey, girls," I say, and my voice has a serious frog in it. "Where is everybody?"

"Good. You alive," a voice says. "You gon' need to be, to pay me back."

Hairy Man Junior carries in a tray of steaming-hot food. He's wearing a chef's hat and an apron that says, "Don't kiss the cook without permission."

He sets the tray on the coffee table. "You need your strength to pay me what you owe me, so I made my specialty, beef hash. I know what you thinking. He made beef hash when he got those?" He lifts one of his hooves for me to see. "I ain't part cow. Just got ugly feet. My hash is vegan. I used the finest jackfruit. You won't be able to tell it ain't real beef."

As good as that hash smells, it was brought in by a red-eyed, hairy monster who eats people. "What are you doing here?"

"I bring you this nice meal, and that's the first thing you say? No 'thank you'? Ungrateful! This the last thing I'll do for you!"

I eye the door. It's not too far. I wanna make a run for it, but when I try to sit up, I'm so shaky and weak I fall back down.

Junior lifts me into a sitting position and shoves a pillow behind my back. "Don't know where you think you going. Eat your food. You obviously need it."

Now my heart is really pounding. "I'm gonna ask you one more time. What are you—argh!"

He just shoved a spoonful of "beef" hash into my mouth. Believe it or not, it's actually delicious, and I can't tell that it's not beef.

"Eat," he repeats.

I'm eating but not 'cause he told me to, but 'cause I'm hungry and it's good. I stop long enough to ask, "What are you doing here?"

"I'm here to collect what's mine! I been on your trail since you left the swamp. I was gonna deal with you real good for destroying my home, but the hellhounds brought you back all banged up yesterday. I can't get nothing outta you if you dead."

It starts to come back to me. "Cleo . . . she brought me."

"Yep. My therapy really paying off. I wasn't as scared of her as I would've been once upon a time. She let me put you in my sack and didn't make a fuss. You was going in and out of consciousness. Looks like you got hit with magic."

"Yeah, by General—" Everything rushes back to me. The wizards' camp, the wand-wood tree, Alex, JP. Then I realize what Junior said. "Did you say this happened yesterday?"

"Yeah. Over twenty-four hours ago."

I hop up and whoa, bad idea. I'm too dizzy to see straight. I fall back onto the sofa. "I gotta save Alex and JP and my dad!"

"I ain't sure that's possible."

"Why do you say that?"

Junior taps his watch, and I just noticed that it has a holographic face—it's Giftech. A mini hologram of a news reporter floats above his wrist.

"Guardians were stunned when they arrived on the scene of the partially destroyed wizards' camp," the woman says. "Several structures were engulfed in flames, thanks to a fire cyclone allegedly drawn by Nichole Blake using illegal wandcraft magic. The twelve-year-old remains on the run with the Msaidizi; however, her brother, Alexander, and an unidentified Unremarkable boy have been taken into Guardian custody. The minors are being detained for questioning. General Sharpe and Elder Aloysius Evergreen had this to say."

The hologram becomes General Sharpe, but the general isn't her usual smug self. There are bags under her eyes, and her chin isn't lifted as high. She looks like she's still spooked from the number Cleo pulled on her.

"We have taken control of the wizards' camp and confiscated their wands," she says. "In the meantime, we are searching the area for Alexis Nichole Blake around the clock. We have every reason to believe that she remains nearby. After all—" General Sharpe seems to look right at me. "She wouldn't willingly leave her brother and her best friend behind. Would she?"

A knot as big as a golf ball forms in my throat. "I . . . of course I . . . I didn't mean—"

The hologram becomes the older balding man with the whiskery chin, Elder Evergreen.

"Do I still think Calvin Blake is guilty? Hah! Do lightning birds fly in storms? He's absolutely guilty! Now he got his child out here, committing crimes too? T'uh! It ain't helping his case a lick. We gon' see to it that he receives maximum punishment tomorrow."

The reporter reappears. "President DuForte is believed to be working with the Guardians regarding the release of her grandson and the Unremarkable boy. As for Nichole Blake, it looks like the young lady truly has abandoned her accomplices, as there is no sign of her yet."

Junior turns off the news. "Told you."

My eyes well up. I picture JP tied up in midair, Alex getting captured, the scared looks on their faces, and guilt rattles me like an earthquake. "I left them. And now Dad's getting sentenced in the morning."

"Actually," Junior says, "he getting sentenced later today. That news report was from last night. Another report said his trial starts at nine a.m. It's around five in the morning now."

"That only gives me four—" I can't say it or I'll bust out crying. "I'm going for a walk."

I hurry off the train before Junior can see me cry.

The abandoned train station of Someplace Safe is the perfect place to mope. It's empty, and I feel empty. We're made for each other.

Sitting on the edge of the platform, I dangle my legs over the train track. I've only ever had two friends, JP and Rebecca, the girl from my homeschool group in Atlanta. Don't get me wrong, she's cool—I'm supposed to go to her bat mitzvah next year—but JP's my *best* friend. Yet when he needed me the most, I left him. Alex isn't what I imagined I wanted for a brother, but he's *my* brother, and I left him too.

Cocoa and Cleo trot over and hop up on the platform. They take turns licking my cheeks.

Junior's hooves clop against the stone. He has his sack slung over his shoulder. He makes sure to keep some distance between him and the hellhounds. I guess he's still not completely over his fear. "You done sulking yet? We got business to discuss."

I use my sleeve to wipe hellhound slobber off my face. I love Cocoa and Cleo, but I'd rather just deal with my tears. "What are you talking about?"

"You owe me a house," he says.

"Huh? I don't owe you a house."

"Yeah, you do. You destroyed my home!"

"No, I didn't. The alligators did."

"You lured 'em when you threw me in the swamp."

"Because you were gonna eat us!" I say. "You said so!"

"That was only to scare y'all. I'm a vegan. Haven't had meat in over twenty years."

"A vegan with bones in his house who threw me in his sack yesterday!"

"I like to collect bones!" he claims. "They make lovely decorations. And my bag is mojoed to carry heavy loads. I wasn't 'bout to break my back, picking you up. And stop trying to change the subject! I ain't got much of anything now, thanks to you! You owe me a house!"

I failed Dad, JP and Alex got captured 'cause of me, and now Junior's telling me I ruined his life too.

The sob comes outta me before I know it.

"Don't you dare!" Junior snaps. "Stop crying and get me a new house!"

"How? I'm only twelve!" I blubber.

"I know who you are!" he says. "I saw the LORE news. You're the president's granddaughter. You're gonna tell her to get me a house or I'm gonna turn you into a meal!"

"I don't know her like that!"

"I don't care!" Junior says as he rummages through his sack. He tosses out a few pieces of damp clothing, pots and pans, a few drenched books, wet photographs of him and his dad, and the map of Jackson before he finally pulls out a G-pen. "You're gonna write to her this instant and tell her to give me a house!"

He holds the G-pen out to me, but his hand is what catches my attention. I didn't see it before 'cause his dad's oversized shirt hung over his hands, but now I see there's a black tree tattooed on the back of his right hand. The trunk is in the center, and the limbs stretch out to his fingers, with little red rubies drawn on them.

The Mark of Eden. The tattoo that High John saw on the Msaidizi thief's hand.

I scoot back, my heart pounding like it'll jump out my chest. "It's you."

"What's me?" Junior sneers.

Blood rushes in my ears. Ms. Lena said the thief was spotted in New Orleans. Junior lived in New Orleans. High John said the thief was short and plump. Junior is short and plump. Then the tattoo—

I scramble to my feet. "Where is it?"

"Where's what?"

"You stole the Msaidizi! Where is it?"

"What?" Junior says loudly. "I ain't steal it!"

"High John saw you with it in New Orleans! He told me himself. He said you had on a mask, but he saw the Mark of Eden tattooed on your hand. It was you!"

"No, it wasn't! I ain't the one Boss Man told to hide it!"

Time comes to a screeching halt.

He's not the one. . . .

"You know what happened to the Msaidizi?"

"I said nothing, you heard nothing!"

This strange feeling seeps into my bones; maybe deeper than that. It's more exciting than excitement could ever be, and it's something I haven't felt in a while: hope.

"Who is Boss Man, Junior?"

"You better leave this alone! You asking for a heap of trouble."

"I don't care! LORE thinks my dad stole the Msaidizi, and they're gonna make him pay in a few hours unless I do something."

"That ain't got a thing to do with me! You don't know who you dealing with. This ain't some storybook villain. You better leave it alone!"

A storybook villain? I can think of someone who might be called that simply because Uncle Ty put him in his books. "Boss Man is Roho, isn't he? He had someone steal the Msaidizi?"

"I ain't telling you squat. Matter of fact . . ." He stalks forward. "I suddenly got a hankering for meat. You either give me a house or pay me with your bones!"

Hope and boldness must go hand in hand. That's the only explanation I've got for what I do. I grab Junior's daddy's clothes. "You come one step closer, and I'll destroy these!"

He goes rigid. "You wouldn't."

"I'll tell Cleo to burn them up," I say. The hellhound stands at my side with a smoky growl to make my point. Cocoa joins with a not-as-intimidating one.

Junior bares his teeth, but he glances at the hellhounds.

He can act as vicious as he wants, he's still scared of them. "I'll have you on a dinner platter 'fore you destroy anything."

"You're too scared of my dogs to try it. Plus if you were gonna hurt me, you would've used the Gift to do it by now, but you won't 'cause you want a house. Well, I want some answers. Talk!"

Junior growls.

That's how he wants to do this? All right, bet. I pull an orange silk shirt from the clothes. Junior wore it the day we met. I hold it in front of Cleo.

"Put that down! That was my daddy's favorite shirt!"

"My daddy won't be able to remember his favorite shirt unless you start talking!"

Junior eyes the shirt more than me. If I didn't know better, I'd say that's some panic in his eyes. "What you wanna know?" he says.

"Why do you and the thief have the same tattoo?"

"Most of us got the Mark of Eden on us."

"Who is us?"

"You figured one thing out already. You can figure that out too."

The Mark of Eden is on the Msaidizi, the weapon that made Roho nearly invincible. It would make sense that a bunch of his followers got it tattooed on them.

"You're followers of Roho," I say.

"We were," Junior grumbles. "Can't follow someone who don't remember who they are."

"How did he order somebody to take the Msaidizi, then? Hadn't he lost his memory by the time it was stolen?"

"Some orders take time to be fulfilled," Junior says. "He gave the order before his battle with Doc Blake. He had a feeling Doc was gonna take him down."

"Why did he order someone to steal it? Who did he tell to steal it?" I ask. "Where did they hide it?"

"I've said more than enough! Give me my clothes!"

"Give me more answers!"

Junior flicks his wrists, and fireballs appear in his palms. "You burn my clothes, and I'll burn that train of yours. Your choice."

I hold the clothes in front of Cleo just to call his bluff. We stare each other down, and the fireballs in his hands double in size.

He means it. I'm not getting anything else outta him.

I hold the clothes toward Junior. He snatches them from my hands and grumbles about house-destroying brats as he stuffs them into his sack.

My hope tries to slip away, but I grip it tight. The pieces of the puzzle are right in front of me. I just gotta put them together.

I fold my hands on top of my head. "Roho had someone steal the Msaidizi from LORE," I mutter. "Where would he have them hide it?"

Junior picks up one of his pots. "You better hope you never figure it out. I told you that you asking for a heap of trouble."

I watch him grab his cast-iron skillet, then I look at the rest of his stuff scattered around. There's more cookware, a teddy bear. Then there's the map of Jackson. Of all the things to save, why that map?

Junior follows my eyes to it. It's only two feet away from me. Unfortunately, that's about the distance between him and the map too.

His red eyes meet my eyes.

We go for it at the same time, but lucky for me, hooves aren't as fast as human feet. I snatch the map up.

"Give me my map!" Junior shouts.

I race toward Bertha, and Junior's hooves clop behind me. Cocoa and Cleo bark and hold him off. The second I'm close enough to the train, I hop on board and slam the door shut.

"Get these dogs away from me!" Junior shouts.

I slide Ms. Lena's recliner in front of the door, then lay the map out on a table. Every inch of me says this map has something to do with Roho. It must.

The map is damp and some of the ink is smudged, making it hard to read. There's a big red smear near the bottom right corner but through the ink I make out one street name near the red smudge: High Street.

"That's downtown," I mutter. I know because Dad takes High Street to get to the governor's mansion when he does handyman work there. He always said that it's called High Street simply because the street goes up a huge roller-coaster-like slope.

"That's that volcano below the city," he'd say. "It makes High Street go so high."

Wait a second.

I stare hard at the map. That smudge . . . it's near High Street, where the underground volcano would be.

What would an underground volcano even look—

My dream comes flooding back to me: it would look like a mountain in a gigantic cave.

"Holy moly," I mutter. "Holy moly, could it . . . could that be where he hid it?"

My hope is now a blazing inferno, burning deep inside me. Problem is, I don't know much about Roho, besides that he wanted to destroy the Remarkable world.

But . . .

I know a lot about a character based on him. In fact, I help run a wiki that has tons of information on that character.

Junior pounds on the door. "I swear, you better give me my map!"

I fumble for my pocket. I've still got JP's phone from when I found it in the woods. Although the screen is cracked, it miraculously comes on.

Uncle Ty said the soul scythe in the Stevie books is Einan's version of the Msaidizi; it makes him almost invincible. In the new book, Stevie, Kevin, and Chloe steal it. In order to steal something, you gotta know where it's kept. I seriously regret not reading the book, but JP read the whole thing and I bet he's put up a summary already.

Unfortunately, his phone is passcode protected. I try 0426 for April twenty-sixth, his birthday.

No luck. The phone gives me a hint: "an awesome date." It also tells me I've got two more tries or I'll be locked outta the phone for an hour.

A heavy force slams against the door, as if Junior hit it with his shoulder. Cocoa and Cleo bark viciously. "I swear, girl, you gon' regret this!" Junior says.

My hands shake, but I manage to type 1225. Christmas. It's JP's favorite holiday. It doesn't work either. One more try left.

I don't know JP's parents' birthdays or his sister's. His other favorite holiday is Thanksgiving, but the date changes every year. I can only think of one other date he might think is awesome.

I type 0527 for May twenty-seventh. My birthday.

It unlocks the phone.

My heart balloons in my chest. I couldn't have asked for a better friend.

But my heart sinks quickly—there's no signal, no way for me to pull up the wiki.

Wait. JP said he was working on a summary of the book. He didn't say he'd put it up yet.

I open his Notes app and scroll through until I find his summary-in-progress of *Stevie James and the Soul Scythe*.

"Get off me!" Junior yells at the hellhounds. "Girl, I swear I'm gonna make this train my new house, and your bones gon' be my first decorations!"

I hastily open the summary and look it over. The book starts out with Einan using the soul scythe to take a teacher's soul. People panic, blah, blah, blah. Stevie, Kevin, and Chloe decide the best way to stop Einan is to take the soul scythe—

I jump at the sound of hooves kicking the door and snarling from Cocoa and Cleo. "When I get through with you, you gon' regret this!" says Junior.

I try to focus on the book summary. With some snooping and sneaking, Stevie, Kevin, and Chloe find out that Einan keeps the soul scythe in his lair, and they find out the lair is in . . .

It's in an extinct underground volcano.

"This is it," I mutter. "This is it!"

The train door bursts open. Junior shoves the recliner outta the way. Cocoa and Cleo hang off his clothes by their teeth, but he ignores them and says, "Give me my map!"

"The Msaidizi is in Jackson!"

Junior stops dead. It's almost as if Cleo and Cocoa are shocked too, 'cause they let go of Junior's clothes. "How you know that?" Junior says.

If I wasn't sure before, that terrified look on his face confirms it.

"I figured it out," I say. "Roho's lair was in the extinct volcano under the city, wasn't it? I bet that's where he told the thief to hide the Msaidizi."

Junior's silence says more than enough.

I tear up. After everything Alex, JP, and I have gone

through, I finally know where the Msaidizi is. "I'm gonna save Dad," I murmur, and I almost can't believe it. "All I gotta do is get to the lair—"

"*All?*" Junior mocks. He laughs, as if there's a joke here that I'm missing. "It's not easy to find, unless you know exactly where to go, and it ain't easy to get into. Till this day LORE doesn't know how to get to it."

"Do you know?"

"If I did, why would I tell you? Especially after what you did to my house."

"But my dad—"

"Not my problem! I told you too much as it is!"

"Are you scared of Roho? Junior, he doesn't even remember who he is."

"You underestimate him," Junior says grimly. "He used the Gift like nobody has. If anybody could get their memory and the Gift back after LORE took it, it would be Boss Man. Plus some folks secretly still faithful to him. I can't have them finding out I helped you get the Msaidizi after he had it hidden."

The thought of Roho or his followers discovering that I took the Msaidizi sends a chill through me. I hope I never face any of them.

"I promise I'll never tell anyone you helped me," I say. "But I'm desperate, Junior. You loved your dad a lot, didn't you?"

Junior's eyes drift downward. "He was the best. Everybody think he was bad, but he was misunderstood. That man loved me with his whole heart. I couldn't have asked for better."

"Everyone is making assumptions about my dad too. Imagine yours no longer remembering who you are. That might be my real life soon, but you can help me keep that from happening. What do I gotta do for you to get me to the lair?"

"You got a house you can give me? That's the only thing I may be willing to help you in exchange for."

"How in the world can I do that? I only have the one I live—" Wait. *I have the one I live in!* "You willing to relocate to Jackson?"

He gives me a suspicious glare. "Why you ask?"

"It's where my house is. You can have it."

"You gon' give me your house?"

I should probably ask Dad before I give it away, but desperate times. "If you help me get to the Msaidizi, I will."

"Yeah right! You tricking me again! First you tricked me into changing into them different animals. Now you gon' pull your second trick. Once you pull the third, you'll be done with me for good."

"Huh?"

"You heard the story 'bout my daddy! That Wiley boy tricked him three times, and after the third time, Daddy had to leave him alone. That's what everybody do to me too. They never want me around."

"That's awful."

"I'm fine!" Junior snaps. "I had it made in the swamps.

250

Didn't have to worry 'bout friends coming, making a mess and disturbing my peace. It was perfect."

I wanna tell him his house was already a mess, but I keep that to myself.

This is mean, but I could see why people might not wanna be around Junior. The guy is terrifying to look at. But I also know what it's like to be the weird kid nobody wants to befriend.

"I was kinda like you," I say to Junior. "Still am, honestly. Unremarkable kids think I'm strange. I never had friends, until I moved to Jackson. That's where I met my best friend, JP. He lives next door, and I bet he'd be your friend too. Then there's Ms. Lena, she's a Visionary. You could hang out at her juke joint. Mr. Zeke and the other regulars are cool. You'd fit in with them."

"What's the catch?" Junior asks. "The house in a gated neighborhood, ain't it? I watched *Desperate Housewives*, I ain't tryna live nowhere like that!"

I have no idea what *Desperate Housewives* is, but okay. "It's not in a gated neighborhood. Dad hates those. There's no catch, and this isn't a trick. I'd give you a thousand houses to save my dad."

Junior studies me hard.

"I'd do the same for my daddy," he says. "I'll take you to the entrance of Boss Man's old colony, that's it. Nothing more, nothing less. Deal?"

He holds his hand out to me.

I shake his hand. "I thought it was a lair, not a colony."

"Boss Man had grand plans. I'll go give the train the directions."

"Wait. I gotta rescue my brother and my best friend first."

Junior gives me an up-and-down look. "Girl, what? How in the world you gon' do that? That juju bag you got might come in handy but—"

I look at him. "What?"

"You got a juju bag somewhere around here. It smells like snow."

At first I have no idea what he's talking about. Then I remember the bag I got on my birthday. I grab my backpack and rummage around till my fingers find the small leather pouch tucked inside, the Miss Peachy's bag.

Junior sniffs hard in its direction. "Yep. That's a blizzard."

"You can figure that out just by smelling it?"

"Sometimes. Miss Peachy hide the smell in a lot of the bags, 'cause us Rougarous can identify what they are easily. Every now and then though, the juju in them be so powerful the smell can't be hidden. I'm almost certain that one there is a blizzard. It'll freeze everything and everyone but the person holding the bag."

"Why is that?" I ask.

"The bag protects you against whatever juju or mojo that's released when you open it. It says so on the fine print."

I turn the bag over, and what do you know, there is a warning on the back in tiny print.

Warning: This bag contains a powerful mojo or juju that will alter your surroundings. Miss Peachy's LLC is not liable for any injury or damage caused by this bag. By opening it, you legally accept full responsibility for your actions. To prevent injury, hold the bag tight as the mojo or juju is released in order to activate the protection mojo. To place the protection mojo on others, touch them with the bag.

"They didn't always have a protection mojo on them," Junior says. "My uncle Larry got knocked out from a mojo bag that rained gold bricks. When he woke up a year later, his wife had spent his winnings. A shame. He got plenty paid from that class action lawsuit, but she ended up taking that in the divorce. Daddy told him not to marry a Banshee."

This is promising. The bag, I mean. Not Junior's uncle's soap opera. "This may work."

"Hah! It's gon' take more than that bag for you to stop them Guardians," Junior says. "They'll light you up the moment you try to open it. You can't trick them like you tricked me."

Trick them, huh?

"Actually," I say to Junior, "I think I can trick them."

SEVENTEEN

THE RETURN OF ROHO

After Cleo drops me off in the woods, I write a G-pen message to General Sharpe.

> TRACK MY LOCATION AND MEET ME HERE. BRING
> ALEX AND JP. I HAVE SOMETHING YOU WANT.

The pinks and purples of the early morning sky gleam overhead. My nerves flutter in my stomach like butterflies on Red Bull. I stuff my hands in my pockets, then take them back out. For the hundredth time, I check to make sure my juju bag is still there.

A strong wind whips through the trees and kicks up dust and leaves. At first I don't see anything but then a Guardian aircraft becomes visible above me, gold and V-shaped and as big as a jet.

The lights illuminate the clearing as it lands. A door

on the side opens, and a staircase descends from the aircraft. General Sharpe emerges, flanked by six Guardians on each side. Two of the Guardians carry a bound Alex and a bound JP.

Two other Guardians point their palms in my direction, but I yell out, "If you want the Msaidizi, you won't bind me."

"Stand down," General Sharpe tells them, and they lower their hands. "Where is it, girl?"

"You know, I'm surprised you found me." I sound bold for somebody who's scared out her mind. "I wasn't sure you were smart enough to locate me. My dad said you couldn't catch rain in a thunderstorm."

"Excuse you?"

"You heard me. Dad and I used to laugh about what a doofus you are. It took you years to catch him, and it took you days just to catch some kids. You're sure you should be a general?"

"Li'l girl . . ." She clears her throat. That did *not* sound like the General Sharpe I'm used to. "I'm not doing this with you. You said you have something I want. Is it the Msaidizi?"

"Chill, Althea," I say. For the record, this is the only time I'd ever call an adult by their first name. Dad don't play that. "Before I give you the Msaidizi, I need to see that my brother and my best friend are okay first."

General Sharpe snaps her fingers, and the two Guardians holding JP and Alex bring them forward. "See? They're fine. We fed them, and they were allowed to bathe, which is more than I can say about you. We could've tracked you by your odor alone."

"Wow, now you're roasting me? You do know I'm only twelve, right? You're what? Fifty? Sixty-five?"

"Not close! I'm the same age as your parents!"

"I wouldn't tell anybody that."

One of the Guardians snorts.

"Laugh, and watch what happens," General Sharpe warns. That "official" voice she's been using is gone. "Look here, you li'l brat—"

"Yo' momma."

General Sharpe sucks her teeth. "You've got thirty seconds to answer my question. What is it that you have for me?"

"I need to hear from JP and Alex that they're okay."

"Unbind their mouths," she orders.

The two Guardians holding JP and Alex wave their hands, and Alex's and JP's mouths unstick.

"We're okay, Nic," Alex says.

"Nic, their big ship is so cool!" JP says. "The showers spray different soaps, and you can ask the microwave thingy for any kind of food and it'll make it and the TV is 4D, which I didn't know was—"

"Bind them again!" says an annoyed General Sharpe, and JP's and Alex's mouths snap shut. "Now. Show me what you have or we'll bind you."

Leaves crunch nearby. It's subtle, and I think I'm the only one who hears it. Good. It's my sign.

"You're absolutely one hundred percent sure you want what I have?"

"Quit stalling and show me what it is!"

If she insists . . .

"All right," I say. I whistle through my fingers.

There's the crunching of more leaves, and General Sharpe and her officers whip around, turning their backs to me. A figure moves among the trees.

"Who's there?" General Sharpe says. "Show yourself!"

A tall, muscular man with a bright gold Glow emerges. Sleek black armor covers every inch of him, except for his eyes; gray as smoke and catlike, they're set on General Sharpe.

The Guardians gasp. JP and Alex make similar sounds behind their zipped lips.

"R-Roho!" General Sharpe stammers.

"Ohhh, that's who this is?" I ask. "I think I've heard of him. I'm not super familiar with Remarkable stuff, living in the Unremarkable world and all."

The Guardians raise their hands. "No, hold your fire!" General Sharpe orders. "How did you find him, girl?"

"He found me. Told me he'd forgotten who he was for a long time and now he remembers."

"W-w-what? How?"

"Beats me. He's a powerful guy. He heard I had the

Msaidizi. He seemed nice enough, so I gave it to him, and it became this suit of armor. Cool, huh?"

"Do you know what you've done?" she shouts.

"You want the Msaidizi, there it is," I say. "Go ahead, take it from him."

Roho stalks forward, and General Sharpe's knees shake. The Guardians raise their hands again, and Roho raises his. I take out the juju bag . . .

"General, on your order!" a Guardian says.

General Sharpe trembles. "F-f-f—"

I snatch the bag open.

An explosion of icy wind and blue light bursts out. I'm knocked flat on my back, and I shield my eyes, expecting screams and shouts.

But everything goes eerily quiet, and it's suddenly freezing cold.

I sit up and open my eyes. The woods have become the North Pole. Snow blankets the ground, and everything is covered in a thick layer of ice. The trees, the Guardians, General Sharpe. JP. Alex. Roho.

I go to him first. He's frozen in place with his hand shielding his eyes. It's the same with the others; whatever they were doing when I opened the bag, that's how they're stuck. Alex and JP have their eyes shut tight, General Sharpe seems to be in the middle of shouting "No!" Icicles hang from their chins and noses. It's like standing in a garden of ice sculptures.

I tap Roho with the bag, and he instantly unfreezes. I

do the same to Alex. The ice and the ropes of light melt away. I guess the protection mojo works on those too.

Alex jolts to. "Roho!"

"Chill," I say. "Get it? Chill? Anyway, that's not him." I nod at Roho. "Go ahead."

Roho shuts his eyes, and the armor disappears. He shrinks as coarse hair grows on his arms and legs, and his feet turn into cow hooves.

"Told you I could shapeshift into anybody!" Junior says.

"What's he doing here?" Alex shouts. "Why did he shapeshift into Roho?"

I knew I needed to distract General Sharpe and the Guardians, and who better than Roho? I asked Junior if he could shapeshift into him. At first he refused to help me until I agreed to ask my grandma to get him a shopping spree at some fancy clothing store in Uhuru. So here we are.

"I'll explain later," I tell Alex. I tap JP with the juju bag. "You okay, dude?"

He hugs himself tight. "Yeah. I'll never eat another Popsicle again."

"Are you okay?" Alex asks.

"Yeah. I'm sorry for leaving you guys."

"It's okay, the Guardians would've taken you too, and what good would that have been?" he says. "I'm just glad you came back."

I smile a little. "Me too."

He gives me one back.

I go up to the Popsicle formerly known as General Sharpe. "Man. I'm cold for doing this, huh?" I crack up. "Cold, get it?"

Her eyes narrow as she makes a muffled sound.

"Well, that doesn't sound very nice," I say. "I'd love to roast you—I bet you wish I literally would—but I gotta go. You should thaw in a couple of hours. Or a day. Who knows? Now if you'll excuse me, I gotta go save my dad."

Back on the Underground Railroad, Alex, JP, Junior, and I board the train. Cocoa and Cleo greet JP and Alex with excited jumps and face licks. Junior goes up front to direct Bertha to the colony while I catch Alex and JP up on things at the kitchen booth. I describe my dream about the cave and how I have a feeling that it's related to the volcano and Roho's colony.

"I can't believe Roho's colony is under Jackson, and there's a volcano under the city," JP says.

I'm surprised myself. Jackson doesn't scream "evil hideaway." New York and Los Angeles? Sure. Dad says the Knicks and the Clippers will drive anyone mad. But Jackson? "It's one place nobody would think of as a hideout," I say.

"That's probably the point," says Alex. "Now the question is . . . what might be waiting for us down there? I doubt it'll be easy to get the Msaidizi."

We get quiet. We could be walking into our grave.

No, I can't put Alex and JP in that kinda danger. "I'll go by myself."

"What? No!" says Alex.

"No way, Nic!" JP adds.

"I've already gotten you guys in enough trouble."

"So?" says Alex. "We're in this together. One of us goes to the colony, all three of us go to the colony. No ifs, ands, or buts about it."

"What he said," says JP. "Kevin and Chloe wouldn't leave Stevie on his own. We're just like them right now, searching for a powerful weapon. It's gonna take all three of us to find it."

This is an odd moment to be grateful I've got them, but yeah. I am. Ugh, here I go, tearing up again. I really hate having feelings.

"All right then," I say. "Let's go get the Msaidizi."

EIGHTEEN

BOOBY TRAPS AND RAPS

We get to Jackson around seven a.m. We have two hours to save Dad and Uncle Ty.

Bertha slows down, approaching a brick wall. A yellow sign hangs from the wall with two words printed on it: Dead End.

"It's not really a dead end, is it?" I ask Junior.

"Not if you know what to do."

He waves his hand, and the brick wall parts open like sliding doors, letting the train through into a tunnel, and the wall slams shut behind us. Mold, moss, and roots have taken over this tunnel. Beyond the glow of Bertha's headlight, it's pitch-black. Super creepy, but hey, that's what I'd expect for the entrance to an evil Manifestor's colony.

Bertha brakes to a stop.

"I got you to the entrance like I promised," Junior says. "You're on your own the rest of the way."

I stare at the darkness ahead and wipe my sweaty palms on my pants. "Go to the colony, find the Msaidizi. Colony, Msaidizi. We can do this." I think. I hope. "Junior, have Bertha take you to Ms. Lena. The train is hers. She can take you to my house."

"We're gonna be neighbors," JP says. "I'll warn you, my parents are gonna invite you to our church. They do that to everyone. They're also gonna try to get you to join."

"Long as I can join the choir, count me in," Junior says. "I been told I got the voice of an angel."

I never would've guessed that, but okay.

Alex, JP, and I get our stuff together. Cocoa happily climbs into my backpack, but Cleo hangs back with Junior.

I motion her with my head. "C'mon, girl. You can come with us."

She barks. I don't speak hellhound but I'm pretty sure she said she's not coming; she's got things to do and places to see. Understandable. After being stuck with those Grand Wizards, of course she wants to venture out and see the world.

She turns to leave, and Cocoa jumps outta my backpack. I wanna call her to me, but as a kid who missed having a mom, I get why she'd wanna be with hers. I can't make her go with me.

But Cleo nudges Cocoa back with her paw. Cocoa whines in response. Her momma lets out an annoyed "this child is testing me" huff and uses her teeth to pick Cocoa up by her scruff. She drops Cocoa at my feet. I don't have to speak hellhound to get this message either: "Take care of her."

"I will," I say.

Cleo rubs her nose against Cocoa's, a hellhound momma kiss, then she dashes off. We watch her momma turn into a streak of smoke that disappears around a bend into another tunnel.

"Don't worry," I tell Cocoa. "We'll see her again."

"Nic?" Alex says. "We should let Mom know where we are in case . . . you know."

In case something really bad happens. I take out my G-pen. Once I send Zoe a message, she can track my location like she did before. I know that the Guardians can too, but hopefully they can't get to the tunnel entrance. I imagine my mom as I write.

WE'RE SAFE. WE KNOW WHERE THE MSAIDIZI IS. YOU CAN FIND US IN JACKSON.

There's so much more I wanna tell her, but a G-pen message doesn't seem like the right way to do it.

I stick the pen back in my pocket. I'm gonna survive and tell her in person. I will *not* die in Roho's colony.

Telling myself that helps me step off the train and into the tunnel.

Bertha starts backing up, and Junior flashes a rascally grin from the door. "Good luck."

The way he says it and that grin of his put a sick feeling in the pit of my stomach. "What are you not telling us?"

He just waves as the train backs through the opening. The brick walls snap shut, sealing me, Alex, JP, and Cocoa in the darkened tunnel.

JP turns on the flashlight on his phone. I can at least see Alex, JP, and Cocoa now, but not much else.

"Is it safe to move?" Alex asks.

I stick Cocoa in my backpack. "Probably not, but we can't just stand here."

"We need to keep our eyes peeled for booby traps," JP says. "The kind you have to outsmart. You can't use the Gift on them."

"What makes you think that?" I ask.

"The Stevie books, of course! When Stevie, Kevin, and Chloe try to get into Einan's lair, they face booby traps that require logic. Evil-guy logic at that."

This is one time I hope he's wrong.

We follow the train tracks and slowly move ahead. Cars hum above us and make that clanging sound that comes with hitting potholes.

The rusted train tracks come to an end, but the tunnel keeps going. JP's arms swing out in front of me and Alex. "There's a wide hole past the tracks. Don't you see it?"

I squint. I only see solid ground. "No?"

"It must be an illusion," Alex says. "You can see through them, and we can't without my glasses, remember?"

"Yeah, but it should've been odd to you guys that the tracks just stop. Logic, people!"

I find a pebble nearby and toss it. It disappears past the

ground, and it's a long while before we hear it hit the bottom. "How do we cross?" I ask.

A low rumble makes us turn around. The wall behind us slowly closes in, and so do the walls on both sides of us.

"Don't panic, don't panic," Alex says, though he's panicking. "What do we do?"

I glance around. I don't know if we are supposed to cross, and I don't see anything that could take us over the pit. No way to get around it either. I look down, and that's when I spot the top of a ladder sticking up out the ground. Since it's not actually ground and an illusion, it must lead into the pit. I point it out to Alex and JP. "We climb down."

"No!" JP says. "Logically, we should climb the ladder, but this is evil-guy logic. We need to jump."

"Into a bottomless pit?" Alex screeches.

"Yes! To get into Einan's lair, Stevie, Kevin, and Chloe had to do the thing that scared them most. Roho wouldn't expect anyone to be brave enough to jump, so that's exactly what we must do."

Alex shakes his head. "No! I'm not jumping into that thing. We don't know what's waiting at the bottom!"

"Those walls will crush us," I say.

He backs up. "I'm not going in that pit!"

I move toward him. Even with everything we've been through, I haven't seen Alex this terrified. "We'll do it together, all right?"

"I can't, Nic!"

"Yes, you can! I believe in you."

The walls move in faster. We're running outta time. I hold my hand out for Alex's.

He stares at it and takes a deep breath. "Okay. I trust you."

It's not "I love you," but it feels close to it.

He takes my hand. JP grabs my other and guides us forward.

"On the count of three," I say. "One—"

"Why did I agree to this?" Alex moans.

"Two!"

"If I die, I'm killing you both!"

"Three!"

We leap together.

I brace myself for immediate impact against solid ground—but it's an illusion, like JP said. I shut my eyes, thinking I'm about to fall into who knows what and possibly splatter on the bottom, but I'm not falling. I'm floating. I open my eyes and see JP and Alex floating alongside me like feathers in a breeze. We gently land on our feet.

Alex opens one eye. "We're not dead?"

"Not yet," I say.

JP points his flashlight, revealing our surroundings. We've landed in another tunnel.

A fork lies ahead of us, where the tunnel breaks off into three more tunnels.

There's a loud *whoompf*, and heat blasts over our heads. We duck, but I manage to glance up. Several jets of flames shoot outta the wall where the ladder is, scorching the metal frame.

"That's why the ladder was a bad idea," JP says. "We would've been burned to crisps."

"Good looking out," I say.

We carefully approach the fork. The three tunnels look the same—made of stone and lit by candles with no end in sight. I can't tell if one is more dangerous than the other. "What's the evil-guy logic here?"

"I'm not sure," JP admits.

Alex gathers up a couple of pebbles and tosses one into each of the tunnels. They ping against the stone. "No motion-activated jujus in place."

"You guys look in those two." JP points them out. "I'll take this one."

"Um, nah," I say. "Do you watch horror movies? You never split up! That's when bad stuff happens."

"Nic, we won't go far," Alex says. "We can yell if we need help. We gotta see which tunnel is the best one to go in, and we'd lose time checking each one out together. We've gotta split up."

I hate that he's right. "Okay, but yell out the second things don't feel right. Deal?"

"Deal," they say.

We carefully approach our assigned tunnels. Mine smells damp and sounds like a gentle ocean breeze, the same way the inside of a seashell does. I hold my breath and step into it.

Nothing happens.

I take one more step.

The candles in the tunnel go out, and complete darkness washes over me.

I turn around. The lighted area I just left is gone, replaced by darkness. "Alex? JP?"

No answer.

My body goes numb. "Alex! JP!"

Complete silence.

My heart hammers against my chest. I can't see my own hands in front of me. It should be impossible, but the tunnel ahead looks darker.

This isn't natural darkness. It's a juju.

I wanna run, but I can't see a way to go. I nearly freak out, but I gotta stay calm.

I stick my arms out and feel around, but my hands never find the tunnel walls. It's as if they've somehow disappeared. It's like I'm in a void.

"This endless darkness, it won't lift, unless you're wise and use the Gift," a cold voice says.

"Who's there?" I demand.

There's no one, only darkness.

"She can't use it, no need to pester," says a higher-pitched voice. "It's a shame to call her Manifestor."

They cackle in unison.

I cover my ears. They're not real. This is similar to the demon trickery DD used on me.

"We are real, your fears we feel, but we're not demons or the dead," raps the first voice. "Our power lies in bravery's demise, we live inside your head."

"Return the way you came, depart," says the higher-pitched voice, "or face those things deep in your heart."

I don't know what this is, but I gotta get outta here, *now*. JP said to use evil-guy logic. In this case, I gotta do the opposite of what the voices say. I run forward, but then outta nowhere, two people appear in front of me.

I stumble back. "D-Dad? Zoe?"

It's hard to explain the relief I feel from seeing them, but it's short-lived—they stare at me with disgust. I move toward them, and they put their hands up, signaling me to stay away, as if they're repulsed at the very thought of touching me.

My parents wouldn't do that. "This is an illusion."

"If only you were an illusion and not our actual daughter," Zoe sneers. "Why did I waste my time searching for *you?*"

"I shouldn't have taken *you*," Dad says. "Your brother is obviously the better twin."

My eyes prickle. "Don't listen to them," I tell myself. "This isn't real."

"It's real, all right."

I whirl around. Alex leans against the wall with a cocky grin.

"Alex!" I hurry to him, but he backs away. "We need to get outta here."

"Why? I like it here," he says, and goes over to our mom and dad. Zoe lovingly holds him close, and Dad looks at him with so much pride.

"Powerless and weak, you have no worth." Those voices speak through my parents. "We deeply regret the day you were birthed!"

The words yank my heart from my chest and stomp it into tiny pieces. "No. No, that isn't true."

"Everything you wanted, I got," Alex says. "Everything I am, you're not."

He and our parents laugh as more people appear. There's my grandma, the president . . . General Blake . . . Sarah. There are others I don't recognize, but I know they're my family. They surround Alex with love and look at him as if he's the crown jewel . . . then they glare at me as if I offend them just by existing. I suddenly don't wanna.

"You're a disgrace!" General Blake says.

"I'm ashamed that you're my descendant!" says Sarah.

"How did I end up with such a failure for a grand-daughter?" says my grandma.

I back up, tears in my eyes. "No! I'm not a failure!"

They shout how awful I am, how much I disappoint them, and I beg and plead for them to stop as I back farther and farther away—

My foot slips off a ledge.

I scream as I tumble through darkness, wind whipping around me, making my eyes water more than they already do. My family is gone, but the voices cackle loudly.

This is it. I'm gonna die, and I can't do anything to save

myself. It might be a good thing Dad won't remember me. Then he won't have to grieve.

I brace myself for impact and pray that it happens so fast, I don't feel a thing.

Except I do feel something. A hand grabs mine.

"Nic!"

Alex stands over me—the real Alex, without a cocky grin or an evil laugh. An orb of light glows in his other hand and illuminates his face.

I gasp for breath. One second, I was tumbling through air, and now I'm sitting on solid ground. "How . . . I fell—"

"No, you didn't. It's a delusion."

He helps me to my feet, but I'm trembling, and he has to hold me up. It's still dark, but Alex's orb helps me see him from the waist up.

"You okay?" he asks.

I nod even though I'm not. "What's a delusion?"

"People call them internal illusions. Instead of seeing what someone else drew like you would with an illusion, a delusion messes with your head and makes you hear, see, and feel the worst things you've ever thought. You thought you were falling, but in reality you were sitting on the ground."

"Oh." I should've known it wasn't real, but it sure felt like it.

"Nic? Are you really okay?"

That wasn't the real Alex saying those mean things, but it's hard to look at him. "Yeah. How'd you get outta your tunnel?"

"'Darkness eventually leads to light.' These traps don't require evil-guy logic. They require wisdom. One reason Roho didn't like LORE is that he thought they had strayed away from tradition. He was big on ancient customs and beliefs and was known to quote Elders Proverbs. They're these old sayings our ancestors brought with them from Africa."

"I don't understand?"

"We jumped into the pit. I now realize that's a reference to the Elders Proverb that says, 'Leap into the unknown to find your way.' These tunnels? 'Darkness eventually leads to light.' That's why it looks like they get darker the farther you go. The delusion makes it hard for you to go forward, which is another proverb, 'Strength is found in the face of fear.' I ran past my delusion and into the darkness. It led me into a lit area. Then I went in your tunnel to find you."

That makes a ton of sense. "We need to find JP."

Alex draws an orb of light in his other palm. He's so good at using the Gift. Unlike me.

I gotta shake this. I follow Alex and his light. We come out into a brightly lit area that the three tunnels lead to. We have to run into darkness again to get to JP in the other tunnel.

His cries lead us to him. We find him curled up and sobbing like a baby.

I bend down in front of him. "JP? It's okay."

He throws his arms around my neck. "I lost everyone!"

I hug him back. "No, you didn't."

"But I did! It got dark, and there was no way out. These voices told me I was alone, then I saw you and everyone else I care about, and you disappeared. I thought y'all were gone like . . . like Leah."

He sobs on my shoulder, and I get teary-eyed. Delusions must work on Seers too.

"You can't get rid of me, dude. Ever," I say.

I let him cry as long as he needs to. After a few minutes, we get him to his feet, and Alex guides us to the lighted area. This time there's only one way to go. Forward.

We quietly trek ahead for what feels like miles. The tunnel starts to stretch wider and wider. The ground slopes upward for a few yards and then it slopes back down, leading right into a humongous pit.

Scratch that, pit doesn't cut it. This is a freaking canyon. There are only two ways to cross it—an old rickety bridge, or a wooden beam. The bridge leads to a narrow tunnel that we could only go through in a single-file line. The wooden beam leads to a much wider tunnel. I'm willing to risk it on that beam to avoid going in that narrow tunnel. I hate closed-in spaces.

A strange hissing noise echoes from the canyon. I peek into it and immediately wish I hadn't. Hundreds—maybe thousands—of snakes slither way below.

I look at Alex. "Got a proverb for this?"

"Why do you need a proverb?" JP asks.

Alex explains the wisdom stuff to him, then squats to check out the canyon. "Definitely can't jump into this one. We've gotta choose a way to cross." He looks from the beam to the bridge, and it's wild how much he looks like Dad when he's thinking hard. He snaps his fingers. "We take the bridge to the smaller tunnel."

"Dude, I am not getting stuck in a tunnel," I say.

"Nic, it's another Elders Proverb. 'Broad is the path that leads to destruction.'"

"I don't care. We should go see if we missed another path."

I try to go back up the slope, but my feet can't gain enough traction, and I slide down, stopping mere inches from the edge of the canyon.

"There's no going back," Alex says. "You do wanna help our father, right?"

Ugh. He had to go there. I love Dad more than I hate closed-in spaces. "Fine."

Alex takes the first step onto the bridge. It creaks under the weight of his foot, and my heart stops as I imagine it giving way.

It doesn't. He lets out a breath and takes another step. JP and I slowly follow his lead. Cocoa barks smoke at the snakes from the safety of my backpack as they hiss.

There's something about having snakes below us that makes us speed up. We hurry into the tunnel and not a second too soon—the bridge gives way into the snake pit.

JP bends over, panting. "Guys, this is a lot."

No kidding. Based on these booby traps alone, this colony feels like a place we should be running from, not running into. I'm terrified of what's waiting for us there.

But we don't have a choice but to keep going. We go into the narrow tunnel. Moss and tree roots brush against us as we squeeze by them. The farther we go, the more the ceiling closes in, and we're forced to crouch and eventually crawl. It feels like the air is being sucked outta the tunnel.

"I'm not claustrophobic, I'm not claustrophobic," I say. I am.

"Think of your dad, Nic," JP says. "You gotta do this for him."

I picture him in my head, and that helps me keep crawling. After a while the tunnel walls aren't closing in as much, and the tunnel expands to the point we can stand instead of crawl.

Up ahead, a rusty elevator door awaits us. The doors part open.

I pause as it hits me that I could be walking into my grave. I didn't see enough in that dream to know how things turn out. But for Dad's sake, I step onto the elevator.

JP and Alex cautiously follow. There are only two buttons on the panel. On one button, an arrow points up. On the other, down. I press down.

The doors snap shut, and with no warning, the elevator violently lurches deeper underground.

NINETEEN

THE TALE OF THE MSAIDIZI

My stomach and my brain get left on the main floor. Alex and JP scream as we plummet with the force of a rocket ship.

Alex's knees buckle. "I'm gonna be sick."

"We're going to hell!" JP cries in a ball on the floor. "I don't wanna go to hell!"

Nobody can ever tell me that boys aren't dramatic.

I shut my eyes tight enough to see stars. Cocoa yawns against my neck. How my dog can be sleepy at a time like this, I'll never know. After several minutes, the elevator slows to a stop and then—

Ding! The doors part, and we gasp.

At once, hundreds of lanterns light up along brick paths, revealing dozens and dozens of stone buildings that dot the rocky landscape that stretches as far and wide as a small town. There are single-story homes as well as massive buildings several stories tall. The brick paths wind around the buildings and lead to the massive volcano that towers over everything at the far end.

"What was Roho planning?" I ask.

"To destroy LORE and start his own government," Alex says. "I bet he wanted this to be the new capital."

I could see that. Strangely enough, the extinct volcano reminds me of a capitol building, the way it watches over the town. Carved in the side of it is a stone staircase that leads to a set of brass doors.

I point them out to JP and Alex. "I bet those doors lead to Roho's lair. We should look there first."

"Uh, did Junior say whether the colony was empty or not?" JP asks.

Now that I think about it, he didn't, but the colony is so still and quiet I doubt anyone else is here. "I mean, it looks pretty empty."

"Looks can be deceiving," says Alex. "Keep close."

Before we leave the elevator, I touch the ground outside it with the toe of my sneaker. Hey, I came this close to falling into a canyon, I ain't doing a repeat. It's solid stone. Not an illusion.

We get out, and a strong scent hits me head-on. It's the same smell that a brand-new belt or pair of shoes might have, or the inside of a fancy car. Leather.

Alex sniffs. "Odd smell."

Agreed. I'm ready to find this Msaidizi and get up outta here *now*.

We follow a brick road into the colony. More lanterns lit by fire come to life as we move along. Motion-detecting Giftech lights, Alex says. The buildings make me believe this is the business area. There's a bank, some stores, and a diner. Some of the roofs are caving in and some of them look charred, as if they were once on fire. This place is starting to remind me of the small towns Dad and I have passed through on our way to a bigger city, the ones he says probably used to be thriving but are now all but forgotten.

"Wonder why Roho's followers abandoned the colony," I say.

"Well, after Grandpa Doc defeated Roho, LORE got most of his followers too. They altered their memories or took the Gift or their power from them for a time. There probably weren't enough left to keep this place going."

"A town under Jackson," JP mutters. "How'd they build it without anyone noticing?"

"I'm sure it wasn't that hard. Unremarkables are super unaware," Alex says. "It's fascinating how they miss things or try to explain them away. Take earthquakes, for instance. Half the time those are caused by Giants."

"They are?" JP says.

"Oh yeah. There's a Giant city in the desert in California. Why do you think they have so many earthquakes there? All it takes is for a few of them to get into a brawl and then bam, earthquake."

"Whoa." JP looks at me. "You think Giants caused that earthquake that day at the museum?"

I forgot about that. "Nah. Giants don't live in this part of the country. It's too humid. They prefer drier, warm climates."

"There was an earthquake here?" Alex asks.

"Yeah. It hit while Nic and I were at the museum with Mr. Blake and Mr. Porter. Weird thing is, though, it was only near the museum. No other parts of town experienced it. We had been cornered by a Boo Hag and—"

"Whoa, whoa," Alex says with a hand up. "A Boo Hag?"

"Yeah. It tried to attack us and then the earthquake hit," I say. "The earthquake didn't last long. I think it was over by the time Dad and Uncle Ty stopped the Boo Hag."

Alex goes, "Huh. That's really strange."

A deep, low rumble shakes the ground. We stop dead.

Ironic we're talking about earthquakes. That felt like a mini one, and it's got me rethinking that whole "it's too humid here for Giants" thing.

"Really, really, really hope that wasn't a Giant," I say.

"Giants have a distinctive odor, and it's nothing like the one we smell," Alex says.

"Then what was it?" JP asks.

"Probably the earth shifting." Alex swallows. "Yeah."

I hope so. I'm kinda scared to move after that, but we turn a corner and make our way into a residential area of the colony. We find quaint houses with rusted tricycles in the front yards. At a playground there are rusted slides and swings. Where four paths meet, a gazebo sits in the center with rocking chairs and tables for playing chess.

"I don't get it," I say. "Roho was evil. This place does not scream 'evil colony for evil Manifestor and his followers.' It's like the suburbs. Just missing a bunch of coffee shops."

"Can anyone understand an evil mastermind?" says Alex.

"I can try. Evil dudes usually want people to be miserable," I say. "There's nothing miserable about this place."

JP points ahead. "What's that?"

There's another park up the brick road. The Astroturf is dusted in blue glitter. In the middle of the park, large stones are stacked on top of each other in a large circle, like a bird's nest made from rocks.

We go check it out. The leathery smell is strongest here, but it also smells like something died, in the stone nest to be exact.

I do and I don't wanna know what that is. I put my foot on one of the stones, pull myself up, and peek inside the nest, and my stomach flips. I look back at Alex and JP. "This thing is filled with bones."

"They're not human bones, right?" JP says. "Right?"

"Too tiny for that. I think they're rat bones."

"Only because whatever ate them probably didn't have other options," says Alex. "Guys, we need to leave."

I climb off the nest, and some of the blue glitter gets on my palms. I look at it closely. It's brighter and coarser than regular glitter, as if it was made with crushed jewels.

"What is it?" JP asks.

"I don't know," I say, though I feel like I should.

An earsplitting roar echoes throughout the colony.

JP jumps. I nearly fall over. Alex squeaks.

"Please tell me that was one of your stomachs growling," JP says.

I straighten, my mind racing. The charred rooftops. The strong leathery smell. The glitter. The stone nest.

"Holy moly," I mutter. "It's a dragon!"

"What?" Alex shouts.

"The roofs are burnt 'cause it breathes fire. The smell? Classic dragon smell. Their skin is like leather, and when it sheds it leaves a glittery dust behind. They live in stone nests, and I think we can figure out what happened to those bones. There's a dragon here!"

The beast roars again, sending dirt raining down on us.

We race toward an abandoned house and hurry inside. The ground shudders as a loud thud rolls through the colony.

We crouch behind a dust-covered sofa.

The beast's footsteps move close, rumbling the ground and kicking up dust along the path. I pray Cocoa doesn't bark and give up our location, but she's more interested in sniffing my hair. Alex whimpers. JP puts his hand over Alex's mouth to muffle the sound.

Maybe I'm too curious, 'cause I decide to peek out from behind the couch.

I bite back a yelp. All I can see are the dragon's scaly

blue legs and feet out the front window, that's how tall it is. One claw alone could crush the three of us at once.

It steps over and around the houses, like a giant monster in an old horror film. I thought it was silly how people in those movies would act like they were too scared to move. Now I get it. Fear weighs my limbs down like an anchor.

The dragon's feet lift off the ground and its wings flap, kicking up dust again. The sound of them quickly fades off into the distance.

JP breathes hard and fast. "Junior didn't mention a dragon."

"Not surprised," Alex says. "We need to go back to the elevator and get outta here."

"Those booby traps aren't made to go back through!" I say. "We need to find a new way out, and if that's the case we may as well get the Msaidizi while we're here."

"This is a dragon we're talking about, Nic! I bet it's protecting the Msaidizi," Alex says. "How are we gonna get past it?"

If there's one creature I know about, it's dragons. "They're vicious, but they can be outsmarted." I'm thinking out loud. "They get confused easily. They're also prone to dizziness, unsteady balance, nausea. Vertigo. Their ears are sensitive, and too much noise causes the vertigo."

"How do you know so much about them?" JP asks.

"I've always wanted one for a pet. Along with a hellhound!" I add, 'cause Cocoa growled at me. This dog . . . "Dad said I'd have to research them first."

"Okay, we make a lot of noise to throw the dragon out of sorts," Alex says. "We could use JP's phone for that and play music loudly while we look."

I shake my head. "No. One of us distracts the dragon. Two of us look." I swallow. "*I* distract, you two look."

"No!" they both say.

"We're not leaving you, Nic," JP says.

"You could get hurt!" says Alex.

I can't explain it to them, I don't understand it myself, but it feels like this is what I'm meant to do—like the real reason I studied up on dragons was for this moment. "I know the most about dragons, it makes sense that I distract it. I'll be okay."

"I don't like leaving you alone," Alex says, and JP nods in agreement.

Oh, *now* they don't wanna split up? I could've sworn they were all about it back at the three tunnels of doom and gloom. "I appreciate your concern, but we don't have time to argue. Dad's trial starts in . . ." I take JP's hand and glance at his phone, but I wish I hadn't. "An hour, and I don't know how long it'll take to get to Uhuru. We can't waste any time."

A roar echoes in the distance. Two guesses as to what that is. I push JP and Alex outta the house. "Go!"

JP leaves his phone with me, and they run down the brick road that winds toward the volcano. It's just me, Cocoa, and the dragon.

Holy moly, it's just me, Cocoa, and the dragon. I glance

over my shoulder at Cocoa, and she rests her head against my neck for a snooze. So basically, it's just me and the dragon. My dog is *not* dependable.

I leave the house and head down a path opposite JP and Alex's, toward the business section of the colony. I search JP's phone for a techno playlist. That's guaranteed to torture even the scariest beast. Once I find one, I put the volume on max and hit play.

I run through the colony, keeping my eyes trained upward. No sign of the dragon yet.

"Your Grace!" a voice calls.

I stumble over a brick but catch myself before I faceplant. "Who's there?"

No answer. "Who's there?" I shout again.

A shadow passes over me, far too fast for me to make out its shape, but I don't need to.

The dragon.

I run faster, but its shadow follows me. The force of its wings kicks up clouds of dust throughout the colony. I can't see the rock ceiling anymore, only the creature's blue glittery underbelly. Its wings are as wide as king-sized beds, and its neck is thick as a tree trunk. I can't crane my neck enough to see its head.

I glance back at the volcano. JP and Alex just started to climb the staircase. Luckily for them, the dragon hasn't noticed them.

Me? Not so much. The techno music doesn't seem to be confusing this thing—it flies with pure determination.

Just my luck that I encounter the one dragon that's been to a rave.

I dart into the abandoned diner.

"Your Grace!"

I trip over a chair but quickly scramble to my feet. I press myself against the wall and mute JP's phone.

The ground shudders from the dragon landing close by. With each step it takes, the building rattles. My knees shake the closer it gets.

But then it sounds like it stops walking. The dragon snarls, and then there's the sound of its wings flapping as they kick up dust. It flies off, like something else has its attention.

Alex and JP.

I race out the diner and search the sky. No dragon, but I spot JP and Alex halfway up the staircase on the volcano. They look my way, and terror takes over their faces.

"Nic, run!" Alex screams. "It's behind you!"

I freeze.

I saw this before, in Ms. Lena's vision.

Warm breath brushes my neck, and I force myself to turn around.

My reflection twinkles in large orange eyes with slitted vertical pupils. The dragon's metallic horns glisten as much as its blue glittery skin. It opens its mouth, and I expect a fiery roar that'll set me ablaze, but the dragon shouts, "Your Grace!"

I stop breathing.

The dragon spoke?

"I am the Helper," it says. "I am the Gift in its purest form."

I fight to breathe as the dragon cranes its head toward me. Tattooed between its eyes is a tree with red specks glistening along the limbs. The Mark of Eden—the symbol we were told we would find on the Msaidizi.

"Yes, I am she," the dragon says. "I am the one your people call the Msaidizi. I have been waiting for you, child."

"M-me?"

"Yes, you, Alexis Nichole Blake. This moment has been destined since before your birth."

She opens her mouth, and a jet of rainbow-colored flames shoots out and surrounds us like a wall. Life-sized outlines of people form in the flames: a mighty man wielding a hammer on a train track, a Giant woman holding a pole on top of a boat, a man pushing a plow across a field. John Henry, Annie Christmas, and High John. There are other outlines I don't recognize, like a warrior fighting a beast with a spear, a soldier covering children with a gigantic shield, a princess fighting an army with a sword.

"For centuries, I have helped Remarkables do great things," the Msaidizi says. "It is the very reason I was created. But some have used me to do much greater than most."

A new figure forms in the flames: tall and muscular with a bald head, the man is surrounded by dozens of other figures. He slips on a black suit of armor and motions his hand. The other figures fall lifelessly around him.

"Roho," I say.

"Our time together was short compared to some," the Msaidizi says. "Roho discovered who I am destined to answer to next. For that reason, he had me stowed away here in this hidden place. I've stayed, for this is where you and I were meant to meet, but I've protected you as best I could."

Outlines of me and JP at the museum form in the flames. The Boo Hag crawls toward us, and the ground shakes violently.

"You caused the earthquake," I say.

"Yes, Your Grace. I always sense when you're in danger, though being here has limited my ability to help you."

I hear every word she says clearly, but my brain is stuck. "Why do you help me?"

Her large orange eyes twinkle with amusement. "I think you know why, Nichole."

The wall of flames dissolves as she lowers her head at my feet.

"I am the Msaidizi," she says, "and I answer to you."

TWENTY
HOMECOMING

I first fell in love with dragons when I was five.

Dad and I lived in Harlem back then. Our block had a park, a bodega, and a pizza parlor. Couldn't get much better than that when it comes to a New York City block. Dad loved it 'cause everyone in our building was exiled like us. Ms. Clayton the Manifestor and her miniature hellhounds lived across the hall. She was a self-exiled librarian who had rooms filled with books on Remarkable history. Next to her were Mr. Sam the Rougarou and Ms. Shante the Vampire and their three teenage kids, Jordy, Jamal, and Jasmine, who drank blood smoothies and changed into Werewolves during full moons. Dad said they were exiled 'cause some Remarkables didn't like "all that mixing of different types of Remarkables."

Then there was Mr. Prince, a Manifestor who lived next door to us. He was a self-exile. He caught creatures to protect the Unremarkables around Harlem under the guise of a handyman. That's how Dad got into the business. One time, a ghoul wreaked havoc in the Apollo in the middle of a show, and Mr. Prince caught it and kept it. He trained it to clean his apartment.

Everyone in the building spent the holidays together like one big family. One Christmas, Mr. Prince proudly showed off his baby dragon, Simeon, that he caught while on a trip to Egypt. At only a few weeks old, Simeon was bigger than Ms. Clayton's mini hellhounds. He tried to bite everyone, except for me. He curled up in my lap as if I was his new home.

Mr. Prince let me play with Simeon every day. Simeon would chase me up and down the stairs, and we'd play catch in the hallways. I'd sneak him raw chicken outta our refrigerator. Unremarkables who saw us together thought I was playing with a kitten.

One evening Dad and I came home from the park, and there was a piece of paper taped to our door. Dad snatched it off before I could see it good, but I do remember catching a glimpse of our faces on it. I was a little kid, so I just figured someone took pictures of us and Dad didn't like them. Now I realize it was a missing and wanted poster.

Dad rushed us inside and said we had to leave. ASAP.

He didn't tell anybody we were leaving except for Mr. Prince, and the older man came and helped Dad pack. I sat on our living-room floor, holding Simeon in my arms, and cried until I got sick.

When it was time to leave, Mr. Prince gently pried the dragon from my hands. I remember it was late at night, but as Dad and I pulled away from our building, I could see Mr. Prince and my scaly best friend under a streetlamp, watching us go. I vowed to one day have a dragon of my own.

John Henry wanted the mightiest sledgehammer in all the land, and the Msaidizi presented itself as that. Annie Christmas longed for a powerful pole for her boat, and the Msaidizi became one for her. I've always wanted a dragon, and the Msaidizi became one, just for me.

I reach for her cheek. She nuzzles it against my palm. Her skin is cool to the touch and much smoother than I would've thought.

"You answer to me." I hear myself saying the words, but they don't seem real. "But—"

"Nic, we're coming!" Alex shouts. He and JP race toward me. Alex has a rope of light in his hand, and JP has a stick he must've found lying around.

He swings it in the dragon's direction like it's a pair of nunchucks. One year of martial arts and he thinks he's Bruce Lee. "Get away from her, you beast!" he says.

Alex whips the rope toward the dragon. "Nic, run!"

"Guys, guys! Chill! It's not just a dragon. It's the Msaidizi."

Alex lowers his rope, but JP swings the stick. Alex grabs it to make him stop.

"Did you say it's the Msaidizi?" Alex asks.

The Msaidizi inches toward them. JP yelps. Alex stumbles back with a frightened squeak and lands flat on his back.

"Calm down, it's cool," I say. "She won't hurt you unless I tell her to." I don't know how I know that, but I do. It's as if I automatically understand how she works.

Alex props himself up on his elbows. "What do you mean, unless you tell her to?"

I don't know how to tell them she answers to me. Honestly, I don't know what to think or *how* to think. My thoughts are jumbled like a big ball of yarn.

"Nic?" Alex says. "What's going—ah!"

"What is—ahh!" I jump as G-pen messages appear in front of me.

NICHOLE!

IT'S MOM!

WHERE ARE YOU?!?!?

I TRACKED YOUR LOCATION BUT I DON'T SEE YOU!

ARE YOU UNDERGROUND?!?

WHY ARE YOU UNDERGROUND?!?!

Alex tries to catch his breath. "She must be really upset if she's using multiple question marks with exclamation points. Mom is a total grammar nerd. We should get up there."

"Exactly how do we do that?" JP asks.

I look to the Msaidizi. "Do you know how to get outta here?"

292

The Msaidizi guides us to another elevator on the other side of the colony. I'm thinking it's impossible for her to fit in, but she shrinks to the size of a lizard, and I put her in my backpack alongside Cocoa. My puppy sniffs her out first, then licks her. In hellhound, that's approval.

The ride up in this elevator isn't nearly as bad as down in the other one, and I make a mental note to kick Junior. I shouldn't be surprised he didn't bring us to the easier entrance. The jerk.

The elevator doors open into a small tunnel with a ladder going up the wall. We climb the ladder and emerge from a manhole cover in the Mississippi Fairgrounds parking lot.

I shield my eyes. I've been underground so long that it takes a second to adjust to sunlight. "You see Zoe?" I ask Alex.

But she sees us first. "Nichole! Alex!"

She and Uncle Ty hurry across the parking lot.

"Mom!" Alex says.

"My babies!" Zoe hugs our necks, then kisses my forehead and Alex's, back and forth, back and forth. "Are you okay?"

"Yeah."

It's not good enough. She pulls us close. "I thought . . ." She gets choked up. She buries her face in my hair. "I can't lose you again."

My throat tightens, though the rest of me relaxes in her

arms. I didn't realize that seeing her would be such a relief after everything we've gone through.

"Are you okay, sweetheart?" she asks JP.

"I'm great! We rode around on the Underground Railroad at like two hundred miles per hour. It was a bit much on my digestive system at first, if you know what I mean, but I got used to it after a while. Getting attacked by a Vampire, Hairy Man Junior, and the Devil's daughter wasn't fun. Having demons turn people against us and getting kidnapped by the Grand Wizards was scary. My arrest wasn't too bad. All in all, this was better than any vacation Bible school camping trip."

Zoe blinks. "You were attacked by who?"

This will be an interesting story to tell. "We're okay. Isn't that what matters?"

"No!" She grabs my cheeks and looks me over closely. "Are you injured? When did you last eat? Or bathe? Oooh, don't answer that. You're musty."

"More importantly," Uncle Ty says, "where did you guys just come from?"

"Roho's colony," I say. "We found the Msaidizi."

I take it out my backpack, and they gasp. Although it's a little dragon, it's still easy to make out the Mark of Eden on the Msaidizi's forehead. I tell them that Roho had someone steal the Msaidizi from LORE. As I talk, the lizard hops onto my shoulder and licks my cheek. I laugh (and ignore Cocoa's growl—jealous much?).

"Oh my God," Uncle Ty says, a grin slowly breaking

out on his face. "You found it. Why is it a dragon, though? I don't need a dragon. I don't think. But who cares! You found it! Zoe, you know what this means? It will answer to me and I can use it to stop the real—"

"We need to go to Uhuru," she says abruptly.

"But Zoe—"

"We'll discuss it later, Ty. Calvin's trial started a few minutes ago—"

That hits me like a punch. "What?"

"—and dare I say it, but the council needs to know the truth, even when it comes to a low-down, dirty, baby-stealing—"

"Zoe," Uncle Ty says, and jerks his head toward us. That's a grown folks' signal for "Remember, there are kids here."

"Right," she says. "Let's go."

All thoughts about the Chosen One and the Msaidizi get pushed out my head, and we hurry to my mom's flying car. She sits in the driver's seat, and Uncle Ty takes the passenger seat. Alex, JP, and I hop on back. I slide my backpack underneath the front seat so Cocoa and the Msaidizi can chill safely. Harnesses automatically wrap over us snugly and lock into place as screens across the dashboard light up.

"Take us home," Zoe says.

The car lifts off the ground. Out my window, I watch us rise higher and higher above Jackson; over the coliseum with its big top, the skyscrapers, the governor's mansion, and churches downtown; the busy interstate, the sleepy suburbs. Soon everything looks like a miniature toy version of itself. We shoot off into the clouds, the morning sun glowing beside us.

The windows darken, then lighten to life like TV screens. The front window shows clear blue skies from a camera outside the car. On the rest, various TV shows play.

"Show us the trial," Zoe says.

All the window screens blink, and my grandmother, the president, appears on them. A large window behind her shows a skyline of a city with cars flying around it.

". . . And that's why you should never challenge a Merperson to a swimming competition," she says.

"I asked Momma to stall the trial while I went to get you three," Zoe explains. "She's running out of stories if she's talking about the time she raced a Merperson."

The camera pans to Elder Aloysius Evergreen, the man I've seen on the news. Dad would call Elder Evergreen in his suit and tie "Sunday morning sharp." His arms are folded tight and he looks ready to blow a fuse.

The camera pans again, showing rows of older Black folks with golden Glows, decked out in their Sunday best; colorful dresses, big decorative hats, suits and silk ties. A couple of their heads bob and weave as they fight to stay awake.

"The Elders are really elders!" JP says. "We have a chance then! Old people love me."

"Don't be so sure about that, kid," Uncle Ty says. "This

is the only thing the Council of Elders does—oversee trials. And they don't take it lightly. They're an old-school bunch. Quick to bring the hammer down."

"Keep stalling them, Momma," Zoe says. "We're almost there."

I don't know which way we go. I don't know how long we fly. It feels like it took a long time and no time at all when we land in a forest.

There's nothing but trees for miles and miles. Not a city in sight. To be honest, it's kinda disappointing, but I remember what Dad once told me: the Gift hides Uhuru.

The car whips around trees and glides over a creek. Uncle Ty takes a deep breath. He runs his hands over his pants. Takes another deep breath, loosens his harness a little.

"Hey." Zoe gently touches his shoulder. "You okay with coming back?"

"Yeah." He nods more confidently. "Yeah. I'm good. Lots of memories, though that may not be a great thing." He gives me a weak smile in the rearview mirror. "But this is worth coming back for."

I try to return his smile, but I can't. The truth is gonna devastate him. Why does the Msaidizi have to answer to me instead of him?

A rhythmic thumping vibrates the floor beneath my feet. It crawls up my legs, into my chest and my ears. I feel it as much as I hear it. Drums. They make me think of tribal dances around a fire, chants in a language I don't know; stuff I've never seen with my own eyes, yet the thought of them feels like home.

"Where's the drumming coming from?" I ask.

"What drumming?" asks Alex.

"Only Nic can hear it," our mom says with a smile. "The ancestors are welcoming you home, baby."

Sunlight glints off something up ahead: tall black onyx columns with a gold gate between them. The metal of the gate twists into regal designs leading up to the Mark of Eden on the very top. Thing is, there's no fence, only a gate.

Two Guardians stand guard in front of the gate. Their faces are hidden by gold-plated tribal masks with lions' faces on them. The taller of the two has long locs, while the stumpy one has cornrows with colorful threads braided into them.

The one with the locs puts a hand up, motioning us to stop.

"Should we hide?" JP says. "We *are* fugitives. Or you could give us an invisibility potion like Chloe took after that embarrassing incident with the ghoul at the school dance. Did that really happen, Ms. DuForte?"

Zoe side-eyes Uncle Ty. "We're gonna have a li'l talk about these books of yours."

"Thanks, JP," he mumbles and watches the approaching Guardian. "*Should* we hide the kids, Z?"

"No. We're gonna be honest. Lying won't help matters."

One Guardian comes around to the driver's side. Zoe's

window automatically rolls down. "Good afternoon, Ms. DuForte," he says.

"Hey, Dante. They got you on gate duty?"

"Yes, ma'am. Got promoted last week. They messed up, letting me and Marlon goof off out here." He points at the other Guardian, the one with cornrows, who's aiming a holographic bow and arrow at a holographic bird whizzing around him.

"I'm sure you're doing great," Zoe says. "Could you let us through?"

"Sure, just let me see who you got in here—yoooo!" he says into his fist, and points at Uncle Ty. "That's the Not-So-Chosen One! Tyran something!"

Uncle Ty sighs. "Saw it coming."

"Tyran Porter is his name, and he's my friend," Zoe says. "I'd appreciate if you didn't call him 'not-so' anything."

"My bad, my bad. Nice to meet you, Mr. Porter. Who else y'all got in here?" Dante stretches his neck to see into the car. "Ain't no way," he says, and lifts his mask. He looks too young to be a Guardian. The pimply brown face is more fitting for a high schooler. "Welcome back, li'l Ms. Blake."

It takes a second for me to realize he means me. Nobody's ever called me Ms. anything. "Thank you."

"Aye, for the record, I don't believe the stuff they been saying on the news 'bout you," he says. "I told Marlon it's gotta be more to it. But ooohwee, you got some explaining to do to the El—whoa!" He jumps back, staring at JP. "Ms. DuForte, that kid don't got the Glow!"

Uh-oh. I forgot Unremarkables aren't allowed in Remarkable cities. Are they gonna arrest us for trying to bring JP in?

Zoe doesn't seem worried. "I know he doesn't. Let us through."

"That's against the—"

"I will speak to my mother and make sure you and Marlon aren't punished. In fact, I may be able to get you a raise."

Dante rubs his wispy beard. "Think you can get us some promotions with them raises?"

And that's all it takes to get JP into Uhuru.

We glide through the gates into a thicket of more trees. The drums beat faster. The line of trees end at what appears to be the edge of a cliff, and we're speeding right toward it. I grip my safety harness and brace myself.

We fly off the edge and tilt up. I only see blue sky until we level out. The river below opens to a broad lake. What I see next takes my breath right outta me.

"Welcome home," Alex says.

In the center of the lake is a vast circular city with a light show flashing above it. Small rivers cut the city up like pieces of a pie, separating four distinct areas from one another. One is covered with fields of colorful flowers, and to the left of it, an area of grassy hills; the garden and the farming districts. The tech district looks more futuristic than I imagined, with glass skyscrapers and buildings that float in midair. The trade district is to its right. From here I see the floating billboards advertising sales.

The four districts all join at an island in the center, the governing district. It's the perfect mix of greenery and stone buildings. A glass-domed building sits in the middle of it, the LORE headquarters I saw on the news. That's exactly where we're headed.

TWENTY-ONE
THE MANIFESTOR PROPHECY

Uhuruan traffic is unlike anything I've seen, and I say this as someone who once lived in Atlanta. I know traffic.

The light show that I thought was flashing above the city is called the skyway. Hundreds of flying cars glide through neon lights shaped like tunnels. Some of the tunnels overlap, and at one point they're above, beside, and below us. Holographic signs flash to tell drivers they're going too fast or to alert them of an exit approaching.

JP presses his face against his window. "How come the cars can't fly where they want? Why do they have to use the tunnel thingies?"

"The sky would be chaos otherwise," Zoe says. "People flying their cars in every direction, hitting one another. The lights are also mojoed to keep the cars from dropping if they experience technical issues. That makes it safer for the fliers."

"Who?" I say.

"Look down a little lower," she says.

I press my face against my window like JP. We're flying over a district filled with shops, stands, and floating billboards—the trade district. Just above the buildings but not as high up as the skyway, people fly. Actual people fly.

"I've seen a lot of stuff in my life," JP says, "but this is the coolest."

I'm with him on that.

The car veers into another light tunnel, and it takes us above the governing district. With its stone buildings, monuments, and perfectly trimmed trees, it reminds me of Washington, DC.

We land in a parking lot beside the LORE headquarters and hurry inside the glass dome. I can't help but look up. Hundreds of levels of floors circle above us, and elevators blur in round glass shafts. Manifestors walk and fly around the lobby alongside Rougarous, Vampires, Azizas, and Remarkables with auras I don't recognize. Everyone has the Glow. JP sticks out big-time.

"Hey! That's an Unremarkable!" a Vampire shouts.

Zoe takes JP by the hand. "C'mon, sweetie."

Uncle Ty leads us to tall iron doors. An electronic sign above them says, "Council Room—Trial in Progress."

A hairy Rougarou in a security uniform blocks our

path. "Whoa! Ms. DuForte, you know better. Y'all can't bust up in there. It's a trial in progress."

"I think I have a good reason to disrupt it, Roy," she says. "We have the Msaidizi."

His eyes practically bug out. "You do?"

"Yes. Now can we go in?" my mom says.

Roy shoves open the doors of the council room for us.

All eyes instantly land on us, and there are dozens of them. The older folks in their Sunday best sit in rows that circle around the room like stands in a coliseum. Where we are would be the arena floor. Behind them we can see the skylines of the other four districts through enormous windows.

"What the hades?" Elder Evergreen from the news says. "We're in the middle of a trial!"

I forget about the trial and the Elders. Standing a few feet away from me, in plain black pants and shirt, is the person I did all this for. "Dad!"

He turns around. His eyes are puffy and dark like he hasn't slept much, but his face lights up. "Alex! Nichole!"

I race to him, and he gives me a crushing hug. Of all the cities I've lived in, none of them felt like home like Dad's hugs do.

He cups my face in his hands, which are covered in silvery gloves that look and feel as if they are woven with steel. "Are you okay?" he asks. "Where have you been?"

I blubber like a little kid. "We found it, Dad. We found the Msaidizi."

"Nichole?" someone calls softly. The president, my grandmother, rises from a seat that's plusher than the rest. As she descends the stairs, she watches me like she's afraid I may disappear.

"Grandma?"

Her smile lights up her face. "Yes, baby girl. Welcome back."

She hugs me tight, and somehow her hug feels like home too. She straightens her shoulders before she faces the Elders. "Good folks of the council, my apologies for the disruption. As you can see, it's for a fantastic reason. After ten long years, my granddaughter, Nichole, has finally returned home."

"Your granddaughter the criminal-in-training!" Evergreen spits. "We oughta put her on trial right now for the mess she's done."

"Elder Evergreen, I'm sure my grandchildren can explain." She sees JP. "Zoe, why is there an Unremarkable boy here?"

Murmurs bubble around the stands.

"He doesn't Glow!" one Elder says.

"Who let him in?" another demands.

JP takes a few steps back, but I go and grab his hand. Alex makes a point to stand beside him. We don't care how upset they are, we want him here.

"I declare! The audacity!" Elder Evergreen shouts. "An Unremarkable in our city? In our headquarters?"

"Calm down, Aloysius," says an older but not elderly

man in the stands. His dark skin has a few wrinkles, and he's dressed casually—jeans, a T-shirt. A baseball cap sits on top of his head.

"That's Grandpa Doc," Alex whispers to me. "Dad's dad."

That's the powerful Manifestor who defeated Roho? I expected someone majestic. You know, flowing beard and hair, glasses, long robe. A wise old man like you see in movies and books. He eyes me and Alex and gives us a curt nod. Alex waves back. I wonder why he hasn't come to hug me like Grandma did? Maybe it's not his style.

"This isn't the first time an Unremarkable's been in this building," he says. "No need to make a fuss over it."

"This boy is a security breach," says Evergreen. "He shouldn't know Uhuru exists!"

"But he's a Seer," I say.

Quiet muttering breaks out in the stands.

Elder Evergreen sneers. "That ain't an excuse. There are laws for a—what in the world?"

The iron doors swing open, and the security guard yells for someone to stop, but a woman marches in.

General Sharpe sets her sights on me, her teeth chattering. "Y-y-you!"

"Althea, how nice to see you," Zoe says.

"D-d-don't! That b-b-brat froze me and my officers with a j-j-juju bag! It t-t-took hours for us to defrost!"

"Geez, that was short," I say. My mom and grandma

shoot me looks. Dad snorts. Grandpa Doc coughs to cover a laugh.

General Sharpe points her trembling finger at me. "You li'l—"

Grandma sets her hands on my shoulders. "Let's hold off on judgment until we have the full story."

"T'uh!" Evergreen fakes a laugh. "I got the full story right here!" He taps his lapel pin, and a holographic scroll rolls out in front of him. "took with the Msaidizi—"

"We didn't have it!" I say. "The scavengers edited the video to make it look like we did."

"Committed arson in New Orleans—"

"The Devil set his daughter's house on fire, not us."

"Illegally used a wand on Unremarkables—"

"I was defending us!"

"Used the Underground Railroad without permission—"

"We didn't know we needed permission!"

"Assaulted Guardians—"

"Assault? I only opened a bag!"

"If disrupting a trial was illegal, I'd add it to the list," Elder Evergreen snips. "The full story is that they're guilty!"

I really don't like him.

Grandma's pursed lips tell me she doesn't either. "An explanation is a great place to start, Elder. Fairness is one of our tenets, is it not?"

"Yes," Evergreen grumbles. "It is."

"Then we will allow my grandchildren and their friend

to explain themselves. The floor is yours, children."

Hah! Take that, Evermean.

The Elders watch with a mix of intrigue and disapproval. Intimidating? Yep. But I step forward. "We haven't been on the run with the Msaidizi. We've been searching for it."

"That's the angle you're going for?" General Sharpe says. "Please! You're clearly covering for your father."

"No, she's not!" Alex says. "I used to think he stole it too, but someone else did. We found out it was spotted in New Orleans."

"Yeah," I say. "So we went there. A Vampire cornered us in the Underground, but the Devil's daughter showed up and . . ."

I tell them everything. JP and Alex add details I miss. I don't tell them Junior's name, just call him an "anonymous source" who told us that Roho had someone steal the Msaidizi. Chatter breaks out when I tell the Elders we found it.

Evergreen sits forward. "You have it?"

"You *found* it?" General Sharpe adds.

"Yeah," I say, "and it can tell you that my dad didn't steal it."

I slip off my backpack and set it on the floor. Cocoa's curled up in a tight ball on the bottom, fast asleep. The lizard Msaidizi climbs up the side of the bag and onto my hand.

"Please, tell them how you disappeared," I whisper.

The Elders stretch their necks and squint to try to see the tiny lizard on my arm. They don't struggle for long. She soon grows to her normal hulking size. The elders shriek.

"Good Lord almighty!" says Evergreen. "That's a dragon!"

"I am the one you call the Msaidizi," it says in a booming voice that rattles the room. "I was stolen by a Manifestor who answered to Roho. He ordered the Manifestor to hide me in his colony."

General Sharpe's eyes look as if they might pop out. Hopefully she's realizing she's been after the wrong person this entire time.

"So you're telling us that Calvin Blake didn't steal you?" Elder Evergreen says.

"No. He had nothing to do with my disappearance."

"I see," Evergreen says with a sour expression. I get the feeling that he was looking forward to punishing Dad for that. "Tell us the name of this Manifestor who stole you."

"I know not their name and did not see their face. I only know their actions."

Elder Evergreen's jaw ticks. "Very well. Then tell us the name of the person who you will answer to next."

Huh? Why does he wanna know that?

"I can only reveal what that person gives me permission to reveal," the Msaidizi says.

Zoe comes and grabs my hand. Tight. "Pumpkin, we should go," she whispers.

"Why?"

"Tell us the name, Msaidizi," Evergreen says.

"I am unable to reveal that unless—"

Evergreen angrily slams his fists against the table. "Tell us the name of the Manowari!"

"The what?" I say.

"Don't you mean the Chosen One?" says Uncle Ty. "That's who it's rumored to answer to next."

"No! We put that rumor out there 'cause people would panic if they knew the truth," Evergreen says. "It's prophesied to answer to the Manowari next! The real one!"

"But—but I thought Roho was the Manowari," Alex says.

"You thought wrong," Evergreen snips. "The real one is to come! And for some reason, the Msaidizi will answer to that person next. Tell us who it is, Msaidizi!"

My body goes cold.

"Elder Evergreen, that's enough," Grandma says, trembling slightly. "These children don't need to hear such things!"

I can't breathe. I can't move.

The Manowari.

The Msaidizi is prophesied to answer to the Manowari.

But the Msaidizi answers to . . .

It answers to . . .

Time remains on pause for me but goes on for everyone else.

Someone mentions taking a recess to discuss Dad and the kidnapping. Grandpa Doc says something about talking to the Msaidizi himself while the elders deliberate. It shrinks to lizard size and lets him pick it up. Elder Ever-green thanks us for retrieving it, though he seems angry still. Then the elders' seats spin around and slide through doors that take them to another room. General Sharpe leaves. My grandparents stay behind, and then it's just me, my family, Uncle Ty, and JP.

Somebody touches my arm. I jump.

"Pumpkin," Zoe says thickly, "it's gonna be okay."

I blink a few times. That's all I can do. "But . . . but the Msaidizi . . . it answers to me."

"I know, baby."

"What?" I look to Dad, and his glassy eyes cut me to pieces. "You knew?"

He bends in front of me. "Hey, hey, hey. Look at me. It's gonna be okay."

I quickly shake my head. "No, no, no, no, no. Dad. I can't. This . . . I can't be . . ."

"This doesn't define you, Nic Nac—"

"You are our wonderful, beautiful baby girl—"

"It doesn't matter what any prophecy says—"

"STOP!" I shout so loud it hurts my throat. "I'm not the Manowari!" I desperately look to Alex. "It's not true. It can't be."

But my brother steps back, staring at me in horror.

"Alex," I croak. I turn to JP, but he doesn't give me that JP smile I'm used to or tell me it's all right. He just stands there, blinking fast.

"Guys, it's me! It's Nic! I'm no different!" I whirl on my

311

parents. "Tell them none of this is true!"

Grandma comes and puts a supportive hand on my mom's shoulder. "Zoe. It's time she knows the truth."

Dad painfully closes his eyes and lowers his head. Zoe puts her hand to her mouth like that's the only thing keeping her from sobbing. They start talking, but I only catch bits and pieces.

"A Prophet came to us when you were a baby . . ."

". . . told us you were the Manowari and would destroy . . ."

". . . didn't know what to do . . ."

". . . I wanted to keep it a secret. I thought LORE would kill . . ."

". . . I wanted to tell my mother. She had just become president . . ."

". . . but I didn't trust her or anyone. So, I took you . . ."

". . . but baby, listen to me. This doesn't change . . ."

"It changes everything!" I scream.

I cover my mouth to keep from puking.

I'm the Manowari.

I'm gonna destroy the Remarkable world.

I wanna jump outta my skin, not be me anymore, or go back to a time where none of this is happening. I'd be cool with going back five minutes to when my parents don't look as if the world just ended.

"Is this why you didn't teach me the Gift?" I ask Dad. "You were afraid of what I'd do with it?"

"I'm not scared of you, Nic Nac, but I didn't wanna take a—"

He stops, but it's too late. It's like a knife ripped through me.

I become a blubbering mess. "I'm a monster. And you took me to protect me from . . ." I look at Zoe but can't see her for my tears. "From you. You wanted to turn me over to LORE?"

"No! No, no, no, baby. I'd never let *anyone* hurt you. I only wanted to tell my mother."

Out of nowhere, Uncle Ty says, "Why didn't either of you tell me?"

My parents and I do a double take. The coldness of his voice raises the hairs on my arms.

"Ty, it's nothing personal," my mom says. "We were scared."

"Too scared to tell your best friend? Who am I kidding? I was always the third wheel with you two."

"Ty, c'mon, it wasn't like that," Dad says.

Uncle Ty holds his head and paces. "'You are chosen to defeat an evil force that will cause destruction.' That's what the Prophet told me. 'You'll one day defeat an evil force.' Of course I didn't defeat Roho. He wasn't the real Manowari." Uncle Ty stops pacing. Eyes me. "The real one was to come."

My parents move in front of me, and that scares me to my core.

"Ty, relax, okay?" Dad says.

Uncle Ty takes slow steps toward us. My parents back up, forcing me to do the same.

"For years, my entire life revolved around those words," he says. "I've been called a failure because people thought I couldn't live up to them. They thought wrong."

"Tyran, stop it. Please," my mom begs. "She's a child."

"She's the Manowari!"

"She's your goddaughter!" says Dad. "We're supposed to be family!"

"Yet neither of you told me the truth about her! You like that I'm known as a failure, don't you?"

"No!"

"Stop lying to yourself, Zoe! Growing up, you especially hated that I was the Chosen One. All that attention I got, and yet as brilliant as you were, you were only known as my best friend. Nobody cared about your accomplishments, and if I fulfilled my prophecy and made a bigger name for myself, you'd be stuck in a bigger shadow.

"Then you. Calvin Blake. You were jealous of me the moment I was brought to Uhuru. You went from being known as Doc Blake's son to Tyran Porter's sidekick. Never thought to be good or great at anything . . . until I became known as a failure. Then you suddenly looked good by comparison!"

"Tyran," Grandpa Doc calls as he slips the Msaidizi into his pocket. His voice is calm yet forewarning, like thunder from a storm that hasn't hit yet. "This isn't the way."

Uncle Ty's face twitches. "Don't you dare say a word to me after what you did! You trained me for years and watched as Roho targeted me again and again. Then the moment I should've proved to everyone who I am, here comes the great Doc Blake to the rescue, taking my moment and my name!"

"I was trying to save you. You were frightened."

"No, you wanted the spotlight! How nice is it, Doc? You get all the glory from stopping Roho but none of the trauma from being targeted by that madman for years. Meanwhile, what did I get? A new name—the *Not-So-Chosen One*. I'm a joke to these people!"

"Ty, the way everyone has treated you is awful, a'ight?" Dad says. "I agree with you a thousand percent on that, man, but you're not thinking straight right now. Nichole is just a kid."

Uncle Ty shakes his head. "Nah, Calvin. Everything makes perfect sense now. I was never meant to defeat Roho." He looks at me. "I'm meant to defeat Nichole."

My brain doesn't process what he's said until the lightning bolt whizzes straight for me.

Zoe yanks me outta the way, and there's a loud bang as the juju hits the wall. A jet of white light zips from my mom's hand and flies at Uncle Ty, but he dodges her juju.

"Zoe, I don't wanna fight you!" he says.

"You'll have to fight us too," my grandma says as she

315

and Grandpa Doc position themselves between me and Tyran Porter. Alex and JP step forward as well.

A shadow crosses Tyran's face. "Then so be it."

He pulls a black stone from his pocket and tosses it into the air.

The council room goes pitch-black.

TWENTY-TWO

THE UNFORTUNATELY CHOSEN ONE

Jujus flash around, and there are screams. An alarm sounds, and dozens of feet pound into the council room.

"Mom! Dad!" I yell. "Alex! JP!"

"Nichole!" my mom says, from my left. No, my right. "Stay behind me!"

"Where are you?"

"Nic Nac!" Dad calls from my right. I think.

"Where is everyone?" Alex shouts from . . . under me? That can't be right.

"I'm right here!" JP says, from behind me, but then when he yelps, it comes from above.

"We have to get Nichole out of here!" Grandpa Doc echoes from far away. Just seconds ago he was near me. That stone did more than just shroud the room in darkness.

It made it hard to tell where anything actually is.

A juju flies at me in the darkness. I duck and barely miss it. "Someone help me!"

Something grabs my hoodie. I'm yanked off my feet and go airborne, high above the chaos. . . .

I land on a scaly back. "Hold on!" the Msaidizi says.

Spikes run down its back like a mane, and I grab hold of one. It rears with a fiery roar and launches through the darkness, toward the sunlight shining through the glass ceiling. I close my eyes and wait for impact.

It never comes. One second we're in the council room, and the next we're soaring through the governing district. The Msaidizi made the glass ceiling disappear.

People run and scream on the streets. The self-fliers hastily land to get outta Dodge as we dart around the stone buildings.

A fireball streaks over my head. Tyran is on our tail. Another zips over me. I duck just before a blast of hot air passes over my head. The fireball missed me by inches, but it sails on and strikes a statue in a park, exploding it into chunks of stone. Little kids on the playground shriek.

Tyran's a danger to more than just me. "Get us outta the city!" I tell the Msaidizi.

It climbs toward the clouds, and my eyes water from the wind whipping my face. Tyran gains on us. Icicles with sharp, pointed tips zip past my ear. They hit the dragon's head, but it doesn't react as it flies past the skyway.

We're above the lake and high enough that I can see

Uhuru in its entirety. I catch glimpses of gold and white streaks shooting into the air from each of the districts. The Guardians.

Ahead of us, the forest stretches wide, and the onyx and gold gate that leads to Uhuru gleams among the trees. We need to get away from Uhuru. Plus, Tyran's gotta get tired from flying at some point, and the farther we go, the—

Red and orange sparks explode in front of me, and searing pain surges up my hands. The fireball hit the Msaidizi's back. It roars in pain, and the fireball hits close enough that I feel the impact. I move my hands, and a second too late I realize I've let go of the spike.

"Your Grace!" the Msaidizi shouts.

I scream as I slide down its back. I reach for another spike, for its skin, but I'm falling too fast to grab hold of anything. I tumble off its tail, and the lake races toward me, Uhuru blurs past me, and the Msaidizi disappears into the clouds.

Help me, I think. Please!

"Kum yali, kum buba tambe!" I hear it say. "Kum yali, kum buba tambe!"

Somehow I know that those are the ancient words that the old man Toby first spoke to my ancestor Sarah. I feel her happiness as the plantation shrank below her, the relief as the cool air rippled beneath her, the hope from seeing a bright blue sky that led to freedom. I stretch my arms in front of me and let the breeze that carried my ancestor carry me.

I'm flying. I'm freaking flying! And it feels . . . amazing doesn't describe it. It's breathtaking. It's happiness. It's freedom. Warmth ripples through my body, from my toes to my fingertips. I suddenly feel as if I'm power itself.

I fly over the lake, and the wind whistles gently in my ears. But then an invisible force swats me. I lose control and tumble over the lake, into the woods.

I land face-first in a clearing. I push myself up and spit out dirt and grass.

The Msaidizi comes and lands nearby, but something's wrong. Its legs give out, and it falls onto her side with a ground-shaking rumble.

I hurry over, and my stomach sinks. Its back is blistered badly from the fireball. A silvery substance oozes out. Dragon's blood.

My mind races. How do I stop the bleeding? What if I can't? What if it bleeds out or gets an infection? What if it dies?

"I will be okay, Your Grace," it says, as if it heard my thoughts. "I shall heal on my own within a few minutes."

But I don't think we have a few minutes.

The trees flicker, and darkness surrounds us. Icicles break through the ground. I yelp and try to get away, but they grab me and the Msaidizi and wrap around us like long, frigid fingers that hold us in place.

I search the sky for the Guardians. "Help! Somebody help us!"

"They won't find you," Tyran's voice says all around me. "My concealment mojo hides us. Anyone passing overhead will simply see the forest."

I fight against the icicles, but they wrap around me tighter. "Uncle Ty, please? Let me go! I need to get help for my dragon."

"Why would I do that?" he asks. "I haven't told you my story."

The trees rustle, and a thin boy emerges from the thicket. He's no older than me, with short twists and a gold Manifestor Glow along his brown skin. His scuffed-up sneakers pound the ground, and his tattered shirt is drenched in sweat.

He runs past me but doesn't see me. He's too focused on what's behind him.

Zzzzap! A lightning bolt whizzes past my ear and hits him with a crack. He falls over.

"No!" I holler.

A shadow of a man forms in the trees. Tall. Muscular. He's hidden by darkness, but I can make out his eyes— gray as smoke and catlike. The same eyes Junior mimicked when he turned into Roho.

"You've heard of memory illusions?" Tyran says. "You dig deep in your mind and draw a past experience. This scene may be familiar to you. In the first Stevie book, Einan lured Stevie into the Realm of Shadows. That was based on a real thing Roho did to me."

The younger version of Tyran groans and weakly gets to his knees. He attempts to crawl away, but Roho zaps him again. He screams out in pain and falls on his face.

"Stop!" I shout.

"Horrible, isn't it?" says adult Tyran. "Roho didn't have the Msaidizi yet, and he was still powerful. This was my first encounter with him, but it was far from the last."

The illusion flickers, and I'm now in a barn filled with straw and bags of feed. The door flies open, and that same thin boy runs inside. He looks a little older than before, and his twists are longer.

Another boy and a girl run in behind him. The boy is taller than young Tyran, and I'd almost think he's Alex except his hair is in cornrows. The girl is practically a replica of me.

Of course my parents were once kids, but seeing them as kids this close is surreal. They shut the barn door and place a wood plank in its handles to secure it more, then back up, watching it closely. Young Dad and young Tyran point their palms toward it. Young Zoe grips a stake.

"While I go for the Vampire, you guys go for the Rougarous," she says.

"It's too many of them!" young Tyran says.

"Ty, we can take 'em!" says young Dad.

The door shakes violently, and Rougarous growl on the other side. My parents and Ty back up more.

"I haven't included this one in a book yet," the voice of adult Tyran says. "Roho sent a small army of Rougarous

322

and a Vampire after me. It's a miracle we survived that day. What kind of person does that to kids?"

The barn door bursts open. Zoe shrieks. Illusion or not, I do too, but the illusion changes again, and I'm back in the forest. Adult Tyran becomes visible in the clearing.

"Imagine getting tortured and attacked year after year, Nichole," he says. "Then everyone expects you to have the mental and emotional capacity to go after the person who put you through such things. It's what you're meant to do, they say. You press on, you train, you prepare yourself—but in the end, the person who should've believed in you doesn't give you a chance to live up to your name."

I fight back tears. Nobody should go through that. "What does this have to do with me?"

"Don't you see? You're the Manowari! Those things Roho did to me, you will one day do, and more. You're one and the same."

"I'm not like him!"

"Not yet. Roho didn't start out as a monster, no. I'd bet he was once a wisecracking, reckless kid. Only difference is, no one stopped him ahead of time."

The icicles crawl farther up my legs, around my waist, my chest, then up to my neck, binding me tightly. The Msaidizi grunts in pain, too weak to break through her own icicles.

Tyran raises his palms. "It'll be fast. You won't feel a thing."

He's wrong. This hurts. Not the icicles so much as

seeing someone who was a hero to me become this. "But you're my godfather! You said you were there when I was born. How can you hurt me?"

"It's not about you! It's what you're destined to become. I'm saving everyone from you!"

"The prophecy could be wrong! Or the Prophet could've mixed me up with another baby. You could be hurting an innocent kid. Then what will everyone call you?"

He tilts his head. "Not like Roho, you say? You tried to play with my emotions. That's a move right from his playbook."

I flinch. "I wasn't . . . that's not . . ."

"I'm mad at myself for not realizing who you are sooner," he says. "As much as I've studied the Manifestor Prophecy, I should've recognized that you fulfilled several of the twelve signs, including the most important one." He looks at my hands. "'For they will harness a power like no other.' That day in your backyard, you touched me and nearly took the Gift from me. Calvin said you touched a Visionary and saw her vision."

"You said that could be a puberty thing!"

"I lied. Nothing about that is normal. You *are* the Manowari. I'm about to do everyone a favor." He points his palms at me. "Goodbye, Nichole."

I search the skies again. Nobody's coming. I gotta save myself. But how? I don't know how to use the Gift, and I can't fly away. The icicles won't let me budge.

I look at my hands.

A power like no other.

I don't know what it is, but right now I need it.

I close my eyes tight, trying to will whatever it is into my hands.

"You're *the only gift you need*," I hear Dad say. *"Everything you need is inside of you."*

I get it now.

The power to save myself, it lies within me.

Literally.

Heat surges in the pit of my stomach and spreads through my body. I open my eyes and see that my hands are glowing brighter than the rest of me.

The icicles break at once. The shadowy illusion around us blinks from darkness to light and back, like someone is flipping a switch.

"What the—" Tyran says. He sends a juju at me.

It gets within inches of me, then ricochets off some invisible force and hits a tree.

I run at Tyran and grab his hands.

A hard jolt passes between us. His aura flickers like the illusion, and the more it flickers, the fainter it gets.

His knees begin to buckle. "Stop," he mumbles. "Stop!"

"I'm not like Roho!" I say. "You are!"

"Nichole!"

I jump, letting go of Tyran, and he collapses. The illusion dissolves, and daylight instantly returns to the forest.

Grandpa Doc hovers above the trees. The Msaidizi weakly stands as the blisters on her back fade slightly.

"The Guardians are on their way, Tyran," Grandpa says. "They only know that you attacked President DuForte's granddaughter, and I doubt that will be taken lightly. We both know this isn't who you are. I think it would be best if you leave while you can."

A wobbly Tyran gets to his feet. "I don't need your help! I'll take them on, I don't care."

"You'd be foolish to try," Grandpa says. "Don't let one bad decision ruin your life."

Tyran narrows his eyes at me as he draws rattling breaths. "I don't know what you did, but you only won today," he growls. "I *will* fulfill my prophecy."

He staggers into the forest. His feet lift from the ground, and he flies off. Seconds later, Guardians in white and gold streak after him in the sky.

I stare at my hands. What kinda power do I have?

I look up at Grandpa Doc hovering above the clearing. The version of him in the Stevie books would have something wise and comforting to say at a time like this. The kinda speech that would stay with me for the rest of my life.

All he says is, "Nice dragon."

TWENTY-THREE

A FATHER'S FATE

Back at LORE in the council room, my mom hugs the oxygen outta me.

"Are you okay?" she says. "You aren't hurt, are you?"

"I'm okay," I say, but she hugs me tighter and kisses me over and over.

She stops long enough for Dad to hug me too. "You good, Nic Nac?" he asks.

"Yeah, I'm good."

He kisses my hair, then turns to his dad. Grandpa Doc kept close and followed me and the Msaidizi back to headquarters. When the dragon shrank to lizard size and I slipped it into my pocket, he went, "Hmm." That's pretty much all he's said to me.

"Thank you," Dad tells him.

"Not necessary."

In the center of the council room, my backpack twitches. I am a horrible dog owner—I totally forgot about Cocoa. I rush over, prepared for the worst, but she peeks her head outta my backpack and yawns. My dog slept through that? Seriously?

I scratch behind her ears. "Silly dog."

Alex and JP hurry over to me. Alex lifts his arms like he's gonna hug me, but then he awkwardly lowers them to his sides. "Glad you're okay, Nic."

"Geez, there's nothing wrong with public displays of affection," JP says, and hugs me super tight. "A hug never hurt anyone."

"Tell that to my organs," I say. He lets go and whew, I can breathe again. "You guys okay?"

"Yeah. We were worried about you. We thought Tyran hurt . . ." Alex's voice trails off. "The prophecy didn't matter after that."

"Does it matter now?"

"No," Alex says. "You're still my sister."

"And my best friend," says JP.

I throw my arms around them. Today I found out the worst news of my life, but I also realized the best: I have more than just a brother and a best friend. In Alex and JP, I have family.

"Ahem, hem!" Evergreen clears his throat extra loud. He and the other elders are back in the stands, along with

my grandparents. General Sharpe is in the room too. "We have important matters to address," Evergreen says. "Starting with Tyran Porter. Has he been caught?"

"No, sir," says General Sharpe. "My officers sent word that he escaped the city. We think he took an invisibility tonic."

"My word. What on earth happened?" Evergreen asks. "Why did he go after the girl?"

My stomach clenches. Dad feared what LORE might do if they knew I was the Manowari. The elders and General Sharpe can't know. There's no way it would go well.

"It was because of me," Grandpa Doc says.

My head snaps up. What?

"What you mean, Doc?" says Evergreen.

"It's no secret that Tyran resents me. I assume he was upset when he found out that Nic found the Msaidizi instead of him. It's my understanding that he wanted to search for it?"

"He did," General Sharpe says. "He begged me to let him go look."

"Well, there you go," says Grandpa. "I'm sure it's hard knowing that yet another Blake 'got in his way.' He had a lapse in judgment."

Strangely enough, his story makes enough sense that I'd believe it too.

Elder Evergreen sadly shakes his head. "May the Most High have mercy on that boy. General Sharpe, please see to it that he's found. Attacking a child ain't a crime to take lightly."

"Hold on," General Sharpe says. "Why did the Msaidizi help *her?*"

I swallow hard. I should've known this was going too well.

"It was fulfilling a sacred contract," Grandpa Doc says. "Help for help. Nichole helped the Msaidizi by retrieving it. It paid its debt by saving her from Tyran. Simple as that."

"Sounds about right," says Evergreen. "Althea, could you please take the Msaidizi and deliver it to the secure facility?"

"Yes, sir," General Sharpe says.

She approaches me, and I carefully set the lizard in her hands, but then she gets in my face. "I don't know what's going on here," she says under her breath, "but I'm gonna find out."

My knees shake, but I straighten as best as I can. General Sharpe can never find out who I'm prophesied to be.

She leaves with the Msaidizi, and the lizard peeks around her and smiles at me. I try to smile back. I know I'll see her again—although I don't wanna think about how and when—but I hoped I'd get to keep her as a pet. We had some fun times . . . okay, we had some traumatic times. But I'm still gonna miss her.

"Now, Calvin Blake," Elder Evergreen says. "Kidnapping is a serious crime. The council took several things into consideration when making our decision regarding your fate. Before we announce it, do you have anything to say for yourself?"

"I thought I was doing what was best for my daughter," he says. "Zoe and I received a prophecy that told us Nichole was in danger. I stand by my reasoning for taking her away, but the way in which I did it was unacceptable."

Zoe hugs herself. "Yeah. It was."

"I know, and I should've discussed things with you instead of making impulsive decisions," Dad says. "I should've trusted you, and I shouldn't have robbed you of ten years with our daughter. My heart may have been in the right place, but it was a cruel choice.

"Alex, baby boy, I'm sorry I wasn't there for you," Dad says. "I'll regret it for the rest of my life. You deserved better than what I gave you. If you don't want anything to do with me, I wouldn't blame you, but I'd love to get to know you and earn the right to be your father."

Alex bites his lip and looks away.

Dad focuses on me. "I'm sorry, Nic Nac. No matter my reasoning, I kept you from having an amazing mom and brother. You deserved better than what I gave you."

I tear up. That's the thing, though. He gave me something amazing: protection. He didn't have a home and a family either, all 'cause he wanted to keep me safe.

How can I be mad at that?

I hug his middle. "I love you too."

He rubs my back and kisses the top of my head.

"Council, what say you?" Grandma calls out.

"Calvin Blake," Evergreen says, in a stiff, official tone, "the Council of Elders hereby sentences you to five years of house arrest. You will be confined to the home of your father, Doc Blake. You must also complete five years of volunteer work. If you do need to leave the property for emergency reasons, you must receive Guardian permission."

"That's all?" Dad says.

"*All?* We can send you to another realm if you'd like!" Evergreen snips. "However, Ms. Zoe DuForte asked the council for some leniency in your sentencing."

"She did?"

"I did," Zoe says. "Sending you to another realm was very, very, very tempting, but no matter what you've done"—she looks at me and Alex—"our kids deserve to have *both* of their parents around."

My heart doubles in size. I throw my arms around her waist, burying my face in her shirt. "Thank you."

"Anything for you, pumpkin."

Grandma dabs her cheeks with a handkerchief. "I think that's all for—"

"Hades nah, it ain't!" Evergreen says. "We gotta discuss this here Unremarkable boy."

JP points at himself. "Me?"

Evergreen keeps talking. "He's seen too much. We need to wipe his memory of the past few days before we send him back to the Unremarkable world."

"No, please don't!" JP says.

"He's a Seer," I add. "He's seen weird stuff his whole life. Tell them, JP."

"Yeah! When I was three, I saw a Fairy, and then at four I—"

"I didn't mean give them your life story, bruh."

"It's not about what he's seen, but what he knows," says Evergreen.

"Hold your dragon, Aloysius. Let's discuss this." Grandpa Doc speaks up. "Harriet Tubman was a Seer, and we named a school after her. The old man Toby was a Seer. We've always considered them and their ability special. The boy could come in handy."

"He has a point," says my grandma. "Seers also possess abilities we're still discovering. This young man may be able to provide us with valuable information."

"Yes! I am very valuable," JP says. "Call me the valuable player most!"

"You mean most valuable player?" I ask.

"Same thing."

I roll my eyes. This guy.

Grandma's mouth twitches, but she holds back her laugh. "I do agree that he could be a security risk," she says. "However, I propose making him sign a nondisclosure agreement."

"Long as it's bound with a juju!" says Evergreen.

JP gulps. "Bound how?"

"If you were to break the agreement and tell anyone about Uhuru or the Remarkable world, you could end up covered in warts or something of the sort for the rest of your life," Grandma says.

"That's a light one," Evergreen sneers. "We can do much worse, boy."

JP quickly shakes his head. "No, no need to do worse! Warts are scary enough. I'll keep my mouth shut."

"I ain't convinced," says Evergreen.

"Then let's take a vote on it," Grandma says. "All those in favor of wiping the young Seer's memory, make yourselves known."

Evergreen and fewer than half the elders raise their hands. General Sharpe raises hers too. Yooo, *less than half*. That means . . .

"Those in favor of allowing the Seer to keep his memory, and for LORE to keep a close eye on him, make yourselves known."

Most of the elders raise their hands. Alex and I join in.

"Then it's settled," Grandma says with a smile.

"All this rule bending," Evergreen grumbles. "Fine! But boy, if you tell a soul—"

"I won't! Nobody would believe me anyway. Flying cars and flying people? My parents would double my therapy sessions."

True.

Grandma chuckles. "Valid point. We will have the contract drawn up, then brief you on security measures before you leave. Elders, we will see to it that you receive constant updates on the Tyran Porter situation. I will personally make sure the Guardians search for him around the clock."

"What if they don't find him?" I ask.

My grandma gives me a smile that tries to hide her concern. "Let's hope that they do. Meeting adjourned."

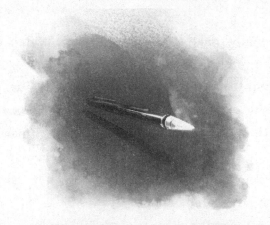

TWENTY-FOUR

IT'S NOT GOODBYE

It's nighttime when we arrive in Jackson.

My mom lands her car a few houses away from JP's, and the newest pothole on the street jostles us around. I wonder if the Msaidizi was creating them to get to me. Now I feel bad for what I've put Jackson's drivers through.

We pull into the driveway of the Williamses' home. The front windows of the house glow bright, and shadows of JP's parents move around behind the curtains.

"Aw, man. Why can't they be at church?" JP whines. "They're always at church! I can't lie to them. Like I literally can't! My mom once prayed that I wouldn't be able to lie, and any time I try, my throat closes and I break out in hives. God works in mysterious ways."

"We can't tell them the truth, JP," I say.

"Nic, I have to. Hiding the truth is a lie in their books."

"You can tell them the truth, sweetie," my mom says.

She pops open her glove compartment. Two shelves holding tiny vials of colorful liquids slide forward. Zoe picks up a lavender vial with silvery glitter shimmers inside.

Alex sits up. "Oh boy Du Bois, that's a memory tonic!"

"Are you gonna erase their memories?" JP asks, and I can't tell if he's scared or excited.

"You're gonna tell them the truth, then I'm gonna *alter* their memories. Are your parents tea or coffee people?"

"My dad can't drink coffee anymore. Caffeine raises his blood pressure, and the church congregation does enough of that. The drama people bring to his office." JP shakes his head. "My mom drinks green tea in the morning and chamomile tea at night. She also likes the occasional sweet tea. Dad doesn't. He's the only Southerner who hates it. Can you believe that?"

"Water it is," Zoe says.

We get outta the car. Next to the Williamses' home, my old house sits in darkness. Uhuruan movers are supposed to go get our stuff later tonight, and I don't know. I should be used to moving thanks to the whole "living on the run" thing, but it's always hard to say goodbye to a home. The only thing harder is getting used to a new one.

I try to take in every detail of the house. The tall pine tree that I could spot a block away to lead me home, the flower bed Dad killed every year, the Visionary sitting on the front porch . . .

The Visionary sitting on the front porch? "Ms. Lena?" I call.

She glances up from a book. "'Bout time y'all showed up!"

We cross the driveway into my old yard. Ms. Lena's bronze Glow lights up the porch. She takes off a pair of bejeweled glasses and sets aside her book, *The Foolproof Guide to Becoming a Rap Star.*

"What are you doing here?" I ask.

"I brought ol' hairy butt like you asked."

She points her thumb back toward a window. Junior happily waves at us from inside the house and holds a hoof for us to see he's wearing Dad's sneakers. Oh, man. Dad's gonna flip when he finds out Junior got his kick collection. Also, who knew Jordans could fit on hooves?

"I figured y'all would come and bring the Seer home," Ms. Lena says. "I wish I had a vision and it would've showed me what time y'all were coming. I been sitting here so long, my butt gone numb."

"Okaaay," my mom says slowly.

Ms. Lena grins, and her gold teeth twinkle in the darkness. "You must be Zoe. Chile, this girl know she stole your face. Leave it to Calvin to mess things up with a beautiful woman."

"Thank you?" Zoe asks more than says. "I'm sorry, I missed your name?"

"I didn't give it, but it's Lena. I run the juke joint over on Farish. It's a regular spot for exiles." She looks at JP and

Alex. "Glad y'all survived. I knew Nic would, but I wasn't sure 'bout you two. Especially the li'l anxious one." She motions at Alex.

"I wasn't sure either," he admits.

"You had a vision that I'd survive?" I ask. "How come you didn't tell me?"

"Calm down, girl. I didn't have a vision. I knew you'd survive because I know what you made of. You a force, Nic Blake. Especially when you hangry. Then it's watch out."

"Truth!" JP says. "You should see her when there's a line at Five Guys."

"The name is *Five* Guys," I say. "Five guys should make the burgers to keep the line moving."

Alex frowns. "Why is it called that if there aren't five guys?"

"The same reason I can't eat an Apple product," Ms. Lena says. "Unremarkables don't make a lick of sense. I didn't come here to talk 'bout that. Bertha told me she took y'all to Roho's colony."

"Your train talks?" JP says. "How come she didn't talk to us?"

"Did you ask her to?"

I raise my brows. "We didn't know we could?"

"Now you know. She said y'all weren't the worst guests she's had, but you could've kept things cleaner. She cut you some slack since you were dealing with so much, but next time act like you got some home training."

A train chastised us, wow.

"Let me get this straight," Zoe says. "Bertha is a train, your train, and you let three kids use her to travel, unsupervised?"

Ms. Lena sets her hand on her hip. "Yeah, what's it to you? They each came back in one piece, didn't they?"

My mom doesn't have an answer for that.

"Mmmhmm. That's what I thought. Y'all find the Msaidizi?" Ms. Lena asks.

"Yes, ma'am," I say.

"Good. You gon' need it."

She takes my hands. Suddenly, images flash through my mind. An underwater city. A building in ruins. Grandpa Doc lying unconscious.

I gasp and snatch away from Ms. Lena.

"My job here is done," she announces loudly. She straightens up with her book and heads off down the sidewalk.

The conversation with JP's parents goes like this: the Williamses are shocked to see JP and ask how he got home. Zoe says she brought him, then introduces herself. The Williamses politely say it's nice to meet her and point out that I "took her whole face," like Ms. Lena said. Southerners. They don't understand why she has their son. JP told them that he traveled out of state with me and Alex to find a powerful weapon.

Cue the awkward silence. The Williamses think this is a "TokTok" prank. Alex asks me what TokTok is. JP tells them it's not and describes our encounter with the Devil's daughter and the Grand Wizards and tells them we found a dragon under Jackson. Pastor and Mrs. Williams silently stand there. Alex gets them some water, and when they aren't looking, my mom pours the memory tonic into their glasses. They sit, take sips, and the tonic immediately puts them to sleep. My mom then whispers in their ears that they picked up JP from his camping trip. When they wake up in a few minutes, that's what they'll remember.

While she tells them lies—I mean new memories—Alex, JP, and I wander out to the front porch and sit on the steps. Crickets chirp loudly, and in the distance sirens and car horns sound off. Dad used to say Jackson can be as quiet as the countryside or as loud as a city, it just depends on what mood it's in.

"Your grandma said I can visit you guys," JP says. "She's gotta work it out with the Guardians, but wouldn't that be cool?"

"Yeah." I try to sound excited, but I'm failing. It's hitting me that JP and I won't be next door to each other anymore.

I think it's hitting him too. "I don't like goodbyes," he says.

My eyes prickle. "Bruh, what? This isn't goodbye. It's see you later."

"Precisely," says Alex. "Grandma keeps her word. You'll visit, and Nic and I will find ways to come see you."

"And I can text you on my tablet every day," I add. "You're not getting rid of me that easy."

341

He bows his head. "It still won't be the same."

I've never had a friend like JP, so this "see you later" stuff is brand-new to me. I don't like it, I'll tell you that.

"Hey, here," Alex says. I rub my eyes and watch him give JP the earpiece that powers his G-glasses. He had an extra one in Zoe's car. "They're on auto-prescription and will adjust automatically to whatever settings you need. You can use them to holo-message us."

JP looks stunned. "You're giving me your G-glasses?"

"It's cool. I have ten more pairs."

"Wow, thanks," JP says. "Hold on, I've got something for you."

He runs in the house, and seconds later comes back with a Magic 8 Ball. "It doesn't use magic or the Gift, but it's as close as us Unremarkables get. You ask it a question, shake it, and it'll give you an answer."

"Hmm." Alex examines the ball. "Will I get straight A's this school year?" He shakes the ball, and gasps. "No? What! That can't be right!" He furiously shakes it again.

"It's not reli—" You know what? Never mind. He can believe it if he wants.

My mom and JP's parents laugh as they come to the front door. It's hard to tell that JP's folks were knocked out by a tonic a few minutes ago.

"I'm so glad we finally got to meet you, Ms. DuForte," Mrs. Williams says. "I'm sorry the visit is short. That drive out to the campgrounds wore us out."

Alex, JP, and I share glances. It worked.

"I totally understand," Zoe says. "We have a long drive ahead of us ourselves. I'm probably gonna crash as soon as I walk into the house."

Pastor Williams tilts his head. "Where are you from again?"

"Small town," Zoe says. "You've never heard of it. Say good night, Alex and Nic."

JP and Alex slap palms. I ignore that it takes them three tries to get it right. Neither of them is coordinated.

JP comes up to me. "I'm deleting the Stevie James wiki and throwing away my books."

I swallow and nod. It feels as if Stevie James died today. I can never read those books again. "Good call."

"We'll talk every day, and you'll tell me the cool stuff you get to do?" JP asks.

"Long as you promise to tell me everything you see and what you and Junior get into."

"Deal." He holds his hand out for a shake.

I look at it and then at him, the bow-tie-wearing, wiki-editing boy from next door. The Msaidizi drew me to Jackson, but I ended up with something much better: a friend.

I throw my arms around him. "Thanks for being the best friend I've ever had."

"Takes one to know one."

I hold my fist out to him. It only takes him one try to bump it.

My mom guides me to her car. JP's parents scratch their

heads as they stare at it, and I hear Pastor Williams say it must be one of those electric cars—a Tessa, he calls it.

We pull away from the Williamses' house. I watch JP and his parents wave on the porch. I think JP points to his G-glasses as if to remind me we'll keep in touch, but it's hard to tell 'cause of the tears in my eyes.

I watch the blur of him till we're too far away for me to see.

Cocoa nips my ear to wake me up in the morning. Some things don't change. Where she's waking me up, well, that's definitely changed.

I yawn and stretch in my bed. It's circular and twice as big as my old one. At the moment it feels feathery soft, but with a simple command I can make it hard as a rock, as airy as a cloud, or as turbulent as ocean waves during a storm. I don't know why I'd want that mode, but it's cool that it can do that.

I scratch Cocoa's back. She hops off the bed to bark at a shooting star that zips past. More stars and planets glow on the walls and ceiling. I decided to sleep in space last night. Kinda like the bed, the way my room looks can be changed to whatever I want.

"Good morning, Nichole," a voice says. "Did you sleep well?"

I sit up, rubbing my eyes. That's Vic-E, the virtual assistant that runs my mom's condo. Zoe said I can ask her to do almost anything.

I didn't realize breakfast was an option. "Can I have caramel cake?"

"I'm sorry, that meal selection would require approval from your mother."

So much for asking her to do "anything."

"Waffles and bacon, then, with a glass of milk."

"What type of milk? Whole, almond, oat, lavender?"

"Uh . . . the kind that comes from a cow."

"I assume that's an excellent choice. I've never had milk or any liquid. It wouldn't be good for my system. Your meal will be ready and waiting for you in the kitchen in the next five minutes. Would you like to see outside? The weather in the tech district is stunning today."

I shrug. "Why not?"

The stars and planets on one wall fade away, and a window showing a sunlit skyline appears. Tall glass buildings tower over the tech district. In the distance, cars fly along the skyway through the colorful tunnels of light.

I go to the window and look out. I can't see the street from up here in my mom's high-rise, only the roofs of shorter buildings. A family splashes in a rooftop pool across the way. Another building has a greenhouse on top, and an elderly couple tends to flowers and plants inside. A holographic billboard floats by, and Alex and I smile back at me with the words ALEX AND NICHOLE BLAKE RETURN HOME WITH THE MSAIDIZI flashing above it. It dissolves, then shows a picture of Tyran with the headline TYRAN PORTER ON THE RUN.

"Quite a view, huh?"

My mom leans against my doorway wearing a smile and a sundress. Her thick ponytail hangs over her shoulder, with gold hair clips glimmering along it.

"Yeah, it's cool."

"Wait until you see the garden district on a summer morning. I've seen it my entire life, yet it never gets old."

I squint at bluish-purple specks way out past the skyscrapers. "Is that it over there?"

She joins me at the window. "Yeah. Those are the indigo fields. Do you know the story of how our ancestors infused the Gift into blue-glass bottles using indigo plants?"

"Yeah, Dad told—" I stop myself. Probably not a good idea to bring up Dad.

"It's okay to talk about him. You're also welcome to go see him anytime you want."

"Really?"

"Absolutely. He's your father, nothing changes that. Although today you may not have time to visit him. Your grandma has declared it a day of celebration, starting with a welcome-home brunch at the presidential palace. Officials from around the world will be there."

Another holographic billboard of me passes my window, and I bite my lip. They wouldn't be doing this if they knew that I'm the Manowari.

"This is a lot for me," I whisper.

Zoe rests her chin on my shoulder. "You're worth this

and more. Don't let anything make you think differently."
She kisses my temple to seal the deal.

"Thanks, Mom."

She sucks in a quick breath.

I look back at her. "You okay?"

She gives me a small smile. "Yeah. Why don't you get dressed and come down for breakfast? Sound good?"

I nod, and she kisses my forehead. As the door closes behind her, I catch a glimpse of her starting to wipe her eyes, and it's then that I realize I called her Mom.

My welcome-home brunch is more of a meet and greet.

A flying limousine brought me, my mom, and Alex to a stone mansion on a grassy hillside. It has more balconies and columns than I can count, and windows that stretch from the floor to the ceiling. The kinda place I'd normally feel like an alien in. But Vic-E helped me pick out this cute flowery dress that's got me feeling as if I belong wherever I go. For a virtual assistant, she's got good taste, although she wasn't a fan of the high-top sneakers. She'll deal.

Grandma Natalie introduces me to one boring official after another. A beefy man with a bushy Afro and a Caribbean accent gives me a firm handshake. He says he's the mayor of the underwater city New Atlantis and that I'm welcome to visit anytime. He offers to shut down the water park just for me, Alex, and JP to have it to ourselves one day, as a reward for finding the Msaidizi. A group of delegates from N'okpuru, an underground city, congratulate me for my "heroics."

"It's sad what happened with Tyran Porter," says a bald, dark-skinned woman. "Upset because you found the Msaidizi? A crying shame. Hopefully the Guardians catch him soon."

I nod and stuff a chicken-and-waffle bite in my mouth.

An hour in, a band of older Manifestors, Rougarous, and a Vampire hop on stage. The Vampire is the lead singer. His band plays some old funk song, and the adults get totally into it. No one notices me slip into the hallway.

I sit on a bench and take out the Unremarkable phone Mom gave me. She said I could use it to talk to JP since it may take him a while to get accustomed to the G-glasses. Also, explaining to his parents why there's a hologram of me in his room is a disaster waiting to happen.

I type a text to him.

Met the mayor of New Atlantis. He offered to shut down the water park for us!

Three dots appear on my screen, then: WHAT?!?

I text Dad next. I'm glad he still has his old phone. The Guardians don't trust him with Giftech. I wish he could be here, but I've been sending him updates all day. I write him another.

Grandma has some old band here.

They're playing a song about fighting funk?

He replies pretty fast.

LOL!

That's Smoky Mack and the Cool Cats.

Your grandma's favorite group.

She went old-school with it.

Too old, I write back.

Alex pokes his head outta the dining hall. He looks both ways before he spots me. "Needed an escape too?"

"ASAP. Is this what it's always like, being the president's grandkid?"

He joins me on the bench. "For official events? Yes. Most days are normal. A Guardian escorts me to school and keeps the paparazzi away. Afterward, I attend whatever extracurricular activity is scheduled. If it's an outdoor activity and Mom is there, a crowd may gather to watch. Our Guardian escort makes sure they don't ask her for photographs and autographs."

"Nothing you're describing is normal."

Alex shrugs. "Normal is subjective. I'll be here to help you deal with everything. That's what twins are for, right?"

"Right."

I hold my fist toward him. He bumps it and we smile. It's gonna be nice having someone who understands.

The dining-hall doors open again, and Mom pokes her head out. "There you are," she says. "It's time, guys."

"Time for what?" I ask.

Alex gets a wide grin. "The fun part."

He pulls me down the hall to glass double doors at the very end that lead to a balcony. A pair of Guardians stand one on each side. Grandma Natalie leaves the dining hall and joins us.

"This is a long time coming, baby girl," she says. "You deserve a proper welcome."

She nods at the Guardians. They open the doors to the balcony, and I hear the cheering crowd way before I see it. My mom, my grandma, and my brother go onto the balcony.

I hesitate. I'm the one they've been warned about for years. Can I face them, knowing that?

But I'm also the kid who's never lived one place for long. The one who's never had a family. Now it seems like there's a family bigger than anything I could've imagined, waiting to greet me. For that, it's worth it to forget who I'm meant to be. At least for a little while. I take a deep breath and step forward—

Large red glowing words suddenly appear in front of me, scaring me so bad I fall on my butt.

YOU THINK YOU'RE GONNA GET AWAY WITH FINDING WHAT I HID?

I try to catch my breath as more of the G-pen message appears.

ENJOY THE CELEBRATIONS NOW.
THEY WON'T LAST LONG.

The messages disappear, and the person finishes by signing their name.

THE APPRENTICE.

I lie on the floor, my heart hammering against my chest as I watch the last letter of the G-message fade away.

Junior warned me that finding the Msaidizi would be dangerous.

I didn't realize how dangerous it could be.

Tyran Porter may be the least of my problems.

"Nichole?" My mom comes back inside and hurries to me. She and a Guardian sit me up. "Baby, what's wrong?"

"I . . ." I try to find the words, but I think about everything she's gone through and how worried she's been about me . . . this would freak her out.

I can't tell her. Not now. I gotta figure out how to deal with it.

I'm *gonna* figure out how to deal with it.

"I'm fine," I say, and make myself smile. "Just nervous."

She brushes my hair back from my forehead. "You have nothing to be afraid of."

If only.

I take my mom's hand and let her lead me onto the balcony to thunderous cheers.

ACKNOWLEDGMENTS

The true gift of this book can be found in those who made it possible.

To God, first and foremost. Thank you for your son, Jesus, and thank you for choosing me to tell this story. I'm excited to see where you take it and me.

My mom, Julia, the Ms. Lena of my life. Thank you for seeing the vision before I do.

My editor, Donna, my own personal Seer who always finds the good stuff. You are truly a remarkable gift.

My agent, Molly Ker Hawn. Thank you for being mojo personified. I hope JP is half as awesome as you. Thank you also to Martha Perotto-Wills, Victoria Cappello, and Aminah Amjad.

My film agent, Mary Pender-Coplan. You're better

than magic could ever be. Thank you for being my guardian.

My cover designers and illustrator, Jenna Stempel-Lobell, Alison Donalty, Setor Fiadzigbey. Thank you for creating something better than I ever could've imagined.

To the remarkable folks at Balzer + Bray/HarperCollins: Paige Pagan, Jennifer Corcoran, Mark Rifkin, Shona McCarthy, Ronnie Ambrose, Dan Janeck, Robby Imfeld, Emily Mannon, Delaney Heisterkamp, Patty Rosati, and Mimi Rankin. I don't need Giftech when I have all of you. Thank you.

My assistant, Marina, and my social media manager, Cody. I literally couldn't get this book done if it weren't for the work you do. Thank you.

To Jackson, Mississippi. Despite everything, you're still a remarkable place. May this book show that to the world. Thank you for making me, me.

And to Kobe, the real Cocoa. You won't even know that I wrote this but thank you for reminding me that life itself is a gift.